COLIN WICKING

The HAUNTING at MANGO FLAT

MURDER. MYSTERY. MANGOES.

Copyright © 2017 Colin Wicking

ISBN: 978-1-925590-37-1
Published by Vivid Publishing
P.O. Box 948, Fremantle
Western Australia 6959
www.vividpublishing.com.au

Cataloguing-in-Publication data is available from the National Library of Australia

Author's note
While primarily a work of fiction, this novel *was* inspired in part by the 'true' story of the Humpty Doo poltergeist.
Google it.

Interview – Part 1

Police interview rooms. Not the happiest places around. Windowless, starkly lit and barely furnished, they're designed for nothing less than maximum discomfort and advertising the idea that there is absolutely no way out unless you start blabbing, which is exactly what I intended to do as soon as the cops came back.

This particular interview room, I had time to notice, appeared recently refurbished but the lingering odour of new paint did not entirely overwhelm the sweet hint of human distress that permeated its worn industrial carpet. Obviously, the renovation budget hadn't extended all the way to the floor. Some of that stench may have been mine. I'd been here before, back when video cameras and recording devices and such were physically in the room with you. Now a single AV unit mounted near the ceiling feeds everything onto a hard drive located somewhere else. I glanced up, knowing that a couple of cops were at that moment hunched in front of a screen somewhere, probably right next door, keeping an eye on things. No fancy two-way cop show mirrors around here. Maybe we can't afford them.

The detectives were taking their own sweet time. They had gone for coffee, leaving me to stew in my own juices for a while. I knew how it worked. It was all part of the little three-way drama we were in the process of acting out. This was serious business. Two people were dead - well, no, make that *three* – and I had a story to tell.

I waited, with nothing to keep me company but the quiet hum of ducted air-conditioning. I studied the backs of my hands. The trembling had subsided and the flecks of blood had dried to a hard black. Under the sharp fluorescent light, the flecks looked like tiny, dark beetles. The bloody spots on my shirt had turned black too. It wasn't my blood so at some point, I supposed, the cops would produce a warrant to seize my clothes, bag them up and send them wherever they had to go, and I vaguely wondered what they would give me to wear instead. Maybe they would simply take me home to change. I had no idea.

I looked at my watch. There was a tiny spatter of blood on the face as well. It was almost 10pm.

My fingers drifted over to my digital recorder. I gave it a couple of spins before picking up my phone. I inspected the blank screen and put it down again. They'd asked me to switch it off. I had yet to ask for my one phone call – you actually do get one - mainly because I wasn't under arrest for anything yet but also because I had no idea who I'd call at this time of night anyway. The only person I *would* call was, I assumed, at that very moment sitting in a room exactly like this one. On the way in, I'd counted six numbered but otherwise grimly identical doors leading off the corridor.

I leaned back in my chair and rolled my neck from side to side for a moment or two, shock finally giving way to exhaustion, and decided to stare up at the ceiling with my bloody hands behind my head until the detectives decided to come back.

A few minutes later the door clicked open with a tiny electronic bleep and Detective Sergeant Knight, a folder tucked under one arm, shouldered through bearing a steaming plastic coffee cup in each hand. Right behind him, Detective Tezuka also carried coffee and a folder.

Unusually (and the name may be a dead giveaway here), Tezuka was Japanese. I hadn't seen him around before. Possibly, he was on some sort of exchange program. His black-rimmed glasses were too big for his face and he was painfully thin. He wore a plain business shirt tucked into trousers that rode way too high. So far, the skinny Japanese detective had had little to say.

Knight I *had* seen around, mostly on evening news bulletins, striding purposefully around this crime scene or that in front of floodlights and news crews the way he had earlier that same evening. At a guess, Knight was slightly younger than me. He wore a faded *Hoodoo Gurus* t-shirt, three-quarter cargo pants and runners. Coincidentally, at that very moment there happened to be a *Gurus* anthology slotted into the player in my car back at the crime scene.

'White, no sugar,' Knight said as he placed a cup on the desk and slid it over.

'Thanks,' I said. 'Did you manage to track down Harry Hollis?'

Knight eyed me as he took his chair. Detective Inspector Hollis was his boss, or one of them at least. I had asked to see him. 'I've left a message for him,' the detective said. 'He's in the building somewhere.'

I glanced up at the camera, imagining that Hollis may, in fact, be one of the cops on the other side of it.

I nodded and waited for them to settle with their coffee and folders. When they were ready, Knight flipped his folder open to the page of notes he'd already started. Tezuka followed his lead and took a sip of his coffee.

'Okay,' Knight said. 'As I said earlier, we need you to run us through tonight's events with a view to establishing exactly what, from your point of view, went on out there, along with anything you can tell us about the events leading up to it.'

'Okay,' I said.

'Now, forensics are still on site and they know their stuff, mate, so you will need to be completely truthful with us. Their narrative needs to match yours and if it doesn't, well, we'll have some problems down the line.'

I nodded and reached for my coffee. 'I know.'

Knight opened his hands. 'Take your time.'

Tezuka suddenly leaned forward, read something and looked up again. 'You have no middle name.'

It was a statement more than a question and it threw me for a moment. I wasn't sure I'd heard him right.

Putting down my cup, I said, 'That's correct. I don't have a middle name.'

Tezuka nodded. 'Japanese people don't have middle names, either.'

'That's very interesting,' I said.

Tezuka smiled, turning to Knight, and said, 'Sorry. Continue.'

Detective Sergeant Knight threw his colleague a doleful look before saying, 'Thank you, detective,' and then looked at me.

After a quick glance at the blood on my hands, I said, 'Right' and proceeded to tell them everything, and for the whole time the screaming woman's words nagged at the back of my mind like bad news I didn't want to hear.

'What have you done?'

1

Jack Jackson.

Looked great in a page one by-line, that name.

But not today.

One of the political reporters had written the front-page splash. Poisonous copper concentrate had spilled all over the port while being loaded onto ships for export. According to an anonymous whistleblower, the powdery substance - containing traces of arsenic, uranium, lead and silica – went straight into Darwin Harbour during the cleanup operation. It wasn't the first time it had happened, either. The whole thing was scandalous and the *Northern Reporter* was going for the jugular.

Sipping coffee, I swung my legs up onto my desk and settled in to read the day's edition: the morning routine. Get in early, scan the news pages and wait for the day to happen. I re-read the only story I'd written the day before, a fluff piece on the hatching of a four-legged chicken, hoping the sub-editors hadn't screwed it up. They hadn't, which was a nice surprise.

And that's me, the hard-bitten hack fretting over a couple of paragraphs in a nothing story on a Tuesday morning when no one else is around.

It hadn't always been like that.

At 46, I'd been with the *Reporter* a little over twenty years, mostly on the police and court rounds. I was damned good at it too. Back then, I smoked two packs a day, grew a moustache and developed a beer belly, so I looked the part as well. But something happened, almost five years ago now, and the cops stopped talking to me. After that I moved over to general news. Didn't have a choice, really. I cut down on the smokes and the beer belly went away. So did the moustache. At first I missed that good old ambulance-chasing adrenalin rush but in the end wasn't that torn up at the way things had turned out, four-legged chickens notwithstanding. At least I could still pay the bills, and I had plenty of those.

Mind you, I *had* been offered better paying gigs around town, mostly in TV and radio newsrooms. I turned them down as a matter of routine. Call me a dinosaur – or worse - but I'm a newspaper man through and through. The things may be doomed but I fucking love them just the same, and it'll stay that way until they die or I do, whichever comes first.

I love Darwin, too. Australia's northernmost capital is home, and it's as screwy as hell, thanks in large part to a dangerous combination of pressing tropical heat and booze. News-wise, she's gold. As a place to live she's not too bad either. It's no Hong Kong or Singapore but we have swaying palms, glorious tropical sunsets and a relaxed lifestyle that allows you to mow your lawn in your underwear without fear of arrest. What's not to like about a place like that?

I finished my coffee and looked out the window.

The view from the *Northern Reporter's* editorial floor is quite something. Situated on a hill overlooking Darwin Harbour, the newspaper office sits halfway between the Central Business District and the city's commercial fishing precinct. Beyond the trawlers berthed at the fishing wharf below, a huge LNG tanker churned through flat green water, heading for the gas plant across the way.

The phone on the front desk rang.

The general editorial line.

I peered over the top of my cubicle, across workstations piled high with old newspapers and filthy coffee cups. Sub-editors are the messiest people on earth. Thanks to them newsrooms look busy even when they're deserted. There's a lingering odour too, of sweat and coffee and newsprint, but after a few years you don't tend to notice it.

The phone rang like an alarm going off. I sighed. It was only ten past eight. I glanced over my shoulder. The chief photographer was wheeling his bicycle towards his office at the back of the newsroom, ignoring both the ringing phone and my friendly good morning wave. Asshat.

I blew out air, folded the paper away, scooped up the handset, stabbed a button, said 'Newsroom' and almost lost an eardrum in the cannon fire of abuse that blasted down the line.

Her name was Nicky Chen and she wasn't happy.

2

'Fucking hell,' Nicky Chen said, blowing out a dense cloud of cigarette smoke. 'That story the cops put in the paper was absolute crap. They made it sound like I was sucking the guy's dick or something. I had my seat belt on, so it's impossible I'd be leaning over going the gobble unless he's hung like an elephant or I've got a neck like a bloody giraffe.'

Laughing, I shifted on the barstool and waved my notebook at the mark across her chest. The notebook was mostly for show. I had a digital recorder running in my front pocket. Despite what you may have heard, the number one rule of journalism is *accuracy, accuracy, accuracy.* Sometimes shorthand isn't enough, especially mine.

'Lucky you had a seatbelt on,' I said.

The deepening bruise ran like a nasty purple tattoo down and across from her left shoulder to the top of her generous right breast. It was almost the same colour as the lurid purple streak in her otherwise jet-black, shoulder length hair.

Nicky Chen whirled her beer bottle through the air. 'Bloody thing almost cut my tits off.'

Scotty took another photo.

'Aw, shit, mate,' Nicky said. 'That'll look fucking great in the paper.'

She laughed. Behind her, the bearded and tattooed barman – his name was Spud, just Spud – offered us a sly wink, possibly agreeing that that would indeed look fucking great in the paper.

'Sorry,' Scotty said.

Scotty wasn't sorry at all. The young photographer was enjoying this. Fresh-faced and fresh out of Melbourne, Scott Larson had been with the *Reporter* just two weeks and had already covered two murders and a non-fatal crocodile attack. The crocodile victim had escaped by poking that sucker right in the eyes, which Scotty thought was fantastic. Now, in a small Northern Territory town with the slightly oddball name of Mango Flat, Scott Larson was staring at Nicky Chen's breasts as though he'd never seen anything like them.

I could understand it. Ms. Chen oozed an almost palpable carnal aura, without even trying. For Scotty, the Chinese ancestry may have added an extra exotic flavour, albeit one that evaporated completely when the absurdly broad Australian accent escaped from her mouth. She was around 30 but she may have been younger, or older. It was hard to tell. She was an out of work hairdresser, which explained the purple streak and why she was at the pub at ten o'clock on a Tuesday morning.

Scotty and I had exchanged a quick this-is-going-to-be-good glance as soon as we'd spotted her sprawled at the bar. Dressed in a too-tight singlet and a faded sarong, she sat tearing open a packet of smokes. Spud didn't seem to mind, despite the smoking ban. Apart from a grizzled truck driver-type devouring a meat pie at one of the tables and a leathery old man in a cowboy hat at the far end of the bar, the place was empty. The truckie and the cowboy didn't seem to mind the smoke, either. Nicky was already on her third beer and that was okay too, because that was the way they did things out here.

Mango Flat is about forty minutes out of town, off the main highway, on the way to Kakadu National Park. It's a service town, mostly, surrounded by five-acre blocks close in and larger farms further out. The population is a mix of proper farmers, market gardeners, retirees, dope fiends and people with quad bikes and dogs the size of ponies. Nicky Chen, despite having all her teeth, looked like she fitted right in.

The beer and smokes and laughter did little to mask her unhappiness. The local cops had issued a press release the previous morning alleging some 'amorous activity' may have led to a single vehicle accident just out of Mango Flat the night before. The driver, they thought, may have been 'distracted' by his female passenger. There was a hint at oral sex. The *Reporter's* hard-arsed police reporter had re-written the release, playing it for laughs. The story had run as an inside page lead, coincidentally on the same page as my deformed chicken story.

Now, Nicky Chen wanted to 'set the bloody record straight', fearing it would take no time at all for the whole of Mango Flat to connect her badly bruised front end to the substantially more damaged front end of a 4WD belonging to local farmer.

'Look,' Nicky said. 'I admit it may have looked a bit suspect when the cops first got there. My boobs were all over the shop and I had ten bucks tucked into my top. They probably thought I was a hooker or something.' She chuckled and then a sudden thought seemed to strike her. 'Ten bucks is a bit cheap for a blow job, though, don't you think?' She let out a hearty, smoky laugh.

Scotty laughed too. 'For sure,' he said.

I could almost feel the hot, lusty blush rising behind his collar.

'And anyway,' Nicky continued, 'if I *was* giving him a blow job I'd just admit it and cop it on the bloody chin, you know.'

Now I laughed. 'I'll quote you on that. Is the guy a friend of yours?'

'Yeah, yeah, yeah. Well, no. Not really.' Nicky chuckled. 'I've seen him around, you know. Poor bastard was just giving me a lift home. I don't have a license at the moment.' She winked. 'Get it back in a month.'

'Well, he doesn't have one now either,' I said, grinning.

'Yeah, and his wife must be giving him all kinds of grief, too.' She laughed again, shaking her head in mock sympathy.

Smiling, I felt for the recorder. This was gold, pure gold. If any of the two hundred pictures Scotty had taken of Nicky Chen's breasts turned out okay, Murray Dowd, the *Reporter's* editor, would splash them all over the front page.

'Nicky?' Scotty said. 'Can I just get a couple more shots of you with -'

'Hang on,' I said.

Over at his table, the truck driver had frozen, the last piece of pie poised mid-air before his open mouth. He had noticed it too - a low, subterranean rumble. We all turned to look out through the doors as the first jolt thudded through the ground beneath the pub. The entire building shuddered, rattling glasses and bottles and furniture. The first bump passed quickly and settled into a deep, almost rhythmic shaking.

'What the hell is that?' Scotty said, blinking.

'Earth tremor,' I told him, getting to my feet to slap a reassuring hand on his shoulder. 'Don't worry. We get them all the time.'

Scotty looked around, gripping his camera gear. Overhead, the whirling ceiling fans chopped from side to side, whining like rotor blades.

'Holy snapping duck shit,' Nicky said, hanging onto the bar.

A second large jolt, as big as the first, coursed through the building. A bottle smashed to the floor behind the bar.

Spud swore.

In a moment, the tremor subsided, rumbling away as quickly as it had arrived. I imagined I could hear it go, grinding away like a giant jet engine fading into the distance. The whole thing had lasted just ten or fifteen seconds. The truck driver scoffed down his pie and pushed his chair back, getting up to leave. The old man in the cowboy hat hadn't reacted at all. He took a nonchalant sip of his beer.

'Shit,' Scotty said. 'Is that it? It's gone?'

'I think so,' I said. 'That was a bigger one than usual, though.'

'Jesus Christ,' Scotty said. 'I knew about the cyclones and crocodiles but nobody told me there'd be bloody earthquakes.'

'Fuck a fucking duck,' Nicky said. 'That *was* a big one. Another beer, Spuddy.'

'Jesus, Nick, I've got to clean this up.'

'You've got all bloody day to do that, mate.'

Spud reached into a chest freezer behind the bar. 'I hope you didn't piss off your ghost, Nick. I told you not to bring him here.'

Nicky shot him a look, waving her cigarette in the air.

'Spuddy…'

I lifted an eyebrow at her.

With an unapologetic smile, Spud handed over the beer, shrugged, and made to clean up the mess. Nicky inspected the bottle briefly before looking back up.

I smiled at her like a shark.

'What ghost?'

'What a woman,' Scotty said when we were back in the car.

'Too much woman for you, my friend,' I said, fiddling with the dashboard vents. The work car's air-conditioning was playing up. Typical.

'You're the one who got her phone number,' Scotty pointed out.

'My interest is purely professional,' I said. I gave up on the vents and started the car.

'She was eyeing you off.'

'You think so?'

Scotty looked at me. 'You missed that?'

'Apparently.'

He glanced back at the pub. 'You believe any of that shit?'

'About the blow job or the ghost?'

Scotty laughed. 'The ghost. I believe her about the blow job.'

'Yeah, me too.' I peered through the windshield at downtown Mango Flat. It wasn't much to look at. Apart from the pub, there was a service station outside of which a stood a tall fiberglass crocodile wearing a cowboy hat, a small supermarket and a bait and tackle shop, all streaky with red dust. I watched as a road-train thundered past on the bitumen, a fuel tanker hot on its heels.

'Well,' I said. 'I've been at this a long time and it's not the first ghost story I've ever heard.'

Scotty frowned. 'Seriously?'

'Sure. We're a tabloid. We love ghosts. And aliens. And babies with tails.'

'Okay. Have you ever heard of a ghost chucking knives around like that? That's a bit special.'

I snorted, nodding at the pub. 'No, but that's probably why she's in there and not at home. Mind you, the *really* interesting thing is that they called in a priest. That's the story right there. We just need to find him.'

'Think she'll come through with his name?'

I winked. 'She has the hots for me. She'll call.'

Scotty laughed. 'Right,' he said, gazing down the road at the cowboy crocodile. 'I'm surprised that thing didn't fall over. Man, this place is fucking unbelievable.'

I put the car in gear and wiped sweat from my face with a sleeve. 'Tell me about it,' I said.

3

'Look, I don't know how many more ways you want me to say this,' the seismologist said on the other end of the line. He was starting to sound irritated. 'The Timor Trench hasn't moved in five million years. The likelihood of Darwin being wiped out in a tsunami, right at this moment, is zip.'

'That's good to know,' I said, thumping out the quote on my keyboard with two fingers, a little disappointed the tsunami angle was going nowhere.

'And again, as I said, the tremors you experience up there, like this one, generally originate in the Banda Sea, and the quakes there are usually quite deep.'

I knew a little about the geology of the Banda Sea. I'd written this same story a dozen times, and spoken to numerous GeoScience boffins. The earthquakes occurred hundreds of kilometres to our north, on the other side of Indonesia, at a distance that would normally make them pass unnoticed on the Australian mainland. However, the weird orientation of the fault-lines in the area allowed seismic waves to funnel very efficiently towards Northern Australia.

'Okay, but this one was larger than usual, though, wasn't it? I can't remember anything over seven before. Just about everyone felt it.' I swapped the handset to my other shoulder and continued typing.

'Not unusually big, no. They really aren't *that* uncommon. As the technology improves, we're getting more precise readings, that's all. And you've got to keep in mind Darwin is growing. A larger population will naturally lead to more people feeling these things. You've also started building a lot of high-rise residential towers and such up there. Tremors from a 7.1 will undoubtedly give them a fair old shake.'

'You've got that right. We heard one of them was evacuated.'

'It would certainly give you a good old rattle, that's for sure.'

I scrolled through the notes on my screen. 'Yeah. Listen, I think that might give me enough to go on for now. Thanks for speaking to me.'

'Not a problem.'

'Just to double check, it's Brian with an *i*, yeah?'

'Yes,' the seismologist said. 'And Smith the way you'd normally spell it.'

I smiled at the sarcasm. 'Okay, Brian. Thanks very much for that.'

'No problem.'

I hung up, rubbed at my forehead and looked out the window. A light haze shimmered in the heat over the harbour. I imagined the tremor may have sent some dust swirling into the air. Beyond the haze, a line of smudgy clouds hugged the horizon.

It had just turned April, which, like September, is a weird kind of month. In April, the monsoonal wet season starts to bleed away into the dry. It's a painfully slow process but eventually the humidity drops, the skies clear, and the chances of a cyclone whirling into action somewhere off the coast get slimmer by the day. Pretty soon, Darwin would be paradise on Earth, at least for a few months. September is the opposite; the humidity begins to climb, paradise becomes a happy memory and by October people are going mad.

Seated at the cubicle next to mine, Beth Harvey swore, then laughed, then stood up. She was in her early 20s, slightly overweight and dressed badly. A swarm of pimples clustered on her chin like tiny red volcanoes. For a kid, Harvey wasn't a bad writer. She rarely spoke to me. She'd probably heard things. Despite that, she looked at me as if she was bursting to talk and anybody would do.

'What's up?' I asked.

She waved at her screen and chuckled. 'Some kid in a takeaway shop stuck his dick in a hot chicken. He's in hospital.'

Not a lot surprises me about the good people of Darwin but that did. 'Run that by me again?'

'He's paying a heavy price for having sexual relations with a hot chook.' Harvey laughed. 'The little sicko's mates have posted the story all over social media.' She laughed one more time and sat down again, abruptly ending the conversation.

My phone bleeped. It was an internal call.

'Yep?'

'Up front for a sec, Jacko,' Murray Dowd said. I peered over my partition towards the front of the newsroom. By now, the place was pumping with bad coffee and worse language. Dowd waved from the front desk. He looked unhappy, which didn't mean much. He always looked unhappy. 'Cantankerous' is not a word I'd use in day to day conversation very often but it suited him to a T.

Murray Dowd was on the other side of 60, short, pudgy and famously old school. He'd written the book on tabloid newspapers and delighted in telling fresh-meat journalism graduates to forget everything they'd ever heard in lecture halls because most of it was crap with no place in the real world. I liked him.

The old man's eyebrows bristled over his sagging, bulldog face like a pair of worn-out scrubbing brushes as I made my way up.

'You're looking very cantankerous today, Murray.'

'Shove your big words up your arse, Jackson,' Dowd said. He gestured at the dozens of thumbnail images filling his screen. 'Why have I got fifty thousand fucking pictures of this head job woman?'

I grinned. 'I think young Mr Larson was quite taken with her bubbling personality.'

'I bet he was,' Dowd said. 'Rankine's got his nose out of joint, by the way. Just so you know.'

I shrugged. 'What's his problem now?'

Paul Rankine was the hard-arse who'd taken over the police round from me. He'd written the laugh-it-up story on Nicky Chen's crash. I didn't like him one bit, possibly due to his supreme over-confidence, which came across as a sort of casual arrogance more than anything else, but also because he reminded me, in some ways, of me. Also, he was a fierce protector of his turf and we'd had more than one explosive newsroom custody battle over this story or that. Usually, I'd let him get so close to boiling point that blood vessels pulsed beneath his forehead like alien worms before giving in.

'He went ballistic as soon as she heard you were out there,' Dowd said. 'Thinks you should've passed it over.'

'It's not exactly a police story now,' I said. 'Do I need to talk to him?'

'Up to you but I'm obliged to remind you we no longer allow fist fights in the newsroom.' He waved back at his screen. 'How are you doing this?'

'As straight as I can,' I said. 'The quotes will carry it. I'll need to censor it a bit, though. She's a very colourful young lady.'

'Right,' he said. 'Pic's going across the top of one, the whole seven columns, pointing to three. Quake's the lead.'

'It was a tremor not a quake.'

'I don't care. Are we all going to die or what?'

'Not today. By the way, you may need to re-think the front. Beth's got a corker on a kid who stuck his dick in a hot chicken.'

'Fuck. I'm burdened with riches today.' The old editor flicked his hand. 'Off you go. Get yours done. Chop, chop.'

'But wait,' I said with a nod at the pictures on his screen. 'There's more. She lives in a haunted house.'

Dowd said nothing.

I shrugged. 'She's sharing some farmhouse out at Mango Flat with a bunch of other people. She said they've had some weird shit going on out there.' I made air quotes when I said *weird shit*. 'Pots and pans moving around by themselves, shoes going walkabout, and one morning they woke up to find a carving knife stuck in a wall. It's freaking them out so much they called in a priest.' I smiled.

'Fuck off,' Dowd said, glancing down at Nicky Chen on his screen. 'Is she for real?'

'Apparently.'

'You get this priest's name?'

'Not yet. She wasn't there when he turned up. One of the other people in the house organized it. And something freaked him out so badly he's refusing to go back.'

Dowd pursed his lips.

'Anyway,' I said, 'she's going to try to con her housemates into talking to us. This thing is already the talk of the Mango Flat pub. TV and radio could get hold of it any time.'

Dowd held up a hand for me to stop. 'Okay. Go for it. Let Mike know what you're doing. Please.'

Mike Cooke. The *Reporter's* Chief of Staff. He was a pain in the arse but I liked him. It was his job to keep tabs on what everyone was doing. Most of the time I was doing my own thing, which sometimes sent him marching in to Dowd to complain. It annoyed him, too, that I made fun of his hair, which was so long and luxuriant he was often mistaken for an arriving rock star at the airport.

I said 'Will do' and headed back to my desk, via the stairs down to the staff canteen.

I needed a sausage roll.

4

I pulled into the driveway just after eight and parked my Toyota Yiros under the house. It wasn't really called a Toyota Yiros, of course. That's what Jessica used to call it. The greasy smell of petrol and freshly cut grass hung in the air as I went up the front stairs. Next door, Eric had mown his lawn again. He was a little OCD that way.

It was too late to call the kids on a school night, although I had an idea they might be all hyped up about the tremor and possibly still awake. I decided to let it go anyway. The in-laws wouldn't be happy if I did get them up. Jessica's parents lived a couple of suburbs away, and they had been very quick to think me capable of murder, so our relationship was not exactly a first-class one. They thought I'd killed Jessica. The cops thought so too, which is why they'd stopped talking to me.

Jessica had been missing for almost five years ago now. Ernie and Margaret had had the kids pretty much ever since. I had them one weekend a month. It was a mutually agreed arrangement, in the best interests of the children, etcetera, blah de blah. Max was 10, Susie 6. They were good kids but the once-a-month thing had already turned them into little strangers. Right then, I knew, there was not a lot I could do about that.

After flicking on the lights and ceiling fans, I locked the front door and dumped the keys, my phone and the recorder into a bowl of household detritus on the side table just inside. My wallet went into a drawer, from which I took a packet of cigarettes and a lighter. I stood there for a moment, looking around.

The house was a stock standard tropical elevated: pretty much a rectangular box set on concrete pillars to catch any meagre breeze that might happen by. They don't build them like that anymore. The bedrooms and bathroom were at one end, accessed by a hallway, with the open plan lounge and kitchen at the other. Each room featured floor to ceiling louvered windows. Downstairs, where I parked the car, were an open laundry and a small bricked-in workshop which doubled as a cyclone shelter.

Nothing appeared to have fallen over during the tremor. Jessica had done most of the interior design and I hadn't bothered changing anything. Bamboo blinds covered the windows. Much of the furniture was teak or mango wood from Indonesia. Scatter cushions from India covered the Balinese daybed we used for a lounge. There were a couple of lamps from Vietnam and Bali, along with an assortment of Buddhas in stone and wood placed strategically around the lounge room, still standing.

The fans weren't doing much more than pushing warm air around so I wandered into the kitchen and selected a beer from the fridge. The humidity had eased off a tad but I'd noticed lightning stuttering in the distance on the drive home. The wet season storms were still hanging around, like troublemakers who wouldn't leave after a party.

I walked over to the daybed, hunted for the television remote under the cushions and flicked on Sky News, more out of habit than anything else. Most evenings I caught the local bulletins at work.

That night, both the local commercial station and the ABC had led with the port pollution story the *Reporter* had broken that morning. Heads were going to roll, quite possibly starting with the one belonging to the port's CEO.

I headed out the back, where a decaying deck overlooked a desperately overgrown palm garden strewn with rotting fronds and thick with mosquitoes. A Balinese *bale* stood in one corner, its thatched roof half rotted away and hanging in shredded clumps. The paved entertaining area was black with mould. The garden had been Jessica's domain too. Now I didn't have the time for it, or I simply didn't care anymore. Something like that.

I *had* thought about selling and moving somewhere smaller. Financially, hanging on to the house was a tough gig. A large slice of my pay went on the mortgage, of course, and I slipped as much as I could to Ernie and Margaret for the kids. A cleaner came in every Friday, but that was okay because I paid her next to nothing. Cam was a Vietnamese refugee who had arrived as a young woman in the first wave of boat people to hit Darwin in the late 70s. That was all I knew about her. I'd found her through one of the sales execs at work. Cam spoke little English, which made her ripe for exploitation, the exec had assured me. Sometimes I worried about that. It wasn't a good look. My exploited cleaning lady was a hunchback.

Despite the obvious financial burden, letting go of the house was a big call. I told myself I was keeping it for the kids and that sounded good enough. In the end, it was all I had to give them.

Slumping into one of the low teak chairs on the deck, I lit my cigarette and blew out smoke. Sirens wailed in the distance, an outboard motor burbled away in somebody's yard, dogs barked and a lone frog abruptly piped up, hoping for rain and sex: the ambient sounds of night-time Darwin.

Next door, Eric slipped into his back yard pool with a splash and started doing laps. He was an old Navy guy, long retired, who also lived alone. He'd lost his wife around ten years earlier to a soil-borne bacterium called *Meliodosis*. It's a tropical thing. It rises to the surface during the wet season to lurk in stagnant puddles and such, and waits to kill people who enjoy gardening, so I was pretty safe.

Eric and I sometimes caught up for a beer but we hadn't in a while. As a young naval rating, he'd been on *HMAS Voyager* when the *Melbourne* had cut her in two in 1964. A while back, after years of legal stoushing, he'd scored over a hundred thousand dollars in compensation. He'd blown half of it putting the pool in. If there's one thing you learn in newspapers, it's that everyone has a story, even the neighbours.

Another part of Eric's story may also have been that he was screwing my wife while my beer belly and moustache were out laughing it up with cops and lawyers every night. I never knew for sure but they were so ... *easy* ... together that I had to wonder. The kids were little. I was never around. Eric was always ready to help out, in one way or another. And despite pushing 70, he was tanned and movie-star handsome, and supremely fit in a no-Viagra-required sort of way. Throw in a slow, steamy night or two with no husband around and ... well, anything could happen.

I'd aired my suspicions to the cops in the days following Jessica's disappearance but I had no idea if they'd followed up. In the intervening years, Eric hadn't raised it with me once, at any rate.

Listening to Eric swim, I realized there was still something in my back pocket. The beer coaster Nicky Chen had scribbled her number on. I had to admit I'd been more than a little intrigued by her bubbling personality myself. I wondered if Scotty had been right, even though she hadn't called back after all.

Flicking my cigarette out into the garden, I went back in for my phone and entered her number under 'Contacts'.

5

'The biggest mistake newspapers ever made,' Murray Dowd had declared after a particularly long lunch one day, 'was jumping on the internet before we even knew what the fucking thing was. We cut our own throats. Five, ten years we're gone. For good.'

He was probably right but despite his misgivings, the *Northern Reporter* had a significant web presence, led by a team of young hipsters who mostly ignored him. By nine the following morning they were on the verge of high-fiving one another over how fast Nicky Chen's profanity laden denial of sexual impropriety had blasted across the internet. (Dowd had decided to hold hot chicken kid for the next edition, and I had no doubt the unfortunate young man and his dick would blast across the internet in similar fashion.) The paper's social media feeds were on fire, and soon the national news sites had picked up the story too. It *was* gold but it probably wouldn't last long. The web measured the lifespan of news in hours, sometimes even less than that. As far as the new media went, Nicky Chen's story had a fair to middling chance of becoming yesterday's news today.

Elbows on my desk, I darkly massaged my temples as I worried that she might not call back after all. Under the headline *Crash Woman Denies Amorous Activities*, Nicky's front-page photograph featured a speech balloon, put there by Murray Dowd, containing the words: *I Did Not Have Sexual Relations with That Man!*

There was a chance, I suspected, that Nicky Chen might not take that very well.

I played with my phone, wondering if I should give her a call. Probably. The Mango Flat ghost story was dead in the water otherwise.

A shadow fell over my cubicle, accompanied by a hefty waft of depressingly familiar aftershave. Paul Rankine was a big guy, with military-cropped hair and, so the story went, a personal trainer. I kind of believed that particular story.

'Paul,' I said with a fuck-off smile.

'Jack', he said, puffing out his chest in a manner that was also depressingly familiar. He leaned in, resting a cylindrical forearm on my wall. He'd swished with a minty mouthwash that morning as well, and for that I was thankful. 'Listen, mate, I know you think you can do whatever the fuck you like around here but enough is enough. Next time you steal a fucking story off me, I'll have something to say and I won't be saying it to Murray. It'll go much fucking higher.'

'No problem,' I said.

That didn't stop him. 'I know the old man has some sort of hard-on for you Jack,' he went on, 'but he's not going to be around forever. Best you fucking keep that in mind, mate.'

I looked away over the top of my cubicle with an exaggerated frown. 'Murray has a hard-on for me? I wish you'd told me that when he was twenty years younger.'

'Fuck you, Jack.'

'Fuck you, Paul. I've got work to do.'

He heaved himself upright. 'Just make sure it's your own fucking work, mate.'

'No problem.' I watched him storm off and then called up Nicky Chen's number on my mobile. Next door, Beth Harvey let out a polite little cough. She had heard the whole thing. Oh, well.

I hit the little green phone icon. Nicky answered after a couple of rings.

'Nicky, it's Jack Jackson, from the *Reporter.*'

'Oh. Fuck. Hello.' She did sound a little pissed off. No surprise there.

'Hi. How are you going? Have you seen today's paper yet?'

'Fuck, no, but I've heard about it. Thanks very much. I didn't expect to be all over the bloody front page.'

I closed my eyes. 'Yeah, sorry about that. I don't get much of a say in what happens to the stories after I've written them. The editors do all that.'

This is the standard reporter's defence. The editor/subs did it. Most of the time people are happy enough with that.

'Right,' Nicky said, somewhat doubtfully.

I decided to dive on in. 'Listen, did you get a chance to find out that priest's name for me? I'd still like to do a piece on you guys, if you'll be in it.'

She didn't reply. For a moment, I thought I'd lost her. Then she said, 'I haven't had a chance to speak to the others yet. I don't think they'd be too keen on it. Things are already fucked up enough around here.'

I heard some commotion in the background, as though someone else had just bustled into the room, and then a baby started crying. Nicky covered the phone with her hand and there followed a brief, muffled conversation.

She came back on and said, 'Kath thinks his name is Charlie or something. Guy's a hundred years old and rode up on some old motorbike, if that helps.'

I blinked in surprise. 'That's great, Nicky. Thanks for that. Can I call you back later? I'd really appreciate it if you could run it by the others for me.'

She thought about that. 'Okay,' she said.

We finished up and I leaned back in my chair.

Father Charlie.

I should have known.

Darwin's Central Business District straddles a peninsular that juts out into the harbour like a misshapen hammerhead. Pretty much surrounded by water on three sides, a leisurely stroll can take you from one side to the other in around ten minutes, weather permitting. I preferred the leisurely stroll option whenever I had something on in town, mostly because it got me out of the office for longer than necessary.

The morning steamed with humidity and I'd worked up a thin sweat by the time I spotted Father Charlie's 1967 Norton Atlas 750 in the tree-lined car park outside Saint Mary's. Sunlight broke through the canopy to flare off the chrome exhaust pipes. Light flared off his polished helmet too, where it rested unsecured on the seat.

Father Charlie Foyle had been Jessica's parish priest. I wasn't Catholic so before he would agree to marry us the old man had insisted I sit through a series of lessons in Catholicism. The experience was good-humoured and mostly bearable but the fun didn't really start until lesson six, which was on how to create more Catholics. Father Charlie thought the Billings Method might do the trick, and he drew an intricate diagram of how it might work. I had to admit the guy drew a mean sperm, if nothing else.

Father Charlie rode a mean bike too. Not long after the wedding, I had written a piece on his passion for motorcycles. There was something quite *spiritual* about going Hell for leather down the highway at 180, he'd said with a wistful grin. He had donned his battered kit for the accompanying photo: leathers, gloves, the works. It was gold.

I pulled up near the front steps and looked at my watch. As luck would have it, Father Charlie was about to head in to the cathedral from his digs out in the suburbs when I'd called. Meeting with the bean counters, he'd explained.

I slid my hands into my pockets and loitered. After a few minutes, Father Charlie emerged with a bulging folder tucked under one arm. He gave me a wave and said goodbye to someone standing just inside the doors. Then he came shuffling down the steps.

'Jack,' Father Charlie said, extending his hand. 'It's great to see you. Your phone call was a very nice surprise.'

I took his hand and said, 'It's been a while, Father.'

It *had* been a while. Father Charlie had aged markedly since I'd last seen him. Six years ago? Maybe more. He seemed smaller than I remembered, hunched over as if something might be pressing down on his shoulders. Behind the thick glasses, the old man's eyes were red-rimmed and glistening. He hadn't shaved in a while either. His face bristled with tough, white whiskers. Father Charlie placed a hand on my shoulder and peered into my face.

'How have you been?' he said.

'Oh. Good.'

'No, really, Jack. *How have you been?*'

The intensity of the question took me by surprise. He genuinely wanted to know. Father Charlie knew about Jessica, of course. Everybody did. I *had* been the talk of the town for a while. In fact, Father Charlie had phoned the house a week or so after Jessica's disappearance to see how I was getting on, even though I may have turned out to be a cold-blooded murderer at any moment. It was the last time I'd spoken to him.

'I'm fine,' I said. 'Really. I'm good.'

'And the children?'

'Good. They're good, too. Growing up. You know.'

The old priest smiled as though that was just what he wanted to hear and dropped his hand. 'I'm always here for you, Jack. You know that. And the children too.'

'I know, Father. I appreciate that.'

Father Charlie nodded thoughtfully and then waved his folder at the street. 'Do you have time to walk with me? My favourite coffee shop is just up the road.' He threw a thumb over his shoulder. 'Just between you and me the stuff they serve in there is rubbish.'

I laughed. 'Of course.'

Despite his age, the old priest set a sprightly pace. 'So, what can I do for you, Jack?'

'I'm chasing a pretty strange story. I've got a feeling you might know something about it.'

I noticed a little hitch in his stride but he pressed on. 'This is about that thing out at Mango Flat, am I right?'

'Yep.'

Father Charlie let out a little chuckle. 'I was wondering how long it would be before somebody from the press got wind of that. This town is too small for secrets.'

'The bike gave you away,' I told him. 'How's the old girl going?'

The priest grinned. 'Like the clappers. How many other people know about this? I mean, media people?'

'Just myself and the editor at the moment, and a photographer.'

Father Charlie stopped for a moment, smiling. 'Well, it was bound to get out sooner or later. Pretty difficult to keep a spinning crucifix quiet, eh?'

I stared at him. 'I beg your pardon?'

6

Squeezed between a tattoo parlour and a seedy-looking Chinese massage place, the cafe was more upmarket than its location might otherwise suggest. Inside was all chrome and terracotta, with trendy recycled timber tabletops and chillout music playing in the background. The display counter offered a range of salads and gluten free cakes. The people behind the counter were young and hip. I hadn't been there before and was a little surprised an elderly Catholic priest would peg it as a favourite hangout joint. Father Charlie was kind of cool, though.

He ordered a cappuccino. I went for an iced coffee. After the Irish backpacker waitress had threaded her way back to the counter, Father Charlie placed his hands flat on his folder where it rested on the table and leaned forward, wet eyes darting about like a conspirator.

'Who told you about it?' he asked.

'I've been speaking to Nicky,' I said. 'She lives out at the house.'

'Sorry. I don't know her.'

'She's on the front of today's paper.'

He looked surprised. 'Talking about their problem?'

'No, no. Unrelated matter. I was interviewing her about something else when the ghost thing came up.'

Father Charlie opened his hands. 'Sorry, Jack. I don't read the paper, and if I did I'd only read the comics.'

I smiled. 'Probably better you don't know about it anyway.'

'Oh,' he said. 'Does she know you're talking to me?'

'Yes, she's okay with it.'

He studied me for a moment. 'How much do you actually know about what's going on out there? You seemed quite surprised about the crucifix.'

'Nicky neglected to mention that. She isn't too keen on going into too much detail until she's discussed it with the other people living out there, which is fair enough. She did tell me their shoes were being lined up on the front steps every night, and that stuff from the kitchen was turning up all over the house. And that they found a knife stuck in a wall.'

Father Charlie thought for a moment, scratching at his stubble.

'Okay. I'll tell you what happened, Jack,' he said. 'As a favour. But I don't want my name in the paper. The Bishop will have conniptions. I haven't mentioned it to anybody.'

'Fair enough,' I said. 'How did you end up out there?'

Father Charlie threaded his fingers together on top of his folder. 'I know one of the young men living out there. Murph. That's not his real name, mind you. It's Harry or Tony or something. First time I met him I told him he looked more like a Murph than a Harry or a Tony. He's short and round. Red hair. Has a long beard these days. Looks a bit like a gnome. He's a Murph.' He laughed. 'Anyway, the nickname stuck and everybody started calling him Murph. A lot of people don't even know that's not his real name.'

'That's funny,' I said.

Father Charlie nodded. 'Indeed. Anyway, I've known him for years. He was a troubled kid. You know the story. Fell in with the wrong crowd. Drugs. Alcohol. All that. Lots of problems at home. When he was 16 or 17, he smashed up his parent's house. That's when the law and welfare people got involved. I met him while he was in juvenile detention.' Father Charlie paused, glancing away out the front window for a moment. 'It took a very long time to win him over, let me tell you.'

'I can imagine.'

Turning back, he said, 'Anyway, eventually we started to click. After he got out, I had him around the church, fixing things up, looking after the grounds, that sort of thing. He fell into the odd job here and there. He's very good with his hands, you know. Helped me strip the Norton one year and put her back together again.'

The waitress came back with our drinks and a wan smile.

'And, what, Murph lives out at the house?' I asked after she'd gone.

'Yes.' Father Charlie dipped his spoon into the cappuccino froth, swirling it around. 'He's the caretaker. Lives on site in a caravan, not in the house itself. I don't know who owns the place but it's probably the biggest mango plantation out that way. Must be five hundred trees out there, at least. Be worth an absolute fortune. The place goes bananas during mango season, apparently. Murph says they get 20 or 30 fruit pickers camping out there for weeks at a time. Last season was quite a good one. Bumper crop.'

I already knew that. I'd written the obligatory official-start-of-the-mango-season story back in October. In a good year, the Territory's mango industry accounts for around half the country's total production, so it's a big deal. I frowned at my iced coffee. It didn't look good. 'How many people actually live out there, do you know?'

'Well, now, I don't really know. The day I visited there were, let's see, a young couple with a baby, a tall fellow covered in tattoos, and Murph. Apparently there are some more but they weren't there at the time. The owner rents out the house so there are people around all the time, you know, for added security. It's a cutthroat business, apparently.'

'Crowded house,' I said. 'So, what, Murph just rang you out of the blue one day and said he had ghost trouble?'

Father Charlie laughed. 'He wasn't that up front about it. He turned up at the church one afternoon and asked me to go out and bless the place. He did seem a little agitated about something but I didn't ask what it was. Murph is the sort of person who won't tell you anything until he's good and ready. Keeps to himself, you know. Anyway, I decided it gave me a good excuse to take the bike for a run. Knock the cobwebs out.'

I watched him try his coffee. It was okay. Father Charlie licked froth from his lips.

'So, what happened?' I asked.

'Oh, I got out there and the story just spilled out of them.' He sipped at his coffee again. 'They *really* needed someone to talk to, I think. It began about three months ago. Somebody started rearranging all their shoes in the middle of the night. Didn't matter if they'd kicked them off in their own rooms or wherever, they'd get up in the morning to find them all collected on the front steps, neatly lined up.' He paused, possibly for dramatic effect. 'Not long after that the thing with the pots and pans started.'

I nodded for him to go on.

Father Charlie went on, 'I suggested someone was probably just fooling around but the young lady - I think her name was Kath - said after the first few times it happened they started locking their bedroom doors at night. Someone was still managing to get into their rooms and take the damned shoes.'

'That's a bit odd.'

Father Charlie held up a hand. 'That's not all. Other objects started moving around in the night. One morning they got up to find all their music discs spread out on the lounge room floor. A few times time they discovered all the kitchen drawers and cupboards open. And then there was that business with the knife. That spooked them more than anything.'

I looked at him. 'No wonder they were freaking out.'

Father Charlie nodded. 'Indeed. Now, up until that point, they were thinking it *was* probably just someone fooling around with them. The house is full of people all the time. I think, going on the lifestyle they lead, it's a bit of a party house, with people coming and going at all hours. That was the impression I had, at least. I suggested it was still possible that it was all a prank. Then Murph told me about the stones.'

'Stones?'

'From the front yard, they said. It's mostly a dirt track down to the house but there's a large gravelled parking area out the front. The gravel's quite loose. I almost lost the bike when I rode into it. Anyway, at first the gravel was landing on the roof, always during the night or early hours of the morning, as though someone was throwing handfuls of it up there. They'd run outside to see what was going on but they could never see anyone.' The priest stopped again, sipping coffee. 'Then the stones started falling from the ceiling. *Inside* the house.'

I leaned back in my chair in surprise. 'What? Out of thin air?'

Father Charlie nodded and opened his hands. 'That's what they said.'

'You're kidding,' I said.

'Jack, I'm a Catholic priest. We don't kid. They'd be sitting around watching TV or having a meal and, ding, next moment there's stones falling on them.'

'Now that's just bizarre.'

'Yes. Very.' He looked into his cup. 'So, that was the situation I found when I got out there. Most of what is going on I can rationally explain in one way or another but those stones, they are something else. I had some very confused young people on my hands, let me tell you.'

I sipped at my iced coffee. It *was* bad but I decided to drink it anyway.

'What happened with the crucifix?'

Father Charlie drained his cup, placed it back on the table and shook his head. 'That I could not explain. At the time, that is. I'd finished doing my thing. I'd gone around the whole house, which took quite a while. The place is huge. It's old, too. Be a fair bit of history there, I think.' He paused for a moment, as if to let me think about that. 'So, afterwards they offered me coffee and we sat in the lounge chatting. I placed my Bible, with the crucifix on top, on the coffee table. We were just sitting there talking when my crucifix started spinning around, right there on the table.'

'Jesus.'

The priest laughed. 'That's what I said. Damnedest thing I've ever seen.'

'Oh. Sorry,' I said.

'That's okay, Jack. Everybody who was in the house at the time saw it happen. One or two of them were doing quite a bit more than using the Saviour's name in vain, let me tell you.'

'How long did it go on for?'

The old priest waved a hand. 'Oh, only a few seconds, really. And it wasn't spinning *that* fast. I was thinking about that on the ride home. It was a hot day. All the ceiling fans in the place were going full blast. It could have been the wind from the fans, which is what I should have told them. But I was caught up in the moment, so to speak.'

I looked at him for a long moment. 'Don't take this the wrong way, Father, but Nicky said you were quite upset about it and you're refusing to go back out there.'

Father Charlie's moist eyes blinked behind his lenses. 'Oh. No. That's not right. It took me by surprise, for sure, but as I said, there *is* a plausible explanation. As for not going back there, well, they may have misunderstood. I had blessed the house. Apart from that, there wasn't much else I could do. I suggested they get in touch with someone with a little more experience in these things.'

'Such as?'

'I mentioned paranormal investigators.'

That was a surprise.

Father Charlie grinned. 'Don't look so surprised, Jack. I've been around for a very long time and I've seen some extraordinary things. I can't explain a good number of them. I've heard a lot of terrific ghost stories too. But in a case like this, you don't just go phone the exorcist. What these young men and women need is for somebody to go out and work out what's really going on.'

'Do you actually know any paranormal investigators?'

The old priest threw up his hands and grinned. 'Not personally, no.'

I eyed him for a moment, toying with my empty glass.

'So, do you know if they've been in touch with anyone?'

Father Charlie leaned forward over his folder. 'No idea, but I strongly advised Murph that they should. A few days after my visit, he turned up at the church again. He'd brought a camera with him to show me a photo.'

I stopped playing with my glass. 'Of what?'

Father Charlie drummed his fingers on his folder. 'A name had appeared on the bathroom floor the night before, made out of the stones from outside.'

'A name?'

'Yes. *Gary.*'

'Gary?'

'Gary,' the old priest said, opening his hands over his folder again. 'And nobody out at that house knows any Garys, alive *or* dead.'

Crossing the road and dodging cars, I was on the phone as soon as I'd handed Father Charlie a business card and said goodbye. Nicky answered after a few seconds.

'Nicky, it's Jack Jackson again. How you going?'

'Yeah, good.'

I made it to the other side of the road alive and headed in the direction of the office. 'Listen, Nicky, I'd really, really like to come out and have a chat to you guys. I just spoke to your priest. It's a wild story. I'm going to knock out a short piece on what happened while he was out there. No names or anything. Nothing that can identify him, you, or anybody else, or where you are.'

She didn't say anything.

'You there?'

'Yeah, I'm here,' she said. 'I still haven't had a chance to talk to the others yet.'

'I'd really appreciate it if you could.'

I heard her let out a sigh. 'Well, after today, I could probably do without any more fucking publicity for a while.'

'I fully understand but I can leave you out of it, if you like,' I said. 'I just need one person, that's all, someone willing to speak to me on the record. Maybe be in a photo.'

Nicky didn't reply.

'Hello? Nicky?'

'Fuck it,' she said. 'Okay. It's my house.'

I had to press the phone hard against my ear as a car with no muffler rumbled by. 'What did you say? You own the place?'

'No, no,' Nicky said. 'But it's my name on the bloody lease. Yeah, come on out. Friday arvo would be best, around five. We should all be here. Come and have a beer with us.'

'Great. That's fantastic. Okay if I bring a photographer with me?'

'Fuck. Sure.'

'Excellent. How do I find the place?'

She gave me a set of complex directions. I thanked her again, said goodbye and slipped my phone back in my pocket.

This was going to be gold.

Back in the office, I thumped out a dozen paragraphs on Father Charlie's spinning crucifix and filed the story in the general news basket. Then I waltzed over to Mike Cooke's desk to fill him in, as per Murray Dowd's instructions.

Surprised that I was actually talking to him, Cooke called up the story and read it, frowning at his screen.

'Ghosts, Jack? You're kidding me.'

'True story,' I said. 'And there's a lot more to it. It's a good yarn.' I nodded at his screen. 'But we should probably hold this one until Friday so nobody else knows we're chasing it. I'm going out there to talk to them proper Friday afternoon. I'll need a photographer.'

Cooke looked at me. 'Okay,' he said. 'Book one now. And thanks for letting me know what you're doing for a change.'

'You're welcome, Mike. One of them is a hairdresser, you know, if you need any help with that,' I said, pointing at his hair.

'Piss off, Jack,' he said with no humour at all.

7

Friday evening. It was getting dark and we were having trouble finding the place. Mango Flat's rural back roads, I learned, do not come with a lot of signage. Maybe the locals had shot them up so often they'd given up replacing them. Rural back roads are like that.

It was raining as well, not too heavily, but enough for the windows to start misting over in the steamed-up evening air. We were in the *Reporter* car with the bad air conditioning, and now it appeared to have clapped out altogether. The wiper blades badly needed replacing too. The windows were down but it wasn't helping. I was starting to think I should have brought the Yiros.

I flicked on the lights, which worked, and pulled onto the shoulder, checked both ways and did a U-turn. The headlights swept through sparsely wooded but otherwise completely empty bush land. It had been a long time since we had seen anything resembling a house. We were in the middle of nowhere and there wasn't a mango tree in sight either. In the passenger seat, Sally North smacked her lips together in annoyance.

'Problem?' I asked. I'd wanted to bring Scotty but it was the kid's day off.

'Nope,' Sally said, which was not entirely true. She was 37, married to a high-up public servant and had two daughters in their early teens. I appreciated how good she was at her job. Impressively, several of her news photographs had picked up national press awards.

Still, there was a tension crackling between us like an invisible arc of electricity. Seven years earlier, we'd had a drunken sexual encounter in a pub car park following a Karaoke night organized by the guys on the Sports desk. At the time, we had both been married, happily as it happened. Things should not have gotten out of hand and we were both pissed off that they had. Afterwards, we tried avoiding each other as much as possible, which was impossible. Even after all this time Sally North, at least, still hadn't forgiven herself. As far as I was concerned, Karaoke nights organized by the Sports guys were bad news. I hadn't been to one since.

I slowed to a crawl as we approached the last turnoff we'd seen. A track wound away into the scrub, snaking by a large, rusting work shed just off the road. I stopped at the entrance. Sally peered out at the letterbox, trying to read the lot number.

'That's not it,' she said. She leaned back and folded her arms. The light was going fast. I knew what she was thinking. This was going to be a shit job, ghost or no ghost. 'Go up to the next one.'

I did as I was told. Again, the photographer searched for the lot number.

'That's it. Eleven oh two. It's so bloody small you can hardly see it.'

'Right,' I said, and swung the car off the road.

The drive was a couple of hundred meters long and full of potholes and deep, muddy wheel ruts. The headlights jolted up and down, stabbing wildly into the overgrown scrub like a pair of bobbing searchlights. Pandanus and cycads and spindly, black-barked native trees emerged from the wild grass like dripping sentinels. We passed by two or three burned out car bodies, and I kind of started wishing I'd never seen *Deliverance.*

Eventually, we caught sight of lights through the trees off to one side. For a moment, I thought we'd taken the wrong turnoff, until the track suddenly swung back towards the lights. After a minute or so, the tyres started crunching in gravel and the ride became a little smoother. A moment later, the house came into full view, lit up like a spaceship. Two powerful floodlights attached high under the front eaves bathed the broad expanse of the yard in glaring white light. The rain had stopped. Overhead, the sky was now completely dark.

I pulled into the broad front yard, which already hosted a jumble of dilapidated vehicles: a battered station wagon, an ancient Holden Commodore with different coloured doors, a small unidentifiable sedan badly in need of some panel beating and an old utility sporting a roll bar adorned with spotlights. I found a space under the huge old frangipani tree that dominated the approach to the house. A stack of dirty plastic chairs leaned against the trunk. Nearby sat a greasy, ancient barbecue surrounded by a scattering of beer cans.

'Oh. My. God,' Sally said, staring through the windshield. 'Somebody should be sitting on the front step playing a banjo.'

I ignored her even though I was thinking exactly the same thing.

'If anybody takes their teeth out in front of me,' she said, 'you'll be taking your own fucking pictures.'

Still ignoring her, I studied the farmhouse. Three or four worn wooden steps led up to the small front porch. There were no shoes lined up on the treads. The door was open.

Father Charlie had been right. The place *was* old, and imposingly large. Two storeys high, not at all designed for the tropics and probably built in the '50s – back when Mango Flat was first being populated – the joint looked a little like an abandoned country cottage. The house had a distinctly *British* feel to it at any rate, and I wondered if the original owner might not have been some English gent seeking his post-war fortune in this far-flung corner of the Empire. Whatever the case, the whole place now sagged with age, as though it might be sinking under its own weight. Dirt and mould streaked the exterior walls. The old-style casement windows were missing glass here and there. Upstairs, some of the windows were boarded up, their lower halves fitted with large, rusted air-conditioning units. A mass of junk piled against the ground floor walls added to the overall rustic charm: oil drums, timber planks, paint cans, an upended trampoline, a half dozen dented metal cupboards, tangled rolls of fencing wire, and a weather-beaten Bain Marie straight out of a 70s fish and chip shop. There seemed to be more of it but it was difficult to make out in the darkness behind the floodlights.

Off to the right and a short distance from the house were more lights. Fluorescents, illuminating the interior of a huge, corrugated iron work shed. One of the three giant roller doors stood open. The longish caravan parked inside had seen better days too. It too was streaked with grime and the tires were flat.

Beyond the house and the shed and the junk, the mango trees marched in wide, perfect rows into the night like some ancient, Tolkien army. They were so massive the canopy merged into a single dark mass behind the house. In the dark, there was no way to tell how far back the plantation went but I guessed it was quite a way. Father Charlie had had every right to be impressed. There seemed to be more buildings back there as well, but from here, they were just low, dark shapes in the general gloom.

A short, pot-bellied man had come out of the shed and was now walking towards us. Dressed in grotty jeans, faded black T-shirt and a leather motorcycle vest, his red hair was almost as long and scraggly as the beard that reached for his navel. Father Charlie's description had been entirely accurate. Murph *did* look like a gnome. He strolled over, crunching through the gravel. I reached into my pocket to switch on the recorder, grabbed my notebook and we got out of the car.

'G'day,' Murph said.

'How you going?' I said.

'Good, mate, good. You the people from the paper?'

I nodded. 'That's right. I'm Jack and this is Sally. You must be Murph. I saw Father Charlie the other day.'

Murph nodded and waved a hand at the house. 'Yeah. I saw your story in this morning's paper. Nicky's inside with the others.' He shrugged. 'Some of them aren't too happy with you.'

'Oh?'

'About the story. You know, doing it without talking to us first.'

I nodded at the open front door. 'Well, that's why we're here now. To get the rest of the story straight from you guys before anybody else does. There's been a bit of interest in it today already.' That much was true, although much of the interest had been from local TV and radio hacks mostly wanting to know what I was smoking.

Murph nodded thoughtfully, but stood his ground and slid his hands into his pockets.

'You're not joining us?' I asked.

Murph glanced over at the house. 'No, no. Few things to do. I'll be in shortly.'

'No worries.'

Murph looked at us for a moment, then turned around, and went back the way he had come.

'He looks like a gnome,' Sally said.

'Behave,' I said. 'Please.'

We headed for the front steps, crunching through the stones. The gravel was a medium-grade blue metal, like the aggregate used in concrete. Each stone was about the size of a thumbnail. It shifted beneath our feet like noisy sand.

As we approached the front door, we heard music. An old Cold Chisel song.

Sally adjusted the camera bag strap slung over her shoulder. 'Barnsey. Excellent.'

'Knock it off, Sal.'

'Right you are.'

A woman appeared at the front door, cradling a baby. She was as short as Murph and a little rounder. Shoulder-length dark hair. Too big T-shirt. Track pants. She turned and called back inside for Nicky. Somebody turned the music off. A second later, Nicky Chen appeared at the woman's shoulder, wearing a sarong. She had a beer in her hand.

'How you going?' Nicky asked.

'Good,' I said.

Sally offered her a thin smile. 'Yeah. Me too.'

Nicky smiled back. 'Come on in,' she said.

We bustled up the steps and went inside.

8

The interior was as shabby as the exterior. A confusion of junk furniture, people and cigarette smoke filled the large front room. I detected a sweet hint of the funny stuff in the air, too, which was no great surprise. They were a rough looking bunch. I had never before seen so many tattoos and broken teeth together in the one room. Sally was probably thinking the same thing but, thankfully, did not spin around on her heels and march right back out again.

The group lounged on a weird assortment of chairs around a coffee table littered with beer bottles and overflowing ashtrays. The four ceiling fans whirling away overhead sent little tornados of ash this way and that around the bottles, and over a couple of freshly used dinner plates.

I smiled. They were all youngish, early to mid-30s, maybe. Apart from Nicky and the woman with the baby, there were three men and another woman in the room, each drinking and smoking.

Every light in the house was on, at least down here. A long, narrow kitchen ran off to the right. On the left, running off the side of the living room, a hallway led, presumably, to more rooms and I could see the bottom three or four treads of a staircase leading upstairs. Another doorway on the left led to another, smaller front room, which may have once been a formal dining area. Now it contained an assortment of dilapidated lounge chairs arranged in front of a large flat screen TV. Toys littered the floor.

'Like a beer?' Nicky asked.

I shook my head. 'No, no. It's a bit early for me. Thanks anyway.'

Beside me, Sally let out a little snort. I briefly considered elbowing her in the ribs.

'Right then,' Nicky said. 'Introductions. Everybody, this is Jack from the paper.'

Their discomfort was obvious. One or two of them shifted uneasily in their chairs, eyeing us with suspicion. I beamed at them as best I could.

'How we all doing tonight?'

A couple of 'goods', two or three raised drinks.

Nicky lifted her beer in Sally's direction. 'I'm Nicky.'

'Oh,' the photographer said. She gave them all a little wave. 'Sally.'

Nicky went around the room. 'Okay, that's Kath with the bub.'

She was still hovering in the doorway behind us, swinging her hips to keep the baby asleep. We gave her a nod and said 'Hi.'

'Guy with the dragon tattoos is Brett, Kath's other half.'

Brett held up his beer and said 'Cheers.' He was a big guy with a shaved head. He wore a neat, thin goatee and a T-shirt and shorts. The dragon tattoos writhed down each forearm, their tails disappearing beneath his shirtsleeves. One of Brett's lower front teeth had gone MIA.

'Next is Lance. You'll have to excuse the smell. He just got in from work.' Nicky smiled at him. Lance smiled back, more gums than teeth. His eyes were red. He wore a grimy fluorescent yellow high visibility vest of the type used by construction

workers. Lance was so painfully thin that the singlet
he wore beneath the vest threatened to slip right off
his bony shoulders. He looked tall, even sitting
down. His arms sported decorations as well. On one,
snakes slithered around a length of chain, on the
other a demon on a motorbike trailed flames. His left
eyebrow sported half a dozen small silver rings. He
swept his hair back in a greasy-looking ponytail.

'And this is Deb and Shane,' Nicky said,
pointing. 'What are the kids doing?'

'Watching a DVD in our room,' Deb said. 'I
don't want them hearing any of this.' She smiled
thinly and began twirling a dark, dangling strand of
hair around her fingers. Like Nicky, she wore a
sarong. A silver stud pierced her lower lip. An
unfinished tattooed sleeve encased her right arm
from wrist to shoulder in an intricate series of cogs
and pistons and levers, like you might find inside a
robot. Sitting down, she looked smaller than she
probably was. Beside her, Shane was getting to his
feet. He offered me his hand. None of the others had
bothered.

'How you going?' he said. He was tall too, and
broad-shouldered. His hair was a bleached sandy
yellow and messed up, like surfer's hair. No tattoos
that I could see and his teeth appeared to be in tiptop
condition. He was still in work clothes, too, and
sweating profusely.

'Good, mate,' I said. We shook hands. I noticed a
thin, wicked scar running from his right temple
down to his cheek.

Nicky pointed her beer at Shane. 'He's such a bloody pisshead he can't remember anything before 1998.'

'Piss off, Nick,' Shane said. Then he turned and shook Sally's hand as well. 'How are you?'

'Oh. Good,' Sally said. I glanced sideways at her, half-expecting her to wipe her hands on her shorts. She didn't.

'Such a bloody gentleman,' Nicky said. 'Where's Murph, by the way?'

'I just met him outside,' I said. 'Said he'd be in later.'

'Yeah, right,' Lance said. 'Murph only comes inside when there's food on offer. Or strippers.'

He let out an unexpected guffaw, so loud I almost jumped. In her seat, Deb *did* jump and she shot him a weird look, as if he had just scared the hell out of her. She drew back into her seat even further. Everyone else laughed along with Lance but I thought one or two of them had to force it. I studied the group for a moment, and then waved my notebook at them.

'So,' I said. 'I guess you all know why we're here.'

Shane glanced at Nicky and then looked back at me. 'Look, let's just get something up front first,' he said. 'We're not really after any publicity with this thing and I'm a little pissed off you've already written a fucking story about it.'

I licked my lips. 'Well, it didn't really say much. It's a couple of paragraphs about a spinning crucifix and a priest telling some people to get some help. That's it.'

Shane shook his head, unimpressed, and then shot a look at Nicky. 'A few people around here know it's us,' he said. 'We already look like a bunch of fucking idiots. Nobody believes this shit. We just want whatever is happening to stop. And *that's* it.'

Thinking fast, I said, 'Well, I fully understand that. But from what Nicky's told me, and from what I've heard from Father Charlie, you guys have a real situation here and a bit of publicity might actually help interest some proper investigators or someone.' I looked around at them. 'All it'll take is one or two of you to go through it with me and be in a photo. We don't even have to name you. If you want to stay anonymous, that's fine. And we can work the photos so you can't be identified.'

'Right.' Shane looked around the room and then back at me. 'I just wanted you to know that one or two of us aren't happy about this, that's all.'

'And that's fair enough but, like I said, a couple of quotes and a photo. That's all it would be.'

'Fuck it. I'll be in it.' It was Brett. He tugged on his goatee and looked over at Kath and the baby. She screwed up her lips briefly but nodded and started stroking the baby's head.

Shane shot him a look and said, 'Mate.'

Brett got to his feet and waved an arm. 'Shane, you weren't here when that priest got the willies and freaked us all out. You're the one who won't let us call anybody like he said. And it wasn't you prowling around the house every night for a week with a fucking shotgun, either.'

I blinked. 'What?'

Brett gestured at Kath. 'She saw something sitting on the end of our bed.'

Kath held the baby closer. 'There was like this dip in our bed,' she said, 'like there was something there. But there wasn't.'

'Screamed her fucking head off,' Brett said.

'Sure fucking did,' Nicky said.

'So I borrowed Murph's gun and sat up all night for a week,' Brett said.

'Until Murph found out and took it off you,' Deb said. There was obvious strain in her voice. Her fingers continued to toy with her hair.

Brett shook his head. 'Yeah, yeah. Like he said, probably not a good idea to have a loaded gun in the house with kids around.'

'Where's the gun now?' I asked.

'Murph locked it away,' Nicky said. 'Out in his van. Good job too.'

Brett ran a hand over his shaved head. 'What else was I supposed to do? None of you arseholes were doing anything. There's something in the fucking room with our kid and you guys all think it's a fucking joke.'

'Hey,' Deb said. 'We've got fucking kids too, you know.'

Now it was Lance who spoke. 'Mate, we're all freaked out, okay? But pinching Murph's gun is going a bit far. Anything could have happened. And it was all the poor bastard needed straight after the dog went missing.'

'I know, okay? I *know,*' Brett said.

'A dog went missing?' I asked.

Lance shrugged. 'Yeah, Murph's dog. Disappeared a couple of weeks ago. I reckon a snake probably got him.'

Nicky glanced at the front door. 'Whatever happened to it was a blessing in disguise. Bloody thing used to bark at anything that moved.'

Ignoring her, Shane waved a hand in Brett's direction. 'I thought you two were moving out anyway?'

'Yeah, well, as soon as we can fucking afford to, mate.'

Now it was Nicky's turn. 'For fuck's sake, settle the fuck down, the pair of you.'

Shane stared at her. 'It doesn't help that you're off down the pub mouthing off every five minutes, Nick. That's why we've got fucking reporters in the house. *Fuck.*'

'Screw you, Shane. I'm not the only one who's been talking about this to people and you fucking know it. Now sit the fuck down.'

Shane glared at her while Brett shook his head in exasperation. Nicky stared them down. After a moment, Brett sat down and Shane huffed back to his seat.

I licked my lips again, momentarily thrown by how abruptly the atmosphere had turned so seriously tense. The bad vibe was there to start with, I supposed, but now the air positively hummed with it. Something was screwed up around here, that was for sure. I looked at Sally, who raised her brow but appeared otherwise unruffled.

'Okay, then,' Nicky said. She turned to me with a rueful smile. 'I'm forever bringing these kids into line. How do we do this?'

I looked around the smoky room.

'How about we run through it from the beginning?'

9

Father Charlie's account of their story had been accurate. The thing *had* started three or four months earlier. In fact, according to Shane the thing with the shoes started happening not long after Brett, Kath and the baby moved into the house just after New Year.

Seated next to Nicky on a low, massively uncomfortable cane settee, I was acutely aware of the bad vibe still passing between the two men. They were stewing.

'Yeah, Father Charlie told me about the shoes,' I said.

Shane frowned. 'I thought priests were supposed to keep their mouths shut.'

'Well, we go back a way. He did insist I not use any names.'

'Especially his, right?'

'Well, yes. He also told me about the stones falling out of nowhere. Is that still happening?'

'No,' Brett said. 'Hasn't happened for a while now. Listen, just so you know, this shit doesn't go on every single night. Happens maybe two, three times a week. We even had a couple of weeks where nothing happened at all.'

'Okay.'

Shane leaned forward, jabbing a finger at the air. 'What else did he tell you?'

'Obviously he told me about his crucifix going for a bit of a spin, and about the pots and pans turning up in odd places. You guys ever see any of this stuff happening?'

'Like things moving around by themselves?' Brett said.

'Yeah.'

'Well, apart from the thing with the crucifix, no. The only one who's seen anything else is Kath.'

I scanned their faces. 'Okay. How about the gravel coming down from the ceiling? You must've seen that happening.'

One or two of them glanced upwards, as if expecting something to happen right then and there.

'Bloody stuff,' Nicky said. 'Falls right out of thin air.' She shifted on the settee so that her knee rested lightly against mine. I didn't move. Sally, parked out of the way at a messy, unusable dining table in one corner, pretended to fiddle with her camera but she had seen Nicky Chen's move and frowned appropriately. Maybe Scotty was right after all.

'But that hasn't happened for a couple of weeks now,' Nicky continued. 'Not since it started turning up on the bloody bathroom floor.'

I looked around.

'And no-one has any idea who Gary might be?'

No-one had any idea who Gary might be.

Kath said, 'We have photos of it. On Deb's computer.'

I looked over at Deb. 'I'd really like to have a look at those. If you don't mind.'

Deb turned her head to Shane, who shrugged. He didn't care, or was pretending not to.

'Computer's in our room,' Deb said, still twisting that dangling strand.

'Right,' Nicky said, slapping a hand on my knee. 'Let's do a quick tour first.'

We started in the kitchen. Like the rest of the house, it was a shambles. Aging appliances, dirty dishes and scattered beer bottles cluttered a long bench top of scarred laminate. Ancient stains spotted the linoleum floor, which in places curled away from the skirting.

Sally stayed quiet, content to peer over my shoulder. Deb did the same. The men had decided to stay right where they were, and Kath continued to waltz around the front room with the baby. A glass panelled door led off the back of the kitchen, out to the rear of the house. It was dark out there but I guessed it might lead to an outdoor laundry area. With a clang, Nicky fished a thoroughly used frying pan out of the overflowing sink.

'So this is our haunted frying pan,' she said. 'Goes off on its own every now and then. Turns up out the front, in the bathroom, stuff like that. A few other bits and bobs wander around as well. Lids and pots and shit. Sometimes in the mornings all the bloody cupboard doors and drawers are open when we come down.'

The frying pan clanged back in to the sink.

'Right,' I said. 'Father Charlie said you found a knife sticking out of a wall. Was that in here?'

Nicky nodded at the light switch just inside the doorway. 'Kath found it one night when she came down to do a bottle for the baby.' She glanced back out into the front room and lowered her voice. 'She's a bit of a screamer, so we all ended up down here to see what the fuck was going on. Sounded like she was being bloody murdered.'

On the wall beside the light switch was a deep, slightly angled slot about four centimetres long. Spidery fault lines cracked through the paint around the edges. At the top, a large flake of paint had chipped away altogether. I ran a finger over the wound.

'Would've taken a bit of force to get it through the wall like that,' I said.

'Yep,' Nicky said. 'Gave us all the heebie jeebies, that did. That's when Murph decided we needed a bloody priest out here.'

'You still have the knife?'

Nicky turned to the bench and slid a large carving knife from a wooden block next to the sink. She waggled it around. 'This is it,' she said.

It was quite a big one. 'Now *that's* a knife,' I said. I looked at it for a moment. 'Would you mind if we quickly stick that back in the wall for a photo?'

Nicky looked at Deb, who shrugged.

'I guess that's okay,' Nicky said, and handed over the blade handle first.

The knife slotted easily back into the wall, meeting little resistance until the blade was a good third of the way in. It *had* been a hefty blow. I looked at Sally and she took a couple of rapid-fire photos, her flash lighting up the kitchen like lightning.

'Anything else in here?' I asked.

'That's it,' Nicky said. I withdrew the knife and handed it back. She slid it back into the block with a thud.

We threaded back through the front room. Watching us, Shane, Lance and Brett continued to smoke and drink in an uneasy silence. We went into the hall. There were two doors on the right and the staircase hugging the wall on the left. Someone had hung a blue tarpaulin over a broken window at the top of the stairs. Down here, there was another back door at the end of the hall but this one was glass free and speckled with mould. Long streaks of white dribbled down the door, as though someone had tried to clean it but given up halfway through.

Deb went ahead and disappeared inside the far room. I heard television noise, which cut off a second or two after she went in.

'Bathroom's in here,' Nicky said, opening the first door. She reached in for the switch and turned on the light. 'Deb and Shane have the room next door. The rest of us are upstairs.'

I poked my head in. So did Sally. I imagined she may have screwed up her nose. It was a large room, tiled in sickly green right up to the ceiling. A stained bathtub/shower combo took up one corner, with the toilet and washbasin against the back wall. A small window at the back overlooked the presumed laundry area. There was a heavy, damp smell in the air, like wet dog or mouldy blanket. A broken exhaust fan hung from the ceiling at the end of a dangerous-looking clump of wires.

'That is one big bathroom,' I said.

'There's another one upstairs,' Nicky said. 'But we haven't had any spooky fucking messages in that one.'

I glanced up at the ceiling. 'Most of it happens down here, then?'

Nicky waved her beer at the staircase. 'Most of it. We *did* find little piles of rocks outside all the bedroom doors upstairs one night a couple of weeks ago. Deb took pictures of those too. Nothing much else has gone on up there, apart from Kath seeing something sitting on her bed.' She paused for a moment, and then leaned closer. 'Brett put a shitload of salt around their bed, you know, to ward off the fucking evil spirits. They looked it up on the internet. It's all around the baby's cot too.'

'Right,' I said. 'The stones are from the driveway?'

'Yep.' She pointed her beer up the hall. 'Let's go look at the pictures.'

'Let's,' I said. I flicked off the bathroom light and closed the door.

In her room, Deb sat hunched at a cluttered desk in front of an ancient computer. The kids had fallen asleep in front of a small television, tangled in bed sheets on a lumpy mattress on the floor. Boy and a girl, probably around three or four, surrounded by toys. Jammed around the double bed were half a dozen cardboard boxes, some open suitcases and a packing crate overflowing with a jumble of clothing. Their whole lives seemed to be crammed into this one small space. It reminded me of the spare room at home, where Jessica's life filled a single room too.

'That's Ellie and Brody,' Deb said with a nod at the kids. 'They've had a big day so they shouldn't wake up.'

Nicky, Sally and I went in, gingerly stepping over the sleeping children. We huddled around Deb to peer at the screen. She worked the mouse with her robot arm, moving the cursor over a dozen small thumbnail images. She clicked on one in the middle of the batch. The processor whirred laboriously. A second or two later the photo filled the screen.

'Jesus,' I said, staring at the name made of stones. The word spread out over most of the bathroom floor. Each letter appeared slightly misshapen, as if a kid had made it, or someone in a hurry.

GARY

I don't believe in ghosts – I'd already decided a real living, breathing human had to be behind what was going on out here - but a tiny electric tingle made the hairs at the back of my neck stand on end anyway. It was the creepiest thing I had ever seen.

'Now *that* is giving me goose bumps,' I said.

'You should have been here when we found it,' Nicky said. 'Fucking unbelievable.'

Deb said, 'We've looked at a lot of stuff about this online. What we have is a fucking poltergeist. You know, a spirit that moves shit around.' She glanced at the kids. 'And they haunt *people* not places. It's got nothing to do with the house.'

I looked at her. It was clear that Deb and Shane had decided Brett and Kath were the haunted people in this case, and that they had brought the trouble with them.

I pointed at the screen. 'How long ago did this happen?'

'This one was a couple of weeks ago,' Nicky said. 'Then it happened again week before last. Same thing.'

'You ever try getting footage of this stuff? You know, set up a camera or something?'

'We don't have a video camera,' Deb said.

Nicky looked at me and shrugged. 'I guess we didn't think of that.'

I said, 'Listen, Deb, we could really use one of these photos in the paper. Would you be okay with that?'

She leaned back in her chair. 'Well, I don't know. I'd have to ask Shane first.'

I dug out my wallet and handed her a business card. 'That's my email address. Could you send them to me at work? If Shane's okay with it?'

'I guess so, but it might take a while. Our connection's a bit hit and miss out here, especially with the storms still around.'

'No problem,' I said. 'Whenever you can.'

I glanced back at the name on the floor. My scalp refused to stop tingling.

10

Murph was sitting in the living room with the others when we came back out. He had showered and changed, and was now wearing an impressively ironed dress shirt and tidy jeans.

'Fifteen minutes,' Nicky told him. Murph waved that that was fine by him. I suddenly wondered if they were a couple, a thought which, given Nicky's little move back on the settee, surprised me. On the face of it, the idea of the Chinese sex bomb and the bearded gnome being an item was preposterous, but there it was.

I offered Murph a nod and clapped my hands together in a down-to-business manner. 'So, who wants to have a bit of a chat about this thing?'

Brett raised an arm, stretching it high like a schoolboy dying to give an answer. 'We'll be in it. Me and Kath.'

'Anyone else?' I looked at Nicky.

'Fuck, no. Not me. I'm famous enough around here already thanks to you and your bloody newspaper.' She raised her beer at me.

'Anyone else? Lance, is it?'

Lance shook his head and blew out smoke. 'Not me, mate. Thanks for asking.'

Shane said nothing.

'Okay, so it's just Brett and Kath. Thanks, guys.'

Brett said, 'No worries.'

I decided to speak to the couple outside while Sally positioned them for photos in front of the house. Nicky joined us, possibly in a supervisory role. By now, the rain had gone for good. Stars were out. Brett held a beer while Kath placated the baby, whose name was Jade, with a bottle. The floodlights on the house cast suitably dark shadows over the wet gravel. It was going to be a top picture.

I jotted down their full names and ages in my notebook: Brett Haverson, 33, Kath Dunlop, 30, baby Jade, seven months.

'Why do you journalists always need to know people's ages?' Kath said. 'That's got nothing to do with anything.'

I laughed. 'Well, it's actually vitally important information if you think about it. For a start, there might be another Kath Dunlop around town. Including your age might head off any confusion.'

'Even with my picture in the paper?'

'Even with your picture in the paper.'

Behind me, Nicky tutted. 'You never asked how bloody old I was.'

'Ah, but there can't be too many Nicky Chen's around, right?'

'No idea,' she said. 'I'm 31, by the way.'

'I'll make sure I include that next time you're in trouble.'

'Good-o,' she said. 'Listen, I've got to go in and have a shower. Carry on.'

We watched her go and then, with a nod at the house, I asked, 'Has either of you experienced anything like this before?'

They both shook their heads.

To Kath I said, 'Okay. Tell me about the night you saw something on your bed.'

She glanced at Brett before speaking. 'Well, Jade woke up for a feed around two o'clock one morning,

69

which is normal, so I went and lifted her out of the cot to take her downstairs to do a bottle. Brett never wakes up so it's always me.' She glanced at him again. He shrugged. 'So anyway, as I turn around again I see this dip in the covers at the end of the bed. It looked kind of weird, you know, so I kind of stared at it. Then it moved.'

'The dip moved?'

'Yeah, it sort of sprang back up, like someone had been sitting there and suddenly stood up.' She nodded her head sideways at Brett. 'So I start calling out to him to get the fuck up.'

'You weren't calling out,' Brett said. 'You were screaming.'

Kath let out a dismissive snort. 'Okay. I was screaming.'

I looked at them both for a moment, and then said to Brett, 'What did you do?'

'Well, I got up and got us the fuck out of the room. We ended up sleeping on the floor down in the TV room.'

'Okay. Sounds like you were both pretty freaked out.'

Brett nodded. 'You have no idea.'

I looked at him. 'So, what, the next night you sat up with the gun?'

He pulled a face and shrugged again. 'Yeah. I was starting to get a bit edgy, you know. There is a lot of weird shit going on around here.' He thought for a moment. 'I just wanted some protection.'

I considered asking him if he thought blowing a hole in the bedcovers might help but decided against it. Instead, I glanced over in the direction of the big work shed.

'So you borrowed Murph's shotgun?'

'Yeah.'

I thought about that for a moment. 'Does he keep it locked up? Like in a gun safe?'

Brett shook his head. 'Not usually. I found it leaning up against a wall. He keeps it handy in case any geese or bats and shit get into the mangoes. He uses it the scare them off. Sometimes he chucks fireworks at them.'

'Okay,' I said. 'I'm just thinking it might be an idea to leave the gun out of things for now. Cops read the paper too. You don't want any of them getting curious about any stray shotguns. Is that okay with you?'

Brett nodded and tugged on his goatee. 'Yeah, sure. I'm kind of embarrassed about it anyway. Thanks.'

I turned my attention back to Kath. 'Did this happen before or after you found the knife in the wall?'

'Oh, before. I think.' She looked at Brett, who nodded. 'There's been so much shit going on around here it's hard to keep track of what happened when.'

'That's understandable,' I said. 'So after the knife thing Father Charlie came out?'

Kath said, 'Yeah. He's a funny old bastard. He couldn't get out of here fast enough once his cross started fucking spinning around.'

'And a while after that the name appeared on the bathroom floor, right?'

Brett let out a loud breath. 'Yeah, and I'll tell you what, that was the fucking creepiest thing of all.' He threw a look over his shoulder back at the house. 'Deb carried on like a pork chop when we found it the first time. She wanted to get the fuck out of here right then and there.' He shrugged again. He was quite good at shrugging. 'But I think they're in the same boat as us. Financially, I mean. We're all stuck here.'

I waved my notebook. 'Shane's got a job, though, right?'

'Yeah, he drives a forklift in some building supplies warehouse or something. Fuck knows what they do with their money.'

'They're saving up for a house, idiot,' Kath said.

'Whatever,' Brett said.

I glanced down at my shorthand, which looks even worse in bad light, wondering if I should ask about the salt around the beds. I decided against it. I didn't want to get Nicky into trouble for blabbing.

'You guys are planning to move out, though, yes?'

Yes, the couple *was* planning to move out, as soon as Brett found work and they could scrape together a security deposit for a flat somewhere. A boilermaker by trade, he had driven his small family up from Adelaide in the clapped out Commodore with the different coloured doors, hoping to take advantage of the Territory's oil and gas boom. Darwin was fast becoming an oily El Dorado, attracting fortune seekers like flies to a barbecue. So far, though, Brett had lucked out.

When we were done, I slipped a business card from my wallet and handed it to Brett, telling them to call me if they thought of anything else. I asked for his mobile number, which he gave to me. Then I asked Sally if she was done as well. She was already packing away her gear, so the grunt in the affirmative wasn't necessary.

'I'll just go inside and say thanks,' I said.

Sally nodded and looked over at our car. She wanted to get the hell out of there. 'Right. I'll wait for you out here.'

By the time we got back inside Nicky had showered and changed. A tote bag hung over one of her shoulders. She raised an eyebrow at me.

'All done?'

'Yeah, it's all good.' I looked around the room. 'Thanks very much for that, guys. And if anyone changes their mind about being in the story, Deb and Brett both have my card. Give me a buzz. I'll let Nicky know when it'll be in the paper. I don't work weekends, so it probably won't get a run until Tuesday or Wednesday next week.' I surveyed the room. 'Like I said, with a bit of luck this may attract the attention of somebody who can help you guys out.'

Lance raised his beer at me. Shane frowned but said nothing and that was it. Nicky touched my elbow.

'Listen,' she said. 'Murph and I are heading into town for a few drinks, you know, if you want to tag along.'

'Oh,' I said. I looked at her. I thought about it. I looked over my shoulder and out through the front door. Sally had already stowed her gear in the car and now stood by the open passenger door tapping a hand on the roof. I reached into my pocket for the keys.

'Yeah, okay,' I said to Nicky. 'Might give us a chance to talk some more.'

'Right.' She looked at the others. 'Behave yourselves, boys and girls. I've got my mobile if anything happens.'

'No worries,' Deb said. To me she said, 'I'll send you those photos.'

I glanced at Shane, who shrugged noncommittally.

'That would be fantastic. Thanks.'

I thanked Brett and Kath again, shook their hands, and said goodbye. Nicky and Murph headed for the beaten-up, unidentifiable sedan in the yard while I went over to Sally. I tossed her the keys. The photographer caught the bunch mid-flight and looked at me and then over at Nicky and Murph as they got into the car.

'Oh, you can't be serious,' she said.

'I'm just going into town for one drink.'

'Yeah, right. She's been eyeing you off ever since we got here.'

'Oh, sure.' What was it with these photographers? Sally scowled. 'I don't want to drive around out here by myself.'

'You're a big girl.'

'And you're an asshat.'

'Yes. Yes, I am. Drive safely.'

'Fuck.' She got in the car, slammed the door and slid over to the driver's side. I gave her a happy wave as she gunned the engine and negotiated her way out of the yard, tires biting disapprovingly into the gravel.

Nicky and Murph were in the front seats. The sedan, which turned out to be Nicky's, was a wreck, outside and in. I slid into the back over torn upholstery as Murph started the car by hotwiring it.

'Don't mind the sparks,' he said with a chuckle. 'It's all part of the service.'

'Uh,' I said as the car shuddered and rattled and backfired twice.

11

'Nice house,' Nicky said after I reached inside to flick on the lights. She kicked off her shoes by the front door and stepped inside. I've always been a ladies first kind of guy. I followed and dumped my stuff in the bowl. It was three in the morning. I badly needed some sleep. We'd hit just about every nightspot in town. Hard. We had lost Murph somewhere in a packed Irish bar a couple of hours earlier and decided to cab it back to my place. I had paid for everything.

'Yep,' I said. 'You want a beer?'

Nicky walked over to the kitchen bench, ignoring me for the moment. She dropped her shoulder bag on the bench top, quickly scanned the living area and then peered down the hall.

'How many bedrooms?'

I slid the glass door closed and locked it with a flick.

'Four,' I said. 'Well, three, really. The first one is useless. Too small to fit a bed in. I use it as an office.'

Nicky nodded as though that made good sense. 'Where are your kids? I thought you said you had kids.'

'They live with their grandparents.'

'So you live in this big fucking house all by yourself?'

'Yep.'

'And where's Mrs Jack? She run away?'

'Something like that.'

She suddenly slapped the side of her face. 'Oh, shit. She's not dead, is she?'

'I don't think so. Would you like a beer or not?'

Nicky looked at me for a long moment, as though she might be sizing me up. Or something. I imagined she might be swaying a little. Or it may have been me. I wasn't sure.

'That Sally chick,' she said. 'She a mate of yours?'

'What? No, not really. We just work together.'

'She's a bit bloody stuck up. Or does she usually look down her nose at everybody like that?'

'Now that you mention it, yes, she is stuck up. Very.' Now I studied her for a moment. 'What's the story with you and Murph?'

She waved a hand. 'Oh, he came with the house. We're mates. He looks after me. Shit, he looks after all of us.'

'Right.'

'No more beer,' Nicky said, rubbing her belly. She offered me a lopsided smile. 'Let's go. I want you to fuck me. Right now. Not up the arse, though.'

I blinked at her. 'Jesus,' I said.

'I need to pee first. Where's the bathroom?'

Ten minutes later, wide awake and propped up on one elbow, I was scribing invisible circles around one of her extraordinary Chinese nipples. Her seatbelt bruise was starting to fade, I noticed. Nicky was smoking in bed, which I thought was disgusting but I let it go. She flicked ash on the floor. I let that go too. The hunchback would deal with it.

I had a question for her. 'Are you related to the Chens who run the electrical stores?'

She waved her cigarette in the air. 'I think you'll find every Chinaman in the joint is related somehow. I've got aunties and uncles and cousins coming out the ying yang. My dad and his brothers own the shops. Any more questions?'

'Yeah. What's a nice Chinaman like you doing living way out in the sticks?'

She dropped her head for a moment. 'Well, sometimes people fuck up, you know. Sometimes *I* fuck up. Apparently, I was born in the year of the black sheep. Better to keep a low profile.' She let out a little snort. 'Christ knows what they thought about me being on the front page of the bloody paper.'

'You don't see them much?'

'Oh, birthdays and Christmas. Chinese New Year. I go home for family dinner once a month. When I've got transport, that is. Next one will be a scream, I'm sure.' She swung out of bed, cigarette finished. 'I'll just chuck this down the dunny.'

I flopped back on my pillow. When she came back she said, 'So, what do you think about Gary the ghost?'

'I don't know.'

She slid back onto the bed. 'Sure you do. You must have a professional bloody journalistic opinion.'

'Well, something's going on.'

'Well, fuck, I know that.'

I looked at her. 'Nicky, there are certainly some odd things going on in your house but it's quite possible one of your mates is doing it.'

'Fuck off.'

'How well do you know them all? I mean, *really* know them.'

'Shit. We all went to school together. Me, Deb, Shane, Lance and Kath. Kath moved down south a few years back so Brett I don't know at all. He's a pain in the arse and he's from Adelaide but I don't hold that against him. He's all over that fucking baby.'

I nodded that I thought she was right about that.

'We were real little shits as kids, let me tell you,' she went on. 'We used to get up to all sorts of crap, especially once Shane got a car. Hit the road, smoke some dope, shit like that.' She snorted again. 'Shane and Deb had their first root out at Mud Point when they were 17, at that old hospital out there. Very romantic. That joint was practically our second home back then.'

'How'd they all end up living with you?'

'Well, Brett dragged Kath back up here looking for work. She tracked me down through mum and dad. They were literally living in their car so I told them they could stay with me as long as they needed to. Shane and Deb couldn't find anywhere else to go either. They had a dog-box apartment in town but the landlord jacked up the rent so high they couldn't afford it. I told them I had a spare room if they needed it and there they were. That was probably two years ago.'

'What about Lance? He seems to be odd man out.'

'Well, Lance is fucking odd all right. Nice enough guy but he creeps me out sometimes. Quiet type, you know, until he laughs that fucking laugh of his. Works on a road crew, so he's out bush a lot.' She thought for a moment. 'He only came back on the scene around six months ago. It was kind of fucked up. Awkward, you know. Shane and him had been best mates as kids until they crashed Shane's car one night. Rolled it and everything, and the fucking thing blew up. Both of them were lucky to get out alive.'

'Christ.'

'Yeah. Shane was pretty badly hurt and it totally fucked up his head. He was in a coma and everything. When he woke up he couldn't remember a fucking thing.'

That explained the scar, I thought. 'Well, that happens sometimes.'

'No, no,' Nicky said. 'He couldn't remember a thing about *anything*. His whole life before the crash was wiped out. He didn't even know who we were.'

'Seriously?'

'Seriously. Everything that was in his head was just *gone.*' She snapped her fingers like a magician making something vanish. 'Deb had a hell of a time convincing him they were together. You know, boyfriend and girlfriend. That whole show was extremely fucked up.'

'What happened to Lance?'

'He got out okay. A few broken bones, I think. He somehow managed to drag Shane out of the wreck before the fire. Or so he says.'

I shook my head. 'Sounds like they were both extremely lucky.'

'Oh, yeah. Anyway, it took a long time for Shane to work shit out in his head. As far as he was concerned, we were all a bunch of bloody strangers, Lance included. Deb stuck with it but we all sort of drifted apart after that. I kept in touch with the girls on and off and that's how we all ended up back together again, I suppose. Then suddenly Lance turns up out of the blue one day to see Shane. None of us had seen him for years and I've got no idea how he found us but there he was. Him and Shane had a few beers together and Lance was talking shit about when they were kids but they didn't really click the way they used to. Like I said, a little fucking awkward.'

'How'd he end up living with you?'

'Well, he said he was looking for somewhere to camp for a few weeks so Shane offered him a spare room upstairs. I guess he was feeling sorry for him or something.'

'And he's still there,' I said.

'Yep,' Nicky said, 'He's still there.'

I ran a hand through my hair. It was difficult to imagine her tattooed and rotten-toothed friends as fresh-faced teens hanging out together. I wondered if they were happy with the way things had turned out for them.

'So, how did you end up out there?'

Nicky screwed up her face and reached for another cigarette. 'I was with a guy who decided we needed to live out in the fucking bush for some reason. He was a bit of a tree-hugger. Murph and him didn't get along too well. Had a few run-ins over fuck knows what. The hippy left. I stayed, got a few other people to move in to help with the rent. Then *they* left and Shane and Deb came along at the right time. Blah blah blah.'

'And Murph looks after the place, right?'

'Yeah. He's been living there for five or six years. Some rich guy owns the joint. I've only met him once, when he came out one mango season to check up on things.'

Nicky lit her smoke. I massaged my temples. A boozy headache was starting to take hold.

Enveloped in a blue cloud, Nicky said. 'None of them is doing this shit, you know. They can't be. I mean, shit, why would they?'

I glanced at the display on the clock on the bedside table, a subtle hint that I was dead tired and ready to crash. Nicky missed it, though, and raised her dark Asian eyebrows at me, expecting a response.

'I have no idea why anybody would be doing it,' I said. She opened her mouth but I held up a hand before she could get any words out. 'But,' I continued, 'it's certainly not Gary the ghost.'

'Well, mister bloody smartarse reporter, how do explain Kath seeing something sitting on her bed?'

'Think about it. You're a smart woman.'

'Fuck. Don't patronize me, Jack.'

'I'm not trying to patronize you. Kath is the only one who has actually *seen* anything ghostly at all. She's just had a baby. She's probably not sleeping too well. She could be so tired she's hallucinating. Who knows? She might be going through post-natal depression or something.'

'Oh, yeah, and a dingo took my fucking baby,' Nicky said.

'A dingo *did* take her baby.'

'So she says.'

'So the coroner says.'

'Whatever,' Nicky said, blowing out a huge cloud of smoke. 'Kath's not the only one who's seen something, you know. We've all seen the bloody rocks fall from nowhere. And what about the thing with the crucifix?'

I told her Father Charlie's ceiling fan theory, after which she said, 'Well, fuck, maybe but the fans aren't blowing rocks around the frigging room.'

I managed a weak smile through my rapidly worsening headache. 'Yeah, I'll have to think about that one.'

'You do that.' She swung out of bed again and headed off to the bathroom to flush away her smoke. 'I need to sleep,' she said when she came back.

'Me too.'

She slipped back into bed and I threw an arm over her. In no time at all she had started to snore, quite impresively.

Morning light smeared through the bamboo blinds in fuzzy horizontal lines. I closed my eyes to block it out before I worked out that Nicky was shaking me awake, which is why I'd opened them in the first place.

'I have to go.'

I rolled over. 'What? What time is it?'

'Almost nine.'

I rubbed at my eyes and struggled to sit up. My head pounded. Nicky had dressed and had her bag over her shoulder, ready to go.

'Oh, oh,' I said.

'Where's the nearest bus stop?' Nicky asked.

'What? You can't catch a bus.'

'I need to get into town,' Nicky said. 'Murph wouldn't have driven home last night. He'll still be floating around somewhere.'

I looked at her. She was out of focus. 'I can drive you.'

'You're still pissed. Your car isn't even here, Jack.' She was right. It was still in the car park at work. 'I can find my own way. I've done it before. Where's the nearest bus stop?'

I had to think about it. 'Go down the end of the street, turn left, then right at the first street. That'll take you to the back of the local shops. Bus stop is out the front.'

She smiled at me. 'Thanks for a top night. I enjoyed myself.'

'What? Oh, yeah. You're welcome.'

'Right. I'm off. Don't get up. I'll let myself out.'

I shook my head, trying to clear it. 'Okay. I'll call you.'

'No worries,' she said.

Nicky wheeled away out of the bedroom with a wave. I listened as she walked down the hall, clicked open the front door, closed it again and went thumping down the front stairs.

12

Monday morning, I was still getting over Friday night. I hadn't been this ill since I'd been poisoned by cocktail-mixing lesbians at a party on the eve of the new millennium. The lesbians were friends of ours but, given they tried to kill me, I think they liked Jessica a whole lot more than they liked me.

I stared at my screen, the Mango Flat story half-written, Brett and Kath's disembodied voices wafting out of the recorder on my desk. I switched it off and rubbed at my eyes. Despite spending much of the weekend slumping around the house popping pills, my alcohol-induced headache hadn't completely evaporated and continued to lurk behind my eyeballs in a dull knuckle of pain.

I sighed and thought about wandering out into the car park for a cigarette. As a rule, I didn't smoke at work, primarily to avoid any spicy car park gossip I might be involved in, but I'd slipped the packet into my trousers on the way out of the house without really knowing I was doing it. Now, staring at the impatiently blinking cursor on my screen, I simply couldn't get my brain to function in its usual happy manner. A smoke might help but probably wouldn't.

I was about to get up and go when Sally North bustled into the newsroom, camera bag slung over her shoulder. She had been out on a job. She took one look at me, shook her head in mock dismay and came over.

'Big weekend?'

'No.'

'You're incredible, Jack,' she said.

'Thanks.'

'You know what I mean. Get a bit, did you?'

'That's none of your business.'

'Right you are.' She considered me for a moment, suddenly frowning. 'You really think it's a good idea getting mixed up with people like that?'

I rubbed at the back of my neck. 'People like what?'

'Trailer trash, Jack.'

'Fuck off, Sal.'

'I'm just saying. That's not a good environment for kids, you know.'

I looked at her. 'The kids seemed okay to me and the baby looked fine.'

'You smelled the ganja, right? That's probably why they're seeing things, you know.'

I didn't respond.

She shrugged, letting it go. 'They send through the photos yet?'

I shook my head. 'Not yet. I'll shoot them over to you as soon as I get them.'

Sally glanced at her watch. 'I'd give them a call but they probably aren't even out of bed yet.'

'Go away.'

She didn't go away. Hovering, she said, 'So, what do you think? You buy any of that shit?'

I sighed again. I really wanted that cigarette now. 'No. Somebody in the house is doing it.'

'That's what I reckon,' the photographer said. 'What about the falling rocks, though? That's a little freaky.'

'I don't know,' I said. 'Maybe someone is just tossing a handful in the air when nobody's looking. I don't *know.'*

'Yeah, you're probably right. What about the cross?'

I waved a hand. 'Probably just the wind from the fans or something.'

'Yeah, probably. Whoever heard of a ghost named fucking 'Gary' anyway? What's that all about?

'No idea.'

Sally shook her head. 'Well, if one of those people out there is behind this shit then that person has a real fucking problem. Mentally, I mean. Normal people don't go around stabbing walls, you know.'

'Obviously.' I fished out the cigarettes and got to my feet. 'I'm going for a smoke.'

Sally stared at me. 'Since when do you bloody smoke? Hope you're not picking up any bad habits, Jack. Or diseases, for that matter.' She gave me a friendly smirk.

'Fuck off.'

'Right you are.'

I watched her head into the glass-walled office at the back of the newsroom, thinking about flying knives and that creepy name on the bathroom floor out at Mango Flat. Sally North was right. Whoever was behind this thing *did* have a problem. That much was obvious. People simply don't do shit like that, and that particular thought sent another little electric message to the hairs on the back of my neck.

Forget ghosts.

Sometimes the scariest things around are your fellow humans.

I went outside for a smoke.

Monday morning bled into Monday afternoon. I slugged out most of the day worrying that my eyes might start to bleed. I informed Mike Cooke I might have an undiagnosed tumour, so he sent through a bunch of press releases and fillers for me to rewrite instead of sending me out anywhere. He was a good guy.

Thankfully, there wasn't much happening anyway, apart from some nut out in the suburbs threatening his neighbours with a running chainsaw, which was a top way to start the week. Rankine was chasing that one. Barring any major death and destruction, the almost chainsaw massacre would lead the following day's edition.

When I was done, I cleared my desk and pulled up Nicky's number on my phone. I looked at it for a long time, drumming my fingers on my desk.

Trailer trash.

Sally was right about that, too. They were most definitely *not* my sort of people, although I had no firm idea whom, exactly, my sort of people might be. But despite the fact I'd known Nicky Chen for less than a week, I liked her. And now, like a protagonist in a Kylie Minogue song, I couldn't get her out of my head. I kept seeing her face, hearing her voice. Imaging her breasts dangling over my face I realized, with some concern, that it wasn't just a sexual thing either. I had genuinely enjoyed her company, and it had been a very long time since I'd let anyone get close enough for that to happen. I wasn't sure how to deal with it. I had no idea if Nicky Chen was simply out for a good time or -

'Fuck it.'

I stabbed the call button. She answered immediately.

'Yeah. Hello.'

'Yeah, Nicky. It's Jack.'

The reply was a long time coming. For one horrifying moment, I thought she might be trying to work out who I was.

'Oh, hi,' she finally said.

My brain did a little flip-flop as it tried to work out a reasonable excuse for ringing her. 'Ah. I was just ringing to make sure you got home okay the other morning.'

'Oh, yeah. Murph got me home safe and sound. Eventually. Couple of pit stops on the way.' She laughed.

'That's good. Listen, what are you up to tonight? I thought we might catch up.'

'Oh.' She sounded surprised.

I winced. *Shit*. 'It's okay,' I said, a little too quickly. 'I figured you'd probably be doing something.'

'Yeah. We're having an early night. Murph's taking me out fishing at the crack of dawn. He reckons I need to get out of the house for a day.'

'Has something else happened?'

'Oh, no. It's just a bit tense around here. You know.'

'Right,' I said. 'No worries. Listen, I'll give you a buzz as soon as I know when the story's running. I haven't actually written it yet.'

'Okay. That'd be good.'

'And I haven't received the photos from Deb yet. Could you give her a nudge for me?'

'Sure. I'll do it now.'

'Thanks. I'll talk to you later then.'

'Yeah. No worries. See you.'

'Okay, bye.'

I disconnected and stared at the phone as if it had just given me an electric zap. A schoolboy blush warmed across my face. I slapped myself on the forehead. Nicky Chen, it seemed, had had her wicked way with me and that, as they say, was that.

Deb's photos landed in my inbox and hour or so later. I forwarded them on to the photographers. That night, I thumped out the Mango Flat ghost story on my home laptop, sure that Murray Dowd would love it so much he would splash it all over the front page.

Which, in the end, is exactly what he did.

13

Dowd held the story until the Thursday edition and bravely dedicated the *Northern Reporter's* entire front page to the ghost house out in the sticks. Sally's photo of Brett, Kath and the baby standing out front was suitably dark and spooky. She'd done a brilliant job, I had to admit. Inset into the main photo was a smaller one, one of Deb's pictures of the name made of gravel on the bathroom floor. The story went bananas, taking over the internet in much the same manner as Nicky Chen and dick kid had the week before. This one, though, had longer legs. Everyone loves a ghost story.

Overnight, the finance editor had fallen off his roof and broken a leg while trying to retrieve his kid's soccer ball, so I was filling in for him and struggling to remain upbeat while churning out stories on the gas boom, the oil boom, the property boom and everything else that goes boom around here. The phone calls that started coming in around mid-morning were a welcome distraction.

In the beginning, the calls were from local newsrooms, mainly, wanting contact details for Brett and Kath. The TV guys already had a crew on the way to the Mango Flat pub, where they were hoping to track down an address. I had a feeling Spud the barman might oblige them, if he knew the way. Meanwhile, I played hard to get, happily telling my media colleagues to fuck off and do their jobs, which went down well.

By lunchtime, I was fielding calls from interstate newsrooms and current affairs shows as well. These

I handled a little differently, particularly the ones from the major networks. Six-thirty shows like *Hard News* and *This Day* had deep pockets. There was a chance they would fork out a substantial sum of money for Brett and Kath's story, although I was in two minds about the idea. On the one hand, there was no doubt at all that they could use the cash. On the other, as far as journalistic ethics went, *Hard News* was bad news. The show was a notoriously tabloid ratings-chaser. There was a distinct possibility any rough-head reporter they sent up would eat them alive.

The producer on the other end of the line was already plucking figures out of the air for me to pass on. I said I would. We swapped numbers. By the way, she said before finishing up, a producer and a reporter were already on their way to the airport, and would hit Darwin that evening, presumably with a blank cheque.

This Day was a little slower off the mark. I told them *Hard News* had beaten them to the punch and already had a crew on a plane heading for Darwin. The producer on the other end of the line swore, made a choking noise and said he'd call me back in five. He didn't.

I called Nicky. As promised, I'd phoned the night before to let her know the story would be running today. I hadn't asked her out.

'This thing is going bananas,' I told her.

'Fucking bananas is right,' Nicky said. 'We've had phone calls coming out our ying yangs all morning.'

'What? From reporters?'

'No, no,' Nicky said. 'Arseholes we know. Most of them taking the piss out of us. A few of them have rocked up out here to do it in person.' She laughed. 'Shane had a bloody meltdown before he even left for work.'

I thought about that. 'Well, he might have an even bigger one when he gets home,' I said. 'You're going to have reporters and film crews coming out your ying yangs fairly soon, too. They're looking for you guys right now. Looks like it might be a bit of a circus.'

'Fuck. That's great.'

'Listen, Nicky, some of these guys may offer to pay you for the story.'

She was silent for a moment. Then she said, 'How much?'

'Depends,' I said. 'Local TV and radio won't offer you anything. Tell them to piss off. There's a lot of interest from the national TV networks and that's where the money is. I've got a figure to pass on to Brett and Kath from *Hard News*, but the rest of you might do okay out of it as well, if you change your minds and talk to them. You just need to play your cards right. Don't jump at the first offer, but don't go too hardball either or they'll walk away.'

'Bloody hell.' She suddenly sounded doubtful.

'I need to give Brett a call. He around at the moment?'

'Yeah, he's around,' Nicky said. 'What are you doing tonight?'

I didn't answer for a moment, letting her think that I had to think about it. 'Tonight? I don't have any plans.'

'Good-o. Let's go to town. I'll get Murph to bring me in. Sounds like I'm going to need a fucking drink or twenty.'

I didn't think I would live through another big night out but I said 'Sure' anyway.

After we'd made the arrangements, I called Brett and told him about the money. He thought about it for two seconds and gave me the go-ahead to pass his number on to *Hard News.*

Gradually, the calls dried up, apart from one more from an afternoon shock jock out of Melbourne. We recorded a short interview, where I ran him through it and shared a few laughs. Afterwards, I finished off the boom town stories and belted out a dozen paragraphs on the nationwide publicity the Mango Flat story had generated, giving Murray Dowd an excuse to rehash it as an inside lead the following day.

After work, I decided to leave my car in the relative safety of the *Reporter's* car park and strolled up to the small bar where Nicky and I had arranged to meet. It was a nice enough place and not too crowded. In a previous life it had been a sweaty little strip club. Looking around, I seemed to recall having seen one or two shows there myself. The waitresses removed their tops during happy hours and flung them at the ceiling fans, I thought. Anyone who caught them received a free drink. Or maybe that was someplace else. Whatever the case, there aren't too many of those sorts of places left now, not that I really care that much.

Murph wasn't with Nicky when she walked in. He'd wandered off to take in a movie. He wasn't happy. The owner of Mango Flat's haunted house had left an increasingly cranky series of messages on his phone throughout the day. He'd seen the place on the front of the paper and wanted to know what the hell was going on out there. Murph still hadn't called him back.

'Guy's name is Fred Kennedy,' Nicky said. 'Apparently he's a really big wheel around town. Murph's not sure how to handle him. He doesn't want to get us all bloody kicked out.'

I whistled. Fred Kennedy *was* a big wheel. The supremely well connected millionaire property developer was the backroom powerhouse behind half the city's major building projects, past and present. It didn't surprise me that he owned property out at Mango Flat as well. Kennedy must be fast approaching 80 by now, I thought. He'd been around forever. I knew him reasonably well, although we hadn't spoken in a number of years.

'I don't think he can just boot you out,' I said to Nicky. 'Not if you're on a lease. Is it through an agent?'

Nicky nodded, looking over at the bar. 'Yeah, yeah. We've still got eight or nine months on the bloody thing. Let's go get a drink and something to eat.'

We went up, ordered beers and steaks, took a number and sat back down again. I was curious to know how they had handled the circling media throughout the day.

Nicky laughed when I asked.

'Well, for a start Murph parked a bloody tractor across the driveway so they couldn't come in,' she said. 'Then he managed to scare off the ones who got in anyway. Murph'll be on the news tonight just for telling the silly pricks to fuck off all day long.'

I laughed and asked if *Hard News* had contacted Brett yet.

'Yeah,' Nicky said. 'They're coming out tomorrow morning, apparently. He didn't talk money or anything, just said we'd work it out when they get there.'

'Just remember to keep your heads. You'll all be fine.'

She held up her beer. 'I hope so,' she said.

After dinner, we hit the city's pub strip, weaving our way from one fine establishment to another through the usual crowd of half-dressed youngsters, horny backpackers, after-work office types and juiced-up defence force personnel taking a little time out from learning to kill. Cops on foot patrol were up and down the street, keeping a wary eye on things.

We finally settled into a place called the Mangrove Club, so named, I theorised, because it was as dank and as fetidly fragrant as a swamp. It was standing room only but we managed to find a spare spot by a beer-barrel table. The music was *doof-doofing* so loudly it rattled my ribcage, and we spent much of the night shouting over it and waving our beers around in frustration.

I was pretty far gone by the time Nicky leaned in close to shout in my ear, *'You're okay, Jack,'* or something very like that.

'You too,' I shouted back. I may have raised my beer at her in salute.

'Want to go for a root in the dunnies?' she shouted.

I banged my beer down on the beer-barrel table and shouted, *'Certainly.'*

It was awkward but we managed. A large Samoan security guard collared me on the way out, demanding to know what the fuck I thought I was doing in the lady's toilet. He started frog marching me through the Mangrove Club towards the front door, creating a chaotic bow wave of spilled drinks and bad language. I didn't put up too much of a fight. These things sometimes end badly.

I tried twisting around to look for Nicky but it was hopeless. I'd lost her. When we reached the entrance, the Samoan gave me a friendly back slap on my way into the street and told me not to come back that night or he would tear my dick off. I believed him, so I decided to lurk a few doors down to wait for Nicky.

Half an hour later, I was still waiting. I dug out my phone. It was 1.30 in the morning. I tried calling her a couple of times but she didn't answer so I gave up and wandered off to find a taxi to take me home.

I paid the driver and waited for him to pull away before I stumbled over to my letterbox, hugged it for support and threw up in the drive. I noticed I had mail. An A4-sized envelope, curled into a half cylinder, protruded from the letterbox lid. After wiping chunks from my mouth with my shirt, I slipped it out and briefly examined it by streetlight. It was unmarked. No address. The postman hadn't put it there. I made my way up the drive and under the house to flick on the fluorescent light over the laundry tubs.

There were three neatly folded *Northern Reporter* front pages inside. Going on the dated style of the layout, two of them were reasonably old. The third, however, was not. It was that day's front page. Someone had circled, in red felt-tip, the name in the smaller photo.

GARY

Confused, I looked at the older pages. They featured red circles as well, and for a while I didn't understand what I was looking at. When I finally *did* understand what I was looking at, I leaned over the laundry tub to vomit again.

14

Once upstairs, I poured myself a large glass of water and took the pages into the office. I turned on the desk lamp, closed the lid of my laptop and laid the pages side by side on the desk in chronological order. Almost perfectly preserved, the first two were fifteen years old. I read and re-read the older front-pages several times, gulping water, picking them up and putting them down again. In places, the red circles were close enough together to look like eyes, which was mildly disconcerting.

That wasn't all.

I had written the stories.

I leaned back in my chair and looked over at the filing cabinet. It held all my old notebooks, including the ones from my crime reporter days. You never throw away your old notebooks. You never know when you might need them again, especially if you're a sloppy journalist who ends up in court a lot, which I was not. The same goes for anything else you may have jotted notes on. Slotted into the bottom draw was a tattered shoebox containing an impressive collection of napkins, beer coasters and menus, and at least one neatly folded paper tablecloth stained with red wine.

I gulped more water. The notes I'd taken that day on the beach in 1998, and all the days after that, would be in there somewhere, like ancient history awaiting rediscovery. I rubbed my forehead. Right then, I couldn't be bothered looking.

I looked back at the front pages.

The beach, I remembered, was a mess.

Thousands of rusted rivets and nails littered the black sand. Further out, towards the shoreline, a jumbled pile of charred timber rose in front of an abandoned bulldozer. The two-man clean-up crew had tossed on a dozen or so ruptured fuel drums and some twisted pipes, like decorations on a burned cake. The workers were sitting quietly on the sand near their machine, looking at their feet and occasionally glancing up at the cops.

Shielding my eyes with my notebook against the glare coming off the water, I looked back at the narrow track leading to the beach. The dozer had churned it up pretty good on the way in, probably obliterating any useful tyre tracks, which is why the cops hadn't closed off the road, I supposed. They'd attached crime scene tape to wooden stakes on the dune overlooking the beach and run it down to the water line on either side of the burned boats.

From behind the cordon, I traced the trail of footprints leading down to the vessels. The investigators were all sticking to the same path, not wanting to mess things up any further. By the look of things, the dozer had already scraped away half the crime scene. I wiped sweat from the side of my face. It had rained the night before and now the morning was steamy with November humidity, and heavy with diesel fumes. Thunder grumbled around inside dark clouds ballooning in the distance, away over the harbour, and the tide was coming in. The cops would have to work quickly.

They had already erected a temporary screen around the dead boy. The body lay in the sandy corridor between the ruined fishing boats. The vessels sat on the beach like a pair of collapsing charcoal skeletons, their sagging sterns crumbling away into the water. One was missing its bow, courtesy of the bulldozer. Australia's maritime authorities had run the boats aground, doused them in fuel and set them on fire. The day before, as it turned out. Moored together in a quarantine zone a couple of hundred meters offshore, more of the confiscated fishing boats bobbed up and down on the incoming tide, waiting their turn.

The little beach hidden in the mangroves was, at a guess, around 20 clicks from town. Despite the haze, I could still make out the low city skyline wavering in the heat away over the water. Only a few years before the illegal fishing boats had burned right on the city's waterfront, on an already polluted beach near the fishing wharf. As the city boomed, environmental pressure saw the operation moved further and further away. Now we were out in the middle of nowhere. It was pure luck we'd managed to find the place before anybody else had, but the TV crews wouldn't be far behind.

I glanced over at my photographer. He'd trudged further along the beach, looking for a wide shot. Bill Garwood was a soon-to-be-dead alcoholic but good at his job. He would get the shot, even if it meant climbing some stinking tree in the mangroves.

I looked back at the huddle of cops near the body, searching for a familiar face. I didn't see one. The investigators were talking in hushed tones, as though they were in church. A dead kid is a hell of a thing.

Then the big cop stepped out from behind the screen. I knew Detective Sergeant Harry Hollis quite well. The Christmas before he'd arrested me for urinating in the street after a party in town. He had just happened to be passing by.

Hollis stopped briefly and said something to the others before heading up through the sand, making for the police vehicles parked on the dune. I walked over as he lifted crime scene tape and ducked underneath.

'Harry.'

Hollis straightened, offered a curt nod of recognition and said nothing. The colour had drained from his face.

'Is it the missing boy?'

'You'll find out same time everybody else does,' Hollis said.

'One question. That's it.'

'No,' the cop said, and started walking off.

I went after him. 'Was he on one of the boats when they blew it up?'

Turned out he wasn't.

Hollis stopped in his tracks, whirled around and grasped my shirtfront with enough force to send me a few juddering steps backwards. I dropped my notebook. We'd eyeballed each other, suspended in the pressing tropical heat like fighters in a one-sided clench, until a startled shout came up from the cops down by the boats.

After an extra little shove for good measure, the big cop finally broke away. Hollis threw three words

over his shoulder as he walked off, and it wouldn't
be the first or the last time I'd ever hear them.

Fuck you, Jack.

15

Murray Dowd was in his office behind the front desk when I went to see him the following morning. Ties are a sartorial oddity in Darwin but Dowd was sporting one today, which meant one of two things: The *Reporter* was going to court or its editor was going to a funeral. I didn't ask which it was.

Dowd was toying with the idea of running bullet hole graphics across the front of the *Reporter's* weekend edition. There had been a wild, high-speed car chase down the highway overnight. The drivers had exchanged gunfire. It was, Dowd announced, straight out of the Wild fucking West. And all over a girl, too, which made the story doubly terrific.

'What do you think?'

'Go with the bullet holes,' I said from the doorway.

'You look like shit,' the editor observed over his glasses.

'I feel like shit. We need to talk.'

'You quitting?'

'Not today.'

'Have a seat.'

I went in and took a seat across from him. The editor's office was, typically, a shambles. Newspapers covered the old man's desk and half the floor. His TV remote sat in a discarded coffee cup. The framed front pages on the wall behind his desk screamed for a first-class wipe over. And a good decade after the office smoking ban had come into effect, the room still reeked of the cigarette smoke blown out by numerous under-the-pump page editors during the afternoon editorial conferences.

I waved the envelope at him just as his phone rang. The editor held up a hand, took the call, and swore throughout the conversation. I waited for him to finish.

When he was done, Dowd nodded down at his phone. 'We need a new photographer. That was McCartney. The Larson kid's girlfriend just called. He's in hospital. Somebody bashed the crap out of him in a pub last night.'

Paul McCartney was the *Reporter's* bicycle nut chief photographer. His parents had been Beatles fans but as far as anyone knew, his ex-wife had both her legs.

'Jesus, is he alright?'

'Jaw's broken in three places. Face is mush. Apparently they're going back to Melbourne.'

'Fuck,' was all I could say. Scotty was a good kid and it was too bad.

'Yes. Fuck,' Dowd said. 'Now, what's your problem?'

I showed him the envelope. 'I found this in my letterbox when I got home last night.'

I slipped out the three front pages and leaned across to hand them to him.

'Okay.' Dowd slipped his glasses off to inspect the pages, pressing them flat with his hands. 'And these are?'

'Top one's yesterday's front page. Excellent job, by the way.'

'Thank you. Get on with it.'

I leaned over and pointed. 'You see someone's circled the name 'Gary' in the photo?'

Dowd looked up. 'Yes, I'm not entirely blind yet, Jacko.'

'Now, the other two are from fifteen years ago.'

He shuffled the pages around. The first featured Bill Garwood's wide shot of the beach, under the headline: BODY ON BEACH MAY BE MISSING BOY. The second featured a black and white photo of a grim-faced Harry Hollis, under a single, blaring word: MANHUNT.

Dowd briefly inspected each page, frowning. 'I'm not going to read it all, Jack.'

'Right,' I said. 'Back in November '98 a kid named Gary Tanner was killed and dumped on a beach out of town. He was 16. He'd been sexually assaulted and had his skull caved in with a brick or something similar.'

'Jesus,' Dowd said.

I took a breath. 'It was pretty fucked up. He went missing on his way home from school. Cops found his bike in a park. No other sign of him until three days later, when he turned up dead. The whole place went nuts.'

'I bet,' Dowd said.

'They never found the killer.'

The old man frowned again, his bushy eyebrows doing a little dance, and he leaned back in his chair. He started twirling his glasses. I could almost hear his mind ticking over. I waited for it to do its thing.

'So,' he said, 'somebody wants you to think a kid who died fifteen years ago is now haunting a house out in the fucking sticks, is that what you're saying?'

'I don't know what I'm saying,' I said. 'It's a little weird, don't you think?'

'Definitely,' he said, suddenly looking serious. 'But the most concerning thing to me right now is that some nut job knows where you live.'

'Well, yeah, there's that too.'

Dowd replaced his glasses and leaned forward to inspect the pages again. 'You want to do something on this?'

'Me? No, although it *has* been a while since we looked at it. I did a piece on the tenth anniversary, the usual unsolved crime thing. I can't recall us doing anything since. Maybe Rankine can have a fresh go at it.'

Dowd nodded. 'That's probably not a bad idea but there's no way in hell we're connecting it to your haunted house, Jack. I'm not that fucking insensitive. Is the kid's family still around?'

'They moved south a year or so after the murder. Gold Coast, I think. I interviewed them over the phone for the anniversary thing. It was pretty tough going.'

Dowd pursed his lips, considering things, and lifted up one of the pages. 'You know,' he said, 'one of the first jobs I went on after I'd finished my cadetship - and this was back in the old *Daily Mirror* days - was to talk to the family of a girl who'd been killed by some fruitcake in a cemetery. Young girl, about 16 or so. She'd gone to put flowers on her grandpa's grave. The guy doused her in petrol and set her alight. He didn't even know her. Turned out he was just some random fucking nut.' He shook his head. 'We should just shoot bastards like that. Seriously. Just shoot 'em.'

He looked up, possibly expecting me to agree with him, so I nodded and said, 'Yep.'

'Hardest thing I ever had to do,' Dowd said. 'I was almost in tears myself.' He glanced back at the pages. 'Okay. I'll talk to Mike about it, see what he thinks.' He collected the pages together and handed them back.

'Right. Thanks,' I said.

'Now, fuck off out of my office and do some work. I suppose I have to organise some flowers or something for Larson.'

'Yeah, no chocolates, Murray. He won't be able to chew.'

'Piss off, Jack. And if you get any more shit in your letterbox you should think about moving.'

I slipped the pages back into the envelope and went back to my desk, where I put in a call to a contact I had at the Licensing Commission.

'I have an anonymous tip-off for you,' I told my contact. 'I think the Mangrove Club has a hidden camera in the lady's toilet.'

'And you know this how?' He sounded sceptical.

'A suspicious lady friend of mine thought she spotted one in there,' I said. 'Said the place was full of underage girls, too. You should raid the joint.'

He laughed. 'I'll look into it, Jack.'

'Thanks, mate. Let me know how you go.'

'Sure.'

I hung up and leaned back in my chair just as my mobile rang. I leaned forward again. It was Nicky, and she wasn't ringing to explain where she'd disappeared to the night before.

'The people from *Hard News* are here,' she said. 'They're offering us five fucking grand. *Each.*'

'That's not bad,' I said.

'You think? This producer chick wants us to sign all these bloody papers and shit.'

'That's fairly standard, Nicky. It's to stop you talking to any other TV networks.'

'Yeah, but we're not bloody lawyers,' she said. 'Brett and Kath have already signed up but I don't know.'

'Okay,' I said. 'I'm coming out. Be about forty minutes.'

As I ended the call, Mike Cooke marched over.

'Have you seen my email yet?'

I threw up my hands. 'About?'

'The cow with a horn growing out of its chin.'

I looked at him for a moment. 'Do cows have chins?'

'Fuck, I don't know. Lower jaw, then.'

'It'd be a bull not a cow.'

'Fuck. Whatever, Jack.' Cooke took a deep breath and spelled it out for me. 'The owners have sent in a photo of it. Their number is on the email. Call them, please, and write it up.'

'Sure,' I said.

Cooke offered me a baleful smile. 'You did such a good job on that fucked up chicken the other week I'm thinking of officially making you our deformed animal writer.'

'Can I put that on my business card?'

'Sure. I need it today, by the way. It's on the list,' he said, and wandered off again with a wave over his shoulder.

'No problem.' I sighed, scratched at the side of my face and grabbed my keys.

16

The house at Mango Flat was somewhat easier to find in the daylight. A rental car and a TV production van had joined the battered fleet parked in the yard. I pulled up behind the van as a middle-aged guy with a ponytail emerged from the side door with a fold-up card table. I'd seen him around town, at various press conferences and such. He was a freelancer, occasionally hired by the hard-pressed local stations when they had to be more than two places at once. I didn't know his name.

Another man, short and pink, hovered by an open rear door of the rental, leaning over an equipment case on the back seat. I'd seen him before, too, but it took me a moment to place him. *Hard News* hadn't sent up one of their foot-in-the-door, chase-you-down-the-street rough-heads after all. Instead, they had flown up a low-level network celebrity – and paranormal investigator – with the unlikely name of Lester Jericho, the host of a reasonably popular ghost-hunting program called *Night Crew*.

'You Jackson?' Ponytail asked as I approached.

'That's me.'

He extended his free hand. 'Gerry Baxter. I think we met at some presser a couple of years ago.'

There was no reason to disbelieve that, so I shook his hand and said, 'Oh, right. How you going?'

'Yeah, good.' Baxter gestured at the house with his card table. 'They're waiting for you inside.'

Jericho looked up, quickly finished what he was doing and strode over, crunching gravel. Despite his obvious discomfort in the oppressive morning heat, he looked upbeat and happy. Jericho was a spiky-haired blonde, probably in his mid-30s, slightly overweight, sweating profusely through his black *Night Crew* T-shirt, and so red in the face he looked about to burst. He wiped a fleshy pink hand on his shorts and held it out.

'Jack, is it? Lester Jericho.'

'Jack Jackson. Good to meet you.'

We shook and then he wiped a sleeve over his face, mopping up sweat. He grinned.

'Is it always this hot up here?' he said.

'Pretty much,' I said. 'First time in Darwin?'

'Oh, yeah. Loved your story, mate. Nice catch.' He waved a stubby hand at his soaked T-shirt. A picture of a ghostly figure rising from behind a gravestone sat beneath the *Night Crew* logo. 'This is right up our alley. Thanks for making it happen. Do you believe in ghosts, Jack?'

'No.'

Jericho laughed. 'Fair enough.' He nodded in the direction of the house. 'I do happen to believe in ghosts and this one's quite exciting. Genuine polt activity is a real rarity, you know. There'd be a hell of a lot of energy involved in putting together that name on the floor. A hell of a lot. Be fantastic if we actually catch it in the act. Most of the time we're chasing shadows and creaky floorboards.'

'Well, good luck with that.' I glanced at Baxter and then back at Jericho's absurdly pink face. 'I thought this was going to be a *Hard News* thing.'

Jericho nodded. 'Oh, yeah. Two birds with one stone, mate, and a tight budget. We'll knock out a shorter segment for *Hard News,* probably three or four minutes, and a longer one for *Night Crew* if we get any decent footage out of it. You wanna do a story on us?'

'Sure,' I said, even though I hadn't given that idea any thought at all. 'There's a lot of interest in this thing. Locally, I mean. It's huge.'

'Excellent,' Jericho said. 'We're just going to set up for some stand-ups, so we can have a chat after that if you like.'

'Sounds good to me,' I said.

Jericho jerked a thumb over his shoulder. 'My producer's inside with the guys. Liz. A couple of 'em have signed on the dotted line but the Chinese lass is waiting for you, apparently.'

I smiled at him and said, 'I'd better go and see what's happening then.'

Lester Jericho nodded and wiped more sweat from his face. 'That'd be great, mate. Sooner we get started the better.'

I left them to it and headed for the front door. Murph rounded the corner of the house before I made the front steps. His hands were in his jeans pockets, which seemed to be their preferred position.

I waved. 'Murph. How you going?'

He glanced at Jericho and the cameraman before answering. 'Yeah. I'm good,' he said, although his expression said otherwise.

'You spoken to Fred Kennedy yet?' I asked. 'Nicky told me he's been giving you grief.'

Murph let out a deep sigh. 'Yeah, he's good for now. Fuck knows what'll happen when he sees this shit on TV, though.' He shook his head, as though he could just imagine how that would go down.

'You coming in?'

One of his hands came out to stroke his beard. 'No, thanks. Nicky's handling it for me. I'm not real good when it comes to money.'

'Fair enough. I'll catch you later then.'

Murph frowned, looking like he was about to say something else and then he did.

'Nicky's a good mate of mine, you know,' he said, shifting from one foot to the other.

'I know.'

'You two seem to be hitting it off.'

'Ah.'

'Just look after her, okay?'

'I will.'

'Okay, then,' he said. And then, 'Sorry, I need to go take a shit.' He turned on his boot heels and went back the way he had come.

I stood for a moment watching Murph go, thinking that he was okay, that he was the sort of good mate you'd want if you wanted good mates, which, when I thought about it, I did not. I went inside.

The usual suspects were crowded around the coffee table in the front room, except for Lance. Cigarette smoke hung in the air in a thick haze. The atmosphere in the room was positively jovial compared to my last visit, although Brett and Kath – she was clutching a baby monitor, I noticed - seemed a little more subdued than everybody else. Shane must have taken the day off. He was sitting on the settee next to Deb, laughing at something she'd just said.

My shadow fell into the room and they all looked up. Nicky got to her feet, and so did a thin, birdlike woman with a *Hard News* ID around her neck.

'Jack, this is Liz,' Nicky said, gesturing the woman forward. She was young, mid to late-20s, red-haired and freckled, and not only looked like a bird but moved like one too. Sweat beaded on her spotted brow. Southerners. They just can't handle the heat. A bony hand flitted out and I leaned forward to shake it.

'Nice to meet you, Jack,' Liz said. Her tiny palm was sticky with sweat. 'Liz McKay. I'm a producer with *Hard News.*' Up close, she had bad skin, the sallow terrain below her cheeks a lunar landscape of acne scars, which was, I thought, probably why she had a backroom career as opposed to an onscreen one.

'We've just been discussing the situation here, Jack,' McKay said. 'It's an amazing story. Just amazing. Just the sort of thing *Hard News* looks for. Unfortunately, Nicky here is holding out on me.'

The producer smiled thinly at that, and so did Nicky, who said, 'Just give us a minute,' and gestured for me to follow her into the kitchen. I held up my hands in apology at McKay and went after her.

'I don't like this, Jack,' Nicky said with a shake of her head.

'What's wrong?'

'I don't know. Murph's a fucking nervous wreck about it. They've agreed to pay him just for letting them be here but he really doesn't want to have anything to do with it. He reckons that Fred whatshisname will throw us out for sure after this.'

I looked at her. 'Nicky, you're going to have five grand in your pocket. No offence but this place is a dump. The money could be your ticket out of here. The others are probably thinking exactly the same thing, you know.'

She pouted. 'I'm not going to just abandon Murph like that.'

'I totally understand that but Murph could probably get out of here too, if he wants. Five grand is five grand. It's easy money. If it was me I'd be jumping at it. Really. And if you decide to stay here there's no easy way to kick you out anyway.'

She looked away through the kitchen window, thinking things through.

'Okay, okay,' she said after a while. 'Money talks, right?'

'Yes, it does.' I waved a hand back at the lounge room. 'Are Brett and Kath okay? They don't seem too happy.'

Nicky huffed. 'Don't worry about them. Got their bloody noses out of joint, that's all. Thought they'd be getting the money all to themselves.'

'Shane's certainly looking a lot happier.'

'Yeah, he changed his tune pretty bloody quick when she started talking in thousands.' A crease furrowed across her brow. 'You're right, though. They all want to get the fuck out of here.'

She looked away out the window again.

'Where's Lance, by the way?' I asked.

Nicky waved a dismissive hand. 'Oh, he bloody stormed out of here this morning as well, fucking dickhead. Said he'd had a gutful of the whole thing and went to fucking work.'

'He's turning down the money?'

'Apparently.'

'Okay. Well, you know, it's his loss.' I tilted my head at the doorway. 'Where are Shane and Deb's kids?'

'At the day-care centre in town. They go three times a week to give us all a bloody break.'

'Right. These TV guys give you any idea how long they're going to hang around?'

'Just tonight,' Nicky said. 'They're going to set up some cameras and record shit while we're sleeping. Care to join us?' She raised an eyebrow at me.

I thought about it. I had nothing better to do.

'Sure.'

Nicky scratched at her chin. 'Okay. Let's go get this party started, shall we?'

We went back into the lounge room just as Lester Jericho, dripping, appeared at the front door.

'We all set, folks?' he asked.

17

After Nicky signed Liz McKay's papers, Jericho led us all back outside. Baxter had set up the card table outside his van, and was erecting a makeshift awning over it to keep the sun off. Jericho's equipment case lay open on the table.

'Just want to run you guys through what we're planning to do tonight,' Jericho explained, 'if my gear doesn't fry in this heat first.'

We gathered around as he ran one by one through his ghost-hunting gadgets. There were a few of them. First Jericho selected a slim digital recorder, not unlike mine, from its foam slot in the case. He held it up.

'Okay, this is your basic digital recorder. I'll use this in the house tonight to see if we can catch any EVPs.'

'EVPs?' Shane was leaning forward for a better look, as though he had never seen a digital recorder before.

'Electronic Voice Phenomenon,' Jericho said. 'There's a theory that some entities, given enough energy, can communicate using normal background noise, like static or radio signals, and that we can capture their voices if we try hard enough to engage them. I've caught some crazy stuff over the years, so I'd like to start off with a session tonight.'

As if on cue, a strange electronic burbling caught us all by surprise, but it wasn't coming from Jericho's recorder. The pink ghost-hunter looked around in confusion.

'Sorry,' Kath said, laughing. 'It's the baby.' She held up the monitor. We all laughed, including Nicky. Kath turned away to trot back inside. I watched her go, thinking she must be supremely confident in the salt-around-the-cot thing to leave the baby unattended.

Jericho patted his chest with a dramatic flourish and said, 'Now *that* caught me slightly off guard. Anyway, as I was saying, I'd like to do a session tonight, to see if we might actually be able to communicate with Gary.'

Beside me, Nicky murmured something I didn't catch. Jericho slotted the recorder into its place and selected a slightly larger instrument from the case. 'Okay, this one is an EMF detector. This'll record any fluctuations in the electro-magnetic fields in the house. Now, there's quite a body of evidence suggesting prolonged exposure to high electro-magnetic fields can cause feelings of discomfort, or unease, if you like, in people.' Here he paused to gesture at the house with his gadget. 'Now, an old place like this is probably going to have really bad wiring. If the shielding is breaking down or anything, you'll likely get some fairly high readings, so that's something we'll need to check out.'

Brett, leaning over the case, said, 'What's that one?'

Jericho set the EMF detector back in the case and said, 'K2 meter.' He lifted it out to show us. About the size of a TV remote, it had a single thumb button below a row of different coloured LED bulbs. 'It's basically a modified EMF detector. The theory goes that spirits themselves produce a magnetic field they can manipulate to give yes or no answers to questions we ask them, via the K2. They might only light up a light or two for a *no*, or the whole row for a *yes.*'

'Right,' Brett said, stroking his goatee.

Jericho slipped the device back into the case and waved at a collection of small video cameras sitting in their slots towards the back. 'We've also got a range of mini DVD cameras we can set up in the hot spots like the kitchen, the front room and the downstairs bathroom. They're all equipped with night vision, so they'll record okay in the dark.'

'You're going to film us in the bathroom?' It was Deb.

Jericho chuckled and quickly wiped away more sweat. 'No, no. We'll set one up in the hallway, looking in. If anyone needs to go, you can just close the door.'

Deb frowned. 'Okay. Sure.'

'Now, we'll hook up the static cameras to some monitors in Gerry's van, and Gerry will keep an eye on them throughout the night.'

Baxter had finished with the awning and now offered us a thin smile.

Jericho scanned our faces, beaming. He was in his element. His exuberance was almost infectious. 'That's basically it. Usually, I've got a whole team with me but we were in a bit of a rush to get here so I had to leave the other guys behind. I'll still be able to film with this, though.' He held up an odd-looking headset with a camera attached to one side. 'I call it Lestercam. It's a high res tactical headset camera with a built in mike, same thing law enforcement uses.'

'That is pretty fucking cool,' Brett said.

'Best investment we ever made,' Jericho said. 'Over the last few years this sort of lightweight gadgetry has changed the face of paranormal investigation. We can pretty much rock up anywhere at a moment's notice and capture absolutely everything and anything on video and audio with no trouble at all. It's brilliant.'

Waiting patiently to one side, Liz McKay cleared her throat and clapped her bony hands together.

'Right,' she said. 'We'll need to get you guys out of here for a few hours tonight while Lester does his thing. Where do you want to go? My shout.'

The Mango Flat pub was the obvious choice, although the wisdom of showing their faces there was the subject of some heated discussion. In the end, the group decided that a free meal was a free meal no matter which way you looked at it. Jericho and Baxter would spend the time conducting the EVP session, setting up the equipment and otherwise having a good poke around.

As Lester Jericho worked out what they would do first – a stand up with Brett and Kath outside, he thought, and then an interview with Shane and Deb in the lounge room, followed by a walkthrough of the 'hot spots' with Nicky – I made ready to leave, explaining I had to get back to work. Jericho and I swapped business cards, and I said I would call him later that afternoon for an interview over the phone, which was fine by him.

He glanced over at McKay, who was on her mobile over by the rental car.

'Listen,' he said. 'Liz will probably shoot me for this, but how would you feel about joining me out here tonight? It's your story, mate, and I could really do with an extra set of hands. We might just find one of those ghosts you don't believe in. Think you could handle one of the mini DVDs?'

'That,' I said, 'would be fantastic. Thanks. What time do you need me here?'

Jericho grinned. 'When does it get dark?'

Nicky walked me back to the car. The only vehicle missing from the yard, I noted, was the utility with the spotlights on the rollbar. It had to be Lance's.

'This'll be a fucking hoot,' Nicky said. Her mood had brightened. Money makes everybody happy. I was kind of jealous.

'Bound to be,' I said, opening the door. We stood there looking at each other for a moment.

'So, you'll be back out anyway?' she said.

'Sure. Listen ...'

'Yes?'

Ever hear of a kid named Gary Tanner?

Instead of asking the question, I looked over at the house. 'Do you know if anybody else went into town last night?'

She gave me a curious look. 'No idea. Why?'

'Oh, it's nothing. Forget it.' I studied her for a moment, and then waggled a finger at her, and then at me. 'Listen, Murph seems to think have we have a thing going.'

She grinned. 'A thing? Bloody looks that way, don't you think?'

'Well, yes, it does.'

'Then we must have a thing going,' she said.

'Will you give me free haircuts?'

'No, and just so you know, I don't usually go for older gentlemen.'

I laughed. 'Well, in that case I'm flattered you've made an exception in my case.'

'So you fucking should be.' A brief frown crossed her brow. 'Jack, I don't put up with crap. Let's just see how it goes. Take it easy. If it doesn't work out, it doesn't work out, okay?'

I considered that, and then nodded. 'Fair enough,' I said. I waved a hand at her. 'You need to stop disappearing on me.'

She smiled. 'Sorry about that. Lost you in the crowd.'

'I waited for you outside.'

'Won't happen again. Probably.'

'Thanks,' I said.

She gestured for me to go. I slipped into the driver's seat. Without saying anything further, Nicky closed the car door and headed back to the house.

18

Two seconds after I walked back into the newsroom Mike Cooke demanded to know where the hell I'd been.

'The house at Mango Flat,' I said, slouching into my chair and dumping the pie and chocolate milk I'd picked up in the canteen on my desk. *'Hard News* has a ghost hunter and a cameraman out there. They're spending the night.'

Cooke looked surprised. 'That was quick. You talking to them?'

'I'm calling the ghost guy back later this afternoon. Lester Jericho, from that TV show.'

'Night Crew? My kids love that show.'

'I'm happy to hear that, Mike. I'm going to be on it. Would you like his autograph?'

'What?'

'Lester Jericho has invited me to join him in the haunted house tonight. I'll have my own camera and everything.'

Cooke whistled. 'That's quite a score, Jack. An autograph would be excellent. In the meantime, can you get that fucking cow thing done? The subs have already laid it on the page. They need thirty centimetres. They're calling it *Unicow.'*

'Thirty? On a cow?'

'Thirty, Jack,' he said. 'Then you need to phone the Adelaide River pub. They had a mini-tornado down there last night.'

'There's no such thing as a mini-tornado.'

'Beg yours?'

'A tornado is a tornado, Mike.'

Cooke rolled his eyes. 'Okay, in that case ring the weather bureau as well.' He trotted away to take a call at his desk, adding as he went, 'And don't go anywhere. I'm a bit thin on the ground today.'

'Right.'

Beth Harvey popped her head over my wall. She had a large glob of food stuck to the corner of her mouth.

'You won't believe this,' she said. 'Some other kid has stuck his dick in a hot chook. It's an epidemic.'

I laughed. 'Unbelievable.'

'Isn't it?'

She disappeared again. It was the second time in two weeks that she had spoken to me. Perhaps I was growing on her.

I scoffed down my pie and called the cow people. In the end, the story turned out okay. The owners probably wouldn't sell it, not with the extra horn and all, and would most likely butcher and eat it themselves instead. Country people.

I plodded methodically through the rest of the afternoon, which was for the most part drama free, apart from reports of a naked man hurling potatoes at a suburban bottle shop which had earlier refused him service. That's Darwin for you.

Later, I called Lester Jericho's mobile. He was back in his hotel room in town, freshening up before heading back out to the house. Everything was set to go, the interviews had gone well, and he was really looking forward to having me on the investigation. The network had groomed him well; the pink man's responses to my questions had the feel of well-rehearsed spiel. The interview turned out okay in spite of that.

I left the office around five, passing Paul Rankine in the corridor leading to the staff car park. He was on his way back in, clutching a greasy bag of takeaway. I wondered if he was aware of the danger inherent in not being home with his wife and kids. I couldn't be bothered pointing it out to him.

We nodded and did not tell one another to fuck off.

I drove home, stopping on the way to pick up my own greasy takeaway. I ate quickly, showered, changed, looked at my watch, selected two beers from the fridge and went next door to see Eric. I knocked on his screen door and called his name.

'Out the back.'

I followed a path that led around the side of the house through a garden that was better than mine. He'd kept at it even after it had killed his wife. The house was a modest low-set brick job that Eric and his wife had purchased during a government fire sale of public housing in the mid-90s.

Dressed only in bright red Speedos, Eric was laying on a white banana lounge by the pool drinking scotch and smoking a fat cigar. His tan was the colour of cinnamon and evenly spread over his splendidly lean body, except for a band of pure white running above the waistband of his swimmers like a narrow sash. The swimmers were pornographically small, which was a little disturbing. The engorged package they contained was much larger than his cigar. I tried not to look at it.

'Jack,' he said, raising his glass. 'How you doing?'

'Good, mate. Thought I'd pop over for a quick one.' I held up the beers.

He grinned - his easy, amiable movie star's grin - and quickly downed the rest of his scotch. I passed him a bottle and pulled up the mouldy plastic chair reserved for guests. We chatted for a few minutes about our health and the weather before I got to the point of the visit.

'You didn't happen to notice any strange cars in the street last night, did you?'

Eric sucked on the cigar and blew out smoke before replying. 'Can't say that I did,' he said. 'Something up?'

'Oh, it's nothing probably. I found something in my letterbox when I got home last night. I've got no idea who put it there.'

'Sounds a bit mysterious, mate. You sure everything's okay?'

'Yeah, yeah. It's sort of work-related. You see yesterday's paper?'

'Sorry, Jack. I don't read the paper.'

'That's okay,' I said. I filled him in on the house at Mango Flat and the *Reporter* front pages about Gary Tanner.

'I remember that,' Eric said. 'Poor kid. They didn't get anyone for it, did they?'

'No, they didn't.'

'I saw a ghost once, you know.'

I looked at him. 'Really?'

Eric nodded. 'Yeah, when I was a kid back in boarding school. You know what kids are like. Place

128

like that is full of ghosts at the best of times. We'd just bunged on an end of year concert and I was packing some gear away in a big old storeroom when I saw this kid standing in a sort of alcove where the fire hose was. He was just standing there, staring at me. There was something about him that gave me the fucking willies, let me tell you. I still have no idea what it was. He was just a normal-looking kid, you know. Anyway, something fell over at the back of the room so I looked over to see what was going on. When I turned back the kid was gone. Thing is, there was no way he could have gotten out of the fucking room without getting past me.'

'Jesus.'

'That's what I said.' Eric took a sip of his beer and then said, 'You think somebody from the house left those pages in your letterbox?'

I shrugged. 'I don't know. The thought has crossed my mind. Two of them were with me last night, so that narrows down the list of suspects a bit. The whole thing is just ... bizarre. If it *was* somebody from the house they would've had to have gone to a bit of trouble to find out where I live.'

'Maybe they followed you home.'

'Maybe.' Another thought crossed my mind. 'You know, these guys are all locals. They grew up here. They were probably just a year or two older than Gary Tanner was when he died. There's no way in hell none of them heard about it. Schoolkid gets abducted and murdered on his way home every kid in town is going to be freaking out.'

'It's pretty fucking strange, that's for sure. But whoever put the thing in your letterbox could just be some old lady with too much time on her hands and an active imagination. You know, someone who kept the papers all these years and put two and two together and came up with five.' He sucked on the cigar. 'Take it from me, you sit around all day with not much to do and your mind goes off in all sorts of weird directions. You have to find something to do.'

I nodded slowly, thinking about that. 'It is a possibility, I guess. I hadn't thought of that.'

Eric raised his beer. 'I'm here to help.'

As always. For a brief moment, an unwelcome image of Jessica clutching at his thrusting, pearly white buttocks crashed into my head. I did my best to make it go away.

We fell silent for a while, until Eric said, 'The kids must be coming over soon, yeah?'

'Yeah. Next weekend.'

'Bring them over for a swim.'

'Sure,' I said. 'Listen, I've got to make tracks. Got a job on.'

'Alright, Jack. Thanks for the beer.'

I forced a smile. 'You're welcome.'

I headed for Mango Flat with the *Gurus* turned low, thinking about Gary Tanner and wondering if I should mention the *Reporter* pages to Nicky or Lester Jericho or anybody else. Dismissing Eric's old lady scenario for the minute, I ran various others around inside my head, thinking things through.

A ghost had not put the envelope in my letterbox. Somebody from the house had. I was convinced of that. Somebody from the house was behind everything that was going on out there. I was convinced of that, too. *Why* they might be doing it was a complete mystery.

The obvious course of action was this: I'd simply waltz in, wave the old news pages at them, and see what happened next. *That* would make good television if nothing else. With a bit of luck the person responsible would simply realise the jig was up and confess. What the hell, we might all end up having a good laugh about the whole thing, except for maybe the individual concerned; the person who had moved the shoes and pots, the person who had left the name made of stones on the bathroom floor - and the person who had stabbed a giant carving knife into a wall with enough force to send paint flakes flying.

Jesus.

Maybe that wasn't such a good idea after all. I suddenly recalled Father Charlie's story about Murph smashing up his parent's house. People, you learn, are capable of anything.

Murph.

He had been in town catching a movie. Or perhaps not. A little film flickered through my brain, of the bearded gnome creeping out of his caravan in the middle of the night to scoop up gravel and hurl it high over the roof of the house. Cut to: Murph lurking suspiciously outside my house in the dark, envelope in hand. Cut to: Nicky leading me by the hand through the Mangrove Club towards the lady's toilet.

Keeping me busy.

Cut to: black.

Interview – Part 2

Interrupting, Detective Sergeant Knight said, 'Did it occur to you at any point prior to this that any of them may have been involved in the death of Gary Tanner?'

'No, it did not.' I drained the rest of my coffee, glancing briefly over the rim at the camera. Was Harry Hollis in the next room? I believed he was. The coffee was cold and went down like grease.

Tezuka leaned forward. 'When did you first suspect?'

It was the first time the Japanese detective had spoken in hours.

'Not until much later,' I said. I put the cup down. 'Look, the only connection I had right then was some old news pages and a name on the floor. And I hadn't actually given much thought as to *why* someone had sent the stories my way.' I thought about it now. 'I guess I was assuming, correctly as it turns out, that whoever it was wanted me to write something about the kid haunting the fucking house. That wasn't going to happen, so I decided to ignore it.' I thought some more and added, 'Someone was screwing with me. I didn't like that.'

Knight: 'So at that time you decided not to confront them with these news clippings?'

'Correct. I suppose in the back of my mind I had an idea that this person simply wanted to up the ante. You know, to freak everybody out even more. Like I said, these guys were kids themselves when Gary Tanner died. At the time, it would have been a huge deal to them. Suddenly being told his spirit was haunting their house ... I don't know.'

Knight thought about that for a moment and then looked down at his notes. 'Okay, back to the Friday night you went back out to the house.'

'I got there around seven.'

Tezuka said, 'Excuse me. Sorry, you thought someone was, in your words, *screwing with you* but you decided to continue?'

'News is news, detective.' I gave a little wave. 'And like I said, everyone loves a ghost story.'

'Yes. You don't believe in ghosts but you went looking for one anyway,' Tezuka said.

I nodded. 'I went looking for one anyway.'

19

By the time I made it to the end of the rutted drive at Mango Flat it was almost dark. The front yard was all but deserted. I'd missed everyone. Murph's battered sedan, the Commodore and the station wagon were gone, as was the rental, probably driven off to dinner by Liz McKay. Lance's utility still wasn't around either.

Gerry Baxter had moved his van a little closer to the house. An electronic glow filled the interior. A couple of thin cables snaked from the open side door across the gravel, over the front steps and into the front room. As I pulled in under the frangipani tree, the cameraman was unwinding another cable from a large spool, trudging carefully backwards through the stones towards the front steps.

Jericho had heard the Yiros. His crimson face popped out of the door and he gave me a wave with a tripod he was holding. The floodlights under the eaves were on but the rest of the house was in darkness. The ghost hunter's black *Night Crew* T-shirt was almost invisible in the gloom, making his pale face appear to bob about like a lonely pink balloon in the doorway. As I waved back, a flash of sheet lightning flared into the sky behind the mango trees. A moment or two later came an ominous rumble. A storm front was moving in. Perfect.

I left the car and headed for the front door, watching as Baxter wound his way inside and disappeared from view. I stood on the porch for a moment, peering inside while my eyes adjusted to the darkness within. Inside, whirls of torchlight swept around the kitchen.

'We're in here, Jack,' Jericho called.

Careful not to trip over Baxter's cables, I threaded my way around the furniture and into the kitchen. At the far end, by the back door, Jericho held a torch as Baxter attached the cable to one of the mini cameras mounted on a tripod.

'Hi, guys,' I said.

Jericho gave me a wave with his free hand. 'Glad you could make it, Jack.' Even in the torchlight, I could see the sweat glistening on his forehead. With the ceiling fans switched off the air in the house was perfectly still and thick as soup. 'We're just finishing up with the static cameras,' Jericho said. 'We've set one up one the other side of the lounge room, looking this way, towards the kitchen door, and the other is trained on the bathroom door, so we've basically got the hot spots covered. You'll have to watch out for them in the dark, and the cables.'

The heat had done little to suppress Jericho's enthusiasm. He spoke rapidly. His adrenaline was pumping. Lester Jericho had a buzz on, which, I guessed, might not be unlike the one I used to get chasing cops and ambulances. Gerry Baxter, though, seemed totally un-buzzed, apparently content with doing the job he'd been hired to do.

'Okay,' I said. 'Why *are* all the lights off, by the way?'

Jericho glanced up at the darkened ceiling. 'It's mainly to eliminate the chances of any false positive readings on the EMF detector,' he said and then, laughing, added, 'plus it also makes the place look spooky as fuck. That's off the record, Jack.'

I laughed too. 'Fair enough.'

Baxter stepped away from the camera and said, 'I'll just go check the feeds,' and went back outside. Pointing his torch at the floor, Jericho led the way back into the front room. His equipment case lay open in a space he had cleared on the dining table.

'The guys'll be back in two or three hours so we're a bit pressed for time,' he said, standing the torch lighted end up on the table. The beam bouncing off the ceiling offered enough light to see.

Jericho slipped another of the mini DVD cameras from the case and handed it to me. 'Apparently one of them took off this morning and hasn't been back, so we'll have to keep an ear out for him in case he turns up.'

'Lance.'

'That's him. Not too happy we're here by the sound of things. You ever used one of these before?'

I turned the camera over in my hands and flipped open the screen. 'Sure.'

'Try not to move it around too fast and you'll be fine. Now because we're lights out the only way you'll be able to see anything is via the screen. It may take a bit of getting used to. Give it a go.'

'Right.' I turned it on, slipped my hand through the strap and tried it out, sweeping around the room. The pinhole light at the front of the camera threw little more than a dim circle but everything on the tiny screen appeared bright and supernaturally green.

'It's got a fresh battery pack so it shouldn't clap out on you. We've had one or two incidents where

the batteries have suddenly drained just like *that*.'
He snapped his fingers. 'The theory is that spirits
may be attempting to use the energy from the
batteries to manifest themselves or communicate in
some way.'

'Okay.'

'Now, and this may make me sound like a bit of a
wanker, try to keep it trained on me as much as
possible, unless something catches your eye of
course. It's okay to swear, by the way, if you *do*
happen to see anything. Adds to the drama. We'll
bleep you later.'

I laughed. 'Fuck. Okay.'

Baxter came back in and gave us a thumbs up.
'Good to go, Lester.'

'Excellent. Thanks, Gerry. We're just about good
to go too.'

The cameraman disappeared again.

'Gerry will monitor the static cameras from the
van while we're in here,' Jericho said. 'Keep the
camera positions in mind so you don't wander out of
shot. Gerry needs to see us at all times.'

'Right. No problem.'

'Excellent,' Jericho said. 'Now, I'll do an intro
back in the studio explaining why you're here with
me but I might get you to say a few words into the
camera anyway. You know, just about how excited
you are to be here or some bullshit. That okay?'

'No problem.'

I handed the mini DVD camera back so he could
film me saying how excited I was to be there.

When we were done, the ghost hunter handed the
camera back, mopped sweat from his face with a

sleeve and reached into his case for Lestercam. He slipped it on. Then he unclipped a two-way radio from his belt. Jericho waved at the camera positioned at the entrance to the hall. Into the radio he said, 'You got us, Gerry?'

The radio crackled. 'All good here, mate.'

To me the ghost hunter said, 'Get the torch off for me, will you? Let's get this investigation underway.'

Jericho started with the EMF detector. He held it at arm's length, methodically waving it first around the lounge room before moving into the kitchen, where he held it close by the light switch next to where the carving knife had hit the wall. The ghost hunter's movements were slow and deliberate, so for the most part I managed to keep his disembodied balloon face in the middle of my screen.

'These readings are all over the shop,' Jericho said. 'That's kind of to be expected with a place this old. Wiring is probably shot to hell. Probably a massive fire hazard too. Might have to mention that to them. How old would this place be, do you think?'

'Probably built back in the 50s sometime,' I said, watching him through the screen. 'Those mango trees out the back have got to be that old, at least. You said this morning that high readings might fool with your mind somehow. How does that work?'

Jericho moved around the kitchen, checking the power points. 'Well, we're all sensitive to EMFs, Jack. You, me, everybody. Our own bodies generate energy fields. High or low frequency electromagnetic radiation can affect those fields in various ways. Now, anything you can plug in to a wall generates electromagnetic radiation. We live with it every single moment of our lives, and people *do* stress out if they're exposed to high frequency fields for any length of time. It does affect you physiologically. That's a fact, and it may explain cases where there isn't any *physical* evidence of paranormal activity, you know, but where people are simply seeing or hearing things, like the young lady who saw something on her bed.'

'Okay,' I said. 'But in this case you do have physical evidence. Allegedly.'

Jericho nodded. 'Yes. Allegedly.' He waved his detector. 'And that's the problem we have here. Nobody has *seen* this stuff as it happens, which is a little odd given the amount of activity they've reported. This is one very active polt.'

'They've all seen the gravel falling from the ceiling,' I said.

The ghost hunter smiled. On screen, his teeth were shiny green. 'Well, I've been thinking about that. Follow me.'

We went back into the front room, where he looked up at the ceiling.

'You know,' Jericho said, 'I grew up in country Queensland. One of our favourite pranks at school was to put flour on the ceiling fans during lunch break. The teacher would come back in, switch them on, and next minute you've got an entire class covered in flour. Hilarious.'

I pointed my camera at one of the fans. The blades were filthy. 'You think someone is putting the gravel on the fans?'

He shrugged. 'It's a possibility we have to consider. Even though I am a believer I still need to look at any other possible explanations, and by that I mean straightforward non-paranormal ones. These fans are hung pretty low. You'd just have to stand on a chair to get up there.'

'Right. How did you become a believer, by the way? Did you see a ghost?'

He gave a little snort of laughter. 'No, I didn't *see* a ghost. I heard one, and it wasn't human.' Jericho extended his arm towards one of the fans and waved the EMF detector around. 'Originally we lived in Brisbane,' he said. 'My folks took us bush when I was about nine or ten. They bought 20 acres, a tractor and five Slim Dusty albums, so they were pretty keen on the country life.' He dropped his arm. 'We lived in a caravan for a few years while the old man decided whereabouts to build us a house. We had a little cattle dog named Scruffy. We found him spewing up blood outside the van one day. Best guess is that he was poisoned. Anyway, the old man took him off somewhere, and shot and buried him. A while after that he started building the house. One night after we'd moved into it my folks left us alone while they went into town to pick up some takeaway. My brother and I were watching TV when we heard a dog panting.' He paused, catching his breath. 'Naturally, we looked around for it but couldn't see a damned thing. It took us a while to work out the panting was coming from *under* the lounge we were fucking sitting on. And there was nothing there.' He paused again. 'Anyway, we were a little creeped out so we told the old man about it

140

when they got back. He thought about it for a while and then told us the lounge was over the exact spot where he'd buried the bloody dog.'

'Okay. That's spooky.'

'Yep, and that's when I decided there must be an afterlife, Jack. Even for doggies.' He glanced down at the EMF detector and then said, 'Let's do some EVP work.'

Jericho placed the K2 meter – the one with the thumb button and row of bulbs – on the coffee table and strolled around the room with his digital recorder asking questions. He held the device in front of him at arm's length, the same way he'd held the EMF gadget.

'Is there anybody here with us?'

'Please come forward and tell us your name.'

'Is your name Gary?'

'Keep an eye on the K2 meter, Jack.'

'Right.'

This went on for a further ten minutes before Jericho stopped to play back the recording. We both leaned in to listen.

'Sometimes these things will pick up stuff that's beyond the normal range of human hearing,' the ghost hunter said, but all we heard was hissing silence after each of his questions.

'What's the scariest thing you've ever heard on one of these?'

'Oh, probably an entity saying my name. That was down in Adelaide, at an abandoned factory. Couple of workers were killed in an industrial accident there back in the 60s. We didn't pick up anything on site but when we went through the recordings in analysis we heard it clear as a bell. *Lester.* It sounded somewhat aggressive too, you know. There's something about personal interaction at that level that sends chills up your spine. It means the thing *knows* who you are.' He pointed the recorder at the hall. 'Let's try the bathroom.'

I asked, 'Have you ever seen anything make words like this before?'

The ghost hunter grinned. 'No. That's what makes this thing so special.'

We went in. Jericho closed the toilet lid and placed the K2 meter on top. We sat with our backs to the sickly green tiles as he repeated his questions. The air was still thick with that wet-dog smell.

'Is your name Gary?'

'Are you here with us now?'

'We aren't here to harm you.'

'Please come forward.'

We heard nothing. Jericho repeated the questions and then he said, 'Whoa, the K2 is going off like a bitch.'

I looked. The row of lights had lit up, bright enough to cast a jumping shadow of the cistern up the wall. The hairs at the back of my neck did an electric little dance. I sucked in air.

The lights flickered, went out, came back on and then went out again. Beside me, Jericho let out a gurgling breath.

'Can you do that again?'

He waited. Nothing happened.

'Can you *please* do that again for us?'

No response.

We sat in silence for a while, staring at the device on the toilet. Suddenly Jericho held up a hand, cocked his head to one side and looked up at the darkness overhead.

He whispered, *'Did you hear that?'*

I shook my head, which he didn't see, so I whispered, *'What?'*

'Sounded like something scraping on the floor upstairs. Listen.'

I listened and, a moment later, there *was* a noise.

'There it is again,' Jericho hissed. *'Is that a door opening?'*

'I don't know.'

'It's above us, right?'

'Sounds like it.'

Without speaking, the ghost hunter got to his feet and motioned for me to follow. We crept from the bathroom into the hall. I pointed my camera up the black staircase, staring at the screen. At the top, lightning threw vague rectangles through the tarpaulin over the window. We listened for a few moments, waiting for the noise to happen again. All we heard was a low grumble of thunder.

'Jeez, I hope we got that on audio,' Jericho said.

Then, as we stood there, one of the upstairs lights came on.

20

As Jericho had promised, what I said next earned a post-production bleep. Above us, pale yellow light fell across the upstairs landing from an unseen doorway, spilling in elongated bars through a rickety-looking timber balustrade and over the top three or four steps. My heart pounded, violently enough to remind me of the way the *doof-doof* music in the Mangrove Club had reverberated deep in my chest the night before. I didn't like that. Not one bit.

'*There isn't anybody else in the house, right?*' I whispered.

Jericho, staring up at the bars of light, shook his head. '*No. I went through all the rooms with the Chinese girl before they left. Keep your camera steady.*'

Lester Jericho, I decided, was not very good with names. I pointed the camera at him, trying to keep it steady.

'*Okay. What do we do?*'

A drop of sweat fell from the tip of his nose. Then he grinned at me, greenly, and for some reason that unsettled me more than the light did.

'*Stay here,*' he said and slowly began to take the stairs one at a time. The timber treads creaked beneath his feet. I kept the camera on him. Two thirds of the way up he stopped to peer through the balustrade. Jaundiced yellow light splashed over one-half of his face.

'*It's the bathroom. I'm fairly certain that door was closed when I was up here before,*' Jericho said over his shoulder, and before he could finish saying *before* the light went out again.

'*Shit,*' Jericho said. His radio suddenly crackled to life, startling both of us. I got bleeped again.

'You're out of shot, guys,' Gerry Baxter said. 'I can't see you.'

Jericho swore again and fumbled for the radio. '*Yeah, yeah,*' he hissed into it. '*Give me two seconds, mate.*'

'Ah. Okay. Roger.'

Jericho now held up the digital recorder once more and said, in a loud, authoritative voice, 'Gary, if that's you could you please turn the light on for us again?'

He waited for a response. The light did not come back on.

'Gary, I know you're trying to communicate with us. Turn on the light again.'

Again, nothing happened. After a minute or so, Jericho retreated down the stairs.

'What do you want to do?' I asked.

'We have to go up there.' Jericho glanced at the cameras positioned at the bottom of the stairs and then spoke into his radio. 'Gerry, can you bring your gear in? We need to take a quick look upstairs.'

'Right. Give me a minute.'

'Do you think it could be the wiring?' I asked.

Jericho thought about it. 'That's a possibility. We need to check it out.'

We heard Baxter coming back towards the house and in a moment jerky white light flooded the front room. By then I'd been peering into my tiny screen for over an hour and Baxter's camera-mounted light appeared so blindingly bright I had to throw my free hand up to cover my eyes.

'What's happening?' the cameraman asked.

'The bathroom light just came on upstairs,' Jericho said. 'Just follow us up while we go check it out.'

'No problem. Looks like it's about to piss down rain, by the way.'

'Okay. Thanks.' The ghost hunter grinned at me again. 'You right, Jack?'

'Sure.'

We went upstairs, cautiously following our own creepy, jerking shadows as Baxter brought up the rear. At the top, Jericho held out a palm for us to stop and called out, 'Hello. Is there anybody there?'

There was no reply. Lightning lit up the tarpaulin again. I could hear the wind picking up outside. A heavy spatter of raindrops coursed across the roof over our heads.

The upstairs landing was L-shaped, turning away parallel to the staircase. There was a closed door in front of us, streaked with mould. Next door, a small recessed alcove contained a towel rack and small side table piled with well-thumbed magazines. The door centred in the back wall of the alcove stood open. The bathroom. Beyond that was the entrance to a dark hallway, presumably leading to more rooms, and then another mouldy door towards the front of the house.

Jericho motioned for us to head for the open door. Floorboards creaked beneath our feet. Baxter's camera threw its white light over our shoulders, lighting up the interior of the room and filling it with long, distorted shadows at the same time. This bathroom was finished in the same sickly manner as the one downstairs, and it smelled the same too. After a brief inspection, Jericho flicked on the light with an emphatic click. He frowned.

'This is really old. Would've taken a bit of force to turn it on,' he said. He flicked the switch several times. 'It's seriously hard to move.'

A stuttering blue flash came through the window at the top of the stairs. Something cracked over our heads and a second later, a thunderous boom shook the house. We all jumped.

'That was close,' Jericho said, peering at the window.

'Lightning capital of the world,' Baxter said.

Jericho looked at him. Baxter lifted his free shoulder.

'Darwin's smack bang in the middle of one of the most lightning-prone areas on earth,' the cameraman said. 'One storm I filmed a couple of years recorded over 5000 lightning strikes in one go. That was a big bastard. This one's a baby.'

Another boom rolled over the house.

'Right,' Jericho said. 'That's good to know. Thank you, Gerry.'

Next, he tested out the door, moving it back and forth. The bottom of it *did* scrape on the floor. He asked, 'Is that the same noise we heard downstairs?'

'Could be,' I said. 'Should we check the other rooms?'

'No,' the ghost hunter said. 'We shouldn't really be up here at all. They only gave us permission to film downstairs.' He turned to Baxter. 'I might do a quick piece to camera while we're up here anyway, Gerry.'

'Go for it, mate.'

I got out of the way as Jericho positioned himself outside the door. The ghost hunter rolled his neck around, as though limbering up for a fight. Overhead, another squally patter of rain hit the roof and a moment later settled into a heavy drumming.

Jericho raised his voice. 'Okay, mate?'

Baxter said, 'Yep. That's good.'

'Right,' Jericho began. 'So, while Jack and I were conducting an EVP session in the bathroom downstairs we heard a noise that sounded like it came from above us. As we went to investigate the source, the light in the room behind me came on by itself and then turned off again. Now, one possible explanation for that is faulty wiring, so we can't at this stage definitively say that it is evidence of paranormal activity.' He stood there for a further five or six seconds. 'All good?'

'It's good,' Baxter said.

Jericho swore anyway. 'Shit. I forgot to mention that the K2 went off just before we heard the noise.'

'You want to do it again?'

'No, no. I'll do it in post when we get back. Let's head back down. I want to get back into that bathroom.'

This time Baxter led the way. He'd just stepped from the bottom tread when he froze. Jericho and I stopped too, almost colliding. All three of us could hear it over the rain. Outside, something was crunching purposefully towards the front door through the gravel. In a moment, it thumped up the front steps and onto the porch. A flash of lightning threw a long shadow into the room. Thunder boomed. Bravely, Baxter took three or four quick steps forward and swung his camera up, pointing it across the lounge room at the front door. A tall figure appeared in the doorway, lit up by Baxter's camera like a blood-drained spectre. Behind the figure, lightning flashed.

'What the fucking *fuck* is going on here?' the figure said.

21

Later, in Nicky's room, in Nicky's bed, Nicky said, 'I bet you almost shit your pants, eh?'

I waved a hand. 'No, I did not almost shit my pants. I knew it must have been Lance coming home all along. We *were* sort of expecting him but we didn't hear his car in the rain. You really do have a way with words, you know.'

Nicky exhaled a near-toxic cloud of cigarette smoke and alcohol fumes. 'Thanks. Sounds like he was happy to see you.'

'Oh, yeah. He stormed around turning all the lights on and then told us he was fucking going upstairs for a fucking shower and then he was going to fucking bed and we could do whatever the fuck we liked. I think he had a bad day at work. Lester sort of shrunk into a little pink ball after that and decided to pack up and wait in the van for Liz.'

'Hide more like it.'

'Possibly.'

Nicky smoked her cigarette for a moment. Although the storm front had blustered through in less than five minutes, rain continued to patter on the tin roof over our heads.

'So,' she said. 'Apart from fat Lester getting all worked up over a bathroom light nothing happened, is that right?'

'Correct. Nothing happened.'

Jericho had, after the return of the decrepit convoy, filled everyone in as quickly as humanly possible in the front room. No, nothing much had happened, and the little that *did* happen wasn't enough to prove anything paranormal was going on. Yes, he was leaving for the night but Gerry would stay in the van monitoring the three static cameras, just in case. Yes, it's somewhat disappointing they hadn't caught too much but you never know. Yes, he would be back first thing in the morning to go through the footage. Yes, he was going now. Goodbye.

'They still have to pay us, right? Even if they get nothing?'

'Yes. How was your night, by the way?'

Nicky snorted. More fumes came out. 'Well, apart from Shane being all super paranoid about people staring at us and the fact that that Liz chick can't play pool for shit, it was pretty okay. Some cowboy rode a horse into the bar, so that was exciting.'

'Does that happen a lot?'

'All the time. You know, that bathroom light has been playing up for ages. It's like a fucking disco in there sometimes.'

'I figured it was a wiring problem of some sort.'

'Sure you did. Murph was supposed to fix it ages ago.'

We fell silent while she continued to puff. A dingy bedside lamp threw a yellow pall over the room, and the air reeked of stale cigarette smoke and perfume, which was not an entirely enchanting combination. Like every other room in the house, Nicky's was crammed with furniture, all of it cluttered with feminine things: perfumes, sprays, hairbrushes, bras, scattered tampon boxes. The floor was a minefield of assorted clothing and kicked-off shoes. A stained sheet hung over the window in place of a curtain. The bed sagged dangerously in the middle, so that our hips pressed together, and it squeaked alarmingly anytime we moved. I vaguely wondered how thick the walls were.

Listening to her breathe, I considered the idea that Nicky might somehow be involved in what was going on here. The whole thing was a fucking hoax for sure and if Nicky was involved in any way she was a damned fine actor. For that matter, they all were. Deep down, the notion that *everyone* in the house might be involved had been with me from the start. Maybe they had cooked the whole thing up over dope and beer and cigarettes around that filthy coffee table one night, although that particular theory presumed they knew how big the story would get. Maybe they did know. Maybe they didn't. I didn't know.

What I *did* know was that if the group had a leader, Nicky was it, and beneath the good time girl veneer there lurked a quiet intelligence she seemed determined to bury. In that regard, she reminded me of Jessica, who was smarter than anyone I knew but had the weird knack of downplaying it, especially in company. I never worked out why she did that. Maybe she didn't want to appear snooty. I have no idea.

I let the thing slide. Nicky was naked.

'Right, that's enough excitement for one night,' she said. She leaned over to stub her cigarette into a disgusting ashtray perched atop a pile of womanly disorder on her bedside table. Turning back, she said, 'Shall we?'

I decided we should, and it was an unnervingly squeaky business.

22

I dreamed of the red circles on the old news pages, the ones that were close enough together to look like eyes.

We woke to an urgent knock on the door and somebody calling Nicky's name. Nicky flopped around unhappily on the bed.

'Go away,' she said.

'Nicky, Lester wants to see Jack.'

There was an anxious edge to Deb's voice, or maybe I imagined that. Still half asleep, I rolled over. A pale rectangle of light had appeared behind the hanging sheet. For a moment, the red eyes of my dream hovered in front of it like a lingering afterimage. I sat up, feeling my wrist, wondering where my watch had gone.

'Deb, it's Jack. What time is it?'

'Nine thirty.'

'Tell him I'll be down in a minute.'

There was no reply. She'd gone. Nicky flopped around some more, wrestling her pillow over her head. In the thin light seeping through the stained sheet I noticed a sickly yellow smudge staining her pillow as well. I looked over my shoulder. A stain smudged my pillow too, and it looked much, much worse. Sally North's crack about catching diseases suddenly came back to me like a dire prophecy. Hell.

'I'm not getting up,' Nicky said. The words were crushed into the bed sheets but I heard them just the same.

Patting her rear, I said, 'I'll go see what he wants,' and swung out of bed. I found my watch in a shoe on top of my clothes. The other shoe was over near the door. I dressed, smoothed out the crumples as best I could and went downstairs after a brief visit to the disco bathroom.

Deb, Shane and Lance were huddled around the coffee table. They had been conversing in hushed tones but clammed up the moment they heard me creak down the stairs. Shane and Deb's little ones were in the TV room, quietly making a mess of their breakfast.

Seemingly over his fit of rage, Lance casually sipped coffee and smoked a cigarette. Deb was smoking as well, only a little more furiously. She *was* edgy. Shrouded in a blue pall, she wouldn't look at me, choosing instead to gaze down at her lap. Next to her, Shane tapped his fingers impatiently on his armrest, not smoking. None of them said good morning to me.

'What's going on?' I asked.

'No idea,' Shane said, and he jutted his chin at the front door. 'They won't tell us.'

I said, 'Ah. Okay, I'll go see if I can find out what's going on.'

Shane nodded and said, 'You do that, mate.'

Outside, Liz McKay was pacing back and forth at the back of the hire car like a woman possessed. On her mobile, she was involved in a deep, heated conversation I couldn't hear. Her bird-like head jerked this way and that, pecking at air. Something was up. Standing beside Baxter's van, Lester Jericho gestured me over with an urgent wave.

'Has something happened?' I asked as I walked up.

'Oh, yeah,' Jericho said. His face was as pink and sweaty as ever but his enthusiasm and good humour had deserted him. He waved at the inside of the van. Seated at a cramped workspace in the rear, surrounded by electronics, Gerry Baxter had a laptop open.

'I want you to see this before we decide what to do,' Jericho said. He glanced over at Liz. 'Set it up again, Gerry.'

The inside of the vehicle reminded me of those surveillance vans you see all the time in movies, all blinking lights and screens and plastic coffee cups. The cameraman had a set of bulky headphones draped around his neck. Baxter tapped a couple of keys, moved his mouse around, and swung the screen towards us. Night vision video ran backwards, so rapidly it appeared little more than a green blur. I couldn't make anything out.

McKay had finished with her call and now stomped over like a tiny storm. 'We have to confront them,' she said. 'That's straight from the boss.'

I stared at her. 'Confront them? What's going on?'

'Watch the video, Jack,' Jericho said.

Baxter clicked his mouse, hitting the play button on the video software's control bar.

I leaned in for a better look. The footage was from the camera positioned at the entrance to the hall, looking across the front room towards the kitchen. On screen, the date appeared at the lower left corner, the time on the right. It began at 04:23:00 AM. Five or six seconds later the picture suddenly jerked, as though the camera had been bumped, and then, a second after that, the image blurred away to one side, only to refocus on a blank wall at the bottom of the stairs.

'Somebody turned it around,' Jericho said.

I looked at Baxter. 'Did you see that happen?'

He screwed up his face for a moment and then said, 'Yes. I did.'

'Did you go inside to see what was going on?'

He shrugged. 'I'm not the ghost hunter around here.'

'Did the other cameras catch anything?'

Behind me, Liz McKay said, 'Play him the other one.'

Baxter exited the screen and scrolled through a menu. He clicked on another file and another green-hued image filled the laptop's screen. This time it was from the camera at the back door in the kitchen. It, too, began at 04:23:00 AM. The cameraman hit play.

Eight or nine seconds after the hall camera had turned around, something flew through the doorway from the front room and across the kitchen. It bounced off the kitchen cupboards and onto the floor, out of view.

'What the hell was that?' I asked.

'It's a toy,' Jericho said. 'As soon as I saw this I went in for a look. It's still on the floor. It's a soft SpongeBob thing. Gerry, go back again and try to freeze it like we did before, right at the moment it appears in the doorway.'

'Right.'

Baxter went back and started running the video frame by frame. I squinted at the screen, waiting for SpongeBob to stick his head through the door again. The cameraman clicked his mouse, freezing the image.

'Zoom in on that, mate,' Jericho said.

Baxter zoomed in. A horizontal line kinked through the middle of the frame but I could still make out a yellow blob with a cartoon eye. I could also see part of the hand that had just let it go, not clearly, but enough to know it *was* a hand and nothing else.

'Shit,' I said.

'Yes. Shit,' Liz McKay said.

'Now zoom in on the window again, mate,' Jericho said.

Baxter shifted the image so that the zoomed-in kitchen window sat in the centre of the screen. I leaned in. The camera had caught a reflection in the window. More than just part of a hand, it was almost an entire forearm, and one decorated with an intricate series of cogs and pistons and levers like you might find inside a robot.

McKay slapped one of her bony hands on my shoulder. 'You've been fucking had, Jack.'

I didn't like her tone, so I said, 'I don't think so, Liz. I'm not the one who flew three thousand miles to be here.' To Jericho I said, 'What are you going to do?'

The ghost hunter wiped sweat from his eyes,

looked from me to McKay and back. He seemed to be shrinking again. He gave it some thought, and then said, 'Liz is right. We have to confront them with this, Jack.'

Over at the house, Brett had appeared at the front door, thoughtfully stroking his goatee. He started to come over.

'That got a webcam?'

McKay had turned her attention to Baxter. She was talking about the laptop.

'Yes,' Baxter said.

'Hit record. Do it now. I want vision of this.' She turned to Jericho. 'If things go pear-shaped just head for the car. It's not locked.'

Jericho had produced a handkerchief and now dabbed it at his slick forehead. 'What?'

'Lester, one of them went psycho at you last night just for being here. Anything could happen.'

'Shit, Liz.'

'I'll let you know when it's time to run.' The producer smiled.

By now, Brett was within earshot so McKay shut up and turned her smirk at him.

'What's going on?' Brett asked.

'We've got something to show you,' Jericho said, still wiping his face. 'Give us a minute to set it up and we'll bring it inside. Can you get everyone together for us?'

Brett frowned, possibly concerned by the look on the ghost hunter's face, or more likely by McKay's smirk, but rubbed the back of his neck and said, 'Yeah, sure.'

He headed back to the house, glancing over his

shoulder once or twice on the way.

'I'm not going to enjoy this at all,' Jericho said, watching him go.

23

The cameraman stayed behind in his van, packing up his coffee cups and preparing to get out of there in a hurry, while McKay marched into the house wearing her deadly smile, Baxter's laptop under one arm and Jericho grimacing at her heels. I followed them in just as unhappily. I don't like scenes either, but, like McKay, I wanted to see how the group reacted to the footage. While not entirely comfortable with filming them without their knowledge, news *is* news. I wondered how best to approach the hoax story, already picturing Murray Dowd's painfully obvious GHOST-BUSTED page one headline. *Hard News,* I suspected, was not going to be very nice about it either. I realised the earliest they could get anything to air was Monday night. I could beat them to it and get the story out Monday morning. *Hard News* might not be happy about that either, but that's how it goes.

Everyone was in the front room now, apart from Nicky, who was still refusing to get out of bed. I asked McKay to give me a minute and went up to get her.

'Fuck off,' Nicky said.

'Nicky, they've got some video to show you guys. It looks like we've caught your ghost.'

She sat up in surprise and rubbed at her eyes. 'What?'

'You really need to come down and see this.'

'Shit. Okay.' She scooped up some clothes from the floor and dressed quickly. We went back downstairs.

'Have a seat,' McKay said with a wave of her scrawny hand.

She had set up the laptop on the coffee table, forcing everyone to crowd on the assortment of chairs on one side. Nicky squeezed in as best she could, parking herself on Shane's armrest. To one side of them, Lance continued to drink coffee, looking bemused by the whole thing. I wondered if he might be stoned. On the other side, Deb had shrunk so far into her chair that she would barely have been able to see the screen, and was twirling that dangling strand of hair again. On the other side of her, Brett and Kath shared the cane settee, he still frowning and playing with his goatee, while she clutched her baby monitor. The producer, the ghost hunter and I stayed on our feet. In the TV room, Shane and Deb's kids were still happily mashing food.

Once Nicky had settled, McKay, still smiling, said, 'Lester?'

Jericho swallowed, loud enough for me to hear. 'Right, okay,' he said. The handkerchief was still in his hand. He wiped it over his lips. 'Folks, it seems we did catch something on the static cameras last night, but it wasn't what we expected. We'd like you to have a look at it.'

'What is it?' Shane said, leaning forward for a cigarette packet. He lit one and waited for Jericho to speak.

'Observe,' Jericho said, rather stiffly, and he abruptly darted forward to hit a button on the keyboard. We watched their faces as the kitchen footage played.

In a few seconds, Nicky said, 'What the hell was that?'

Brett shook his head, and then leaned forward, looking down at the screen as though he was trying to see the object on the kitchen floor. Shane and Lance leaned forward as well.

'What *was* that?' Kath said.

'That,' Liz McKay said, 'was somebody throwing a kid's toy across the room. And we have identified the person who threw it. We caught her reflection in the kitchen window. Would you like to see again?'

The producer gave Deb a death stare, probably expecting her to immediately leap to her feet and confess. We all followed McKay's gaze.

'What the hell are you saying?' Shane said, looking around in confusion.

McKay pointed at Deb. 'Your wife here, or whatever she is, faked it, mate.'

Shane turned to Deb. She was shaking her head, twirling her hair, looking around.

'What did you do?' Shane asked.

Deb opened her mouth, thought better of it, and closed it again.

'What the *fuck* did you do?'

I was watching Nicky. The look on her face suggested she had no idea what was going on, which was kind of a relief. We waited for Deb to say something.

Finally, she said, 'Nothing was happening.'

Shane stared at her. 'What the fuck does that mean?'

Deb, still shaking her head, threw up an arm. 'Nothing was happening,' she said. Her voice cracked. She pointed at Lester. 'They said nothing was happening.'

'So fucking what?' Shane shot back. Now he shook his head, waving at the screen. 'Why the hell would you do that?'

Deb suddenly leaned forward, shouting. *'So they would fucking believe us!'*

The sudden ferocity of her words hit Shane like a slap. He jerked back in his chair, stunned. For a moment, everyone in the front room was too astonished to speak.

Then Kath suddenly leapt to her feet and waved the baby monitor in Deb's face. 'Christ, this is bullshit, Deb. Fucking hell. What were you thinking?'

Deb shook her head, shrinking back.

Kath stood before her for a second or two longer, before abruptly turning away. She waved her baby monitor at the rest of us. 'I really have had enough of this fucking shit!' she said. She pushed past Brett, who sat on the settee with his mouth open like a bewildered fish, and stormed off, into the kitchen.

McKay twisted the knife. 'Let me tell you something,' she said. 'This makes me think you people concocted this whole story. And I'll tell you something else. *Hard News* takes a very dim view of that sort of behaviour. The money is off the table. Deal's off, people.'

Nicky said, 'You can't do that. We signed a contract.'

McKay turned the death stare on her. 'Did you actually read it? You people *lied* to us. That negates the deal, honey. You have a problem with that, take us to court.' She turned to Jericho, who was shifting grimly from foot to foot. 'Get the laptop, Lester. We're leaving.'

Jericho gave me a sorry-about-this look and moved to get the computer, but before he could scoop it up an ear-splitting scream came from the kitchen, blasting out so loudly it seemed to carry its own shockwave.

Shane moved first.

Deftly crushing out his just-lit cigarette on the coffee table, he sprang to his feet, so quickly he almost knocked Nicky from her position on the armrest. He flew for the kitchen entrance. A microsecond later Brett followed suit, desperately scrabbling to his feet and slamming a knee into the edge of the coffee table along the way, so hard that the laptop juddered across the surface. A moment after that, the rest of us surged at the kitchen in a chaotic mass. In the rush, one of Lester Jericho's shoes came down on my own, crushing it like a brick. A chair fell over. Liz McKay may have squeaked like a girl.

Crammed in the doorway, we heard Shane shouting at Kath, *'What? What?'*

She had pressed herself hard against the kitchen bench opposite the window and was now pointing the baby monitor at the glass with a ramrod-straight arm, her other hand at her chest.

'There was some crazy looking black guy at the window!'

'Where?' Brett shouted.

Kath waved at the back door. *'Out the back! He*

ran around the back!'

Shane took off, hurling himself past her to wrench open the back door. Once outside, he was off and running, his head turning this way that as he sprinted in the general direction of the mango trees. Brett ran after him and, after having a good think about it, so did I. There *was* an outdoor laundry on the other side of the back door, I noticed.

The ground sloped deceptively away from the back of the house, making it easier to run, but the mango trees were further away than they looked. Mostly hidden from view from the front of the house, a series of small corrugated iron work sheds sat in a cleared, muddy yard at the bottom of the slope. Hundreds of timber pallets stood around the sheds in unevenly stacked towers. Disintegrating cardboard packing boxes littered the ground. Brett disappeared between the stacks in front of me, running hard. Mud flicked from his boot heels.

Already past the sheds, Shane suddenly veered to his right without missing a beat, as though he'd locked onto his target, and he headed into the broad, shadowed corridors beneath the trees. Then Brett reappeared, pounding after him. I thudded after them both through the mud between the pallets, already breathless. By the time I caught sight of them again they were way ahead of me, deep under the trees.

Scanning ahead, I caught a fleeting glimpse between tree trunks of dark, running legs blurring beneath a flash of red shirt, which may have been a football jumper with a white number 13 on the back. Or maybe it was an 18. He was too far ahead to know for sure. The guy could *run*. He was already miles away. There was no way Shane and Brett would catch him – which was probably a good thing - but they ran as hard as they could anyway.

I slowed to a trot. A crushing pain filled my lungs. Another, sharper pain stabbed at one side of my abdomen. Sweating, I glanced over my shoulder, back at the house. Everyone had come outside now, including the kids. Murph had turned up too, no doubt attracted by the scream, and was slowly walking down to the sheds, waving back for everyone else to stay where they were. I noticed Gerry Baxter there as well, camera on his shoulder. He must have moved pretty fast too.

I trotted into the trees. They *did* go on forever. The air beneath the dense canopy was cloying and still. Far ahead, a couple of rows over, Shane had given up the chase, propping against a thick trunk with his hands on his knees. Brett had passed him by, dodging around trees, but was rapidly losing steam. By now, the running man was nowhere to be seen.

I slowed to a walk, trying to catch my breath. The ground beneath my feet was sodden and, apart from some tough-looking clumps of grass, completely barren. There was something else on the ground near the base of a tree in the next row. A grey, leathery mound, about the size of a dog. I glanced back at Shane. Brett had given up too, and was now trudging back to him.

I looked back at the grey lump.

I walked over to it.

It *was* a dog, so badly decomposed that the smell of death was long gone. Stringy tufts of fur still clung to its dead-black skin in little islands. The skin had stretched tight over the ribcage. In places, it had cracked open, revealing bones. One of the back legs was missing, probably gnawed off by some passing animal. The dog's skull had been smashed flat. In places, I could see fractured bone, shattered into dozens of pieces like broken glass.

Raised voices came through the trees, muffled by the thick air. The tree blocked my view of Shane and Brett, so I had to step away from the dead dog to see what was going on. The two men were arguing. Brett waved his arms, shouting. Shane shouted back and gave him a little shove in the chest. I stood there for a moment, wondering what to do. Then Brett raised a fist. Shane leaned back, dodging the intended blow, and swung a forearm up, slamming it into Brett's chest and forcing him back into a tree trunk.

Despite the pain, I ran. I shouted, too, but they ignored me. I watched as Shane let loose two rapid punches to Brett's stomach, dropping him. Brett slid down the trunk like an empty sack.

'Hey! *Hey!'*

Shane looked at me, and then back at Brett. He took a few steps away and stood there opening and closing his fists, ready to go again if Brett managed to magically spring back to his feet. It took me a good thirty seconds to reach them, and when I did, I couldn't speak. I leaned against the trunk over Brett, gasping down at him. Curled up on the ground, his breath heaved in and out. Shane's breath exited his nostrils so forcefully I could hear it whistling. I looked over. His face was red with anger, and the scar that ran from his temple to his cheek was as white as the dead dog's bones.

The three of us stayed that way for a bit, collecting ourselves in the shadows under the trees. Then Shane shook his head, turned away without a word and headed slowly in the direction of the house. At my feet, Brett rolled over. I helped him up. He wavered unsteadily for a moment and then said, 'Fuck.'

'You okay?'

'Yeah, sure.'

'What the hell was that about?' I asked.

He gulped air and waved after Shane. 'Mate, it's been ... on the cards ... for fucking ... months. The guy ... is an idiot.'

I wiped my dripping face with a sleeve and looked towards the house. Murph waited at the edge of the trees, hands on hips instead of in his pockets. Even from here, I could tell he wasn't too impressed. Behind him, by a stack of pallets, Deb and Kath were exchanging words as well, but they were too far away for us to hear anything.

I pointed. 'More trouble,' I said.

Brett looked and said, 'Fuck. Great.'

Gerry Baxter passed the women without a second look, heading back to where Jericho and McKay hovered by the back door. He had run down to film the chase. Now Jericho was waving at the cameraman to join them up at the house. I couldn't see Nicky anywhere but Lance was hanging in the background, keeping an eye on them.

Up ahead, Shane emerged from the trees and brushed past Murph with a fuck-off wave, marching towards Deb and Kath. Before he got there, Deb broke away to meet him, leaving Kath staring at her back. In a moment, Kath raised the baby monitor to her ear, and then waved it in the air so Brett could see. He waved back and she waddled back up the slope in a half-run.

Brett and I started back in silence, each of us doing our best to recover. On the way, I looked for the dead dog but couldn't find it again. Everywhere under the trees looked the same. I decided to shut up about it.

24

By the time we made it back to where Murph was waiting my calf muscles were tight with pain. Of everything that hurt, though, my chest was giving me the most grief. My lungs burned. Maybe I needed a personal trainer too.

'You okay, mate?' Murph said to Brett.

'Yeah, mate. Just had the wind knocked out of me. No major damage.'

Murph nodded as though that was an acceptable answer but said, 'I swear to God if any shit like that goes down again I'll be asking people to fuck off out of here. I mean it.'

Brett nodded at him. 'Fair enough, mate. Fair enough. I have to go find Kath.'

We watched him head up the slope. Everybody else had disappeared. Shane and Deb. Nicky. Lance. Jericho, Baxter and McKay were nowhere to be seen either.

'Nicky tell you what happened?'

Murph didn't look at me. Staring up at the house, he said, 'Yeah.'

I studied him for a moment. 'Crazy stuff.'

'Yeah.'

'You think Deb could be behind this whole thing?'

He finally turned my way, slipping his hands into his pockets. 'No. I don't. Listen, I think Nicky is upset. She ran back inside.'

It took me a moment to work out what he was saying. 'Oh. I'll go find her.'

Murph nodded, and turned to look back into the

mango trees. 'What were you looking at down there?'

'Pardon?'

'You stopped to look at something.'

I rubbed my fingers under my chin. 'Oh, some dead animal. Possum, I think.'

'Okay. Right.'

'I'll go look for Nicky.'

Murph didn't move. He kept looking down at the trees. 'Right.'

I started up the slope, looking once over my shoulder. Murph was walking slowly down to the tree line.

Shit.

'Jack!'

Jericho had come around from the side of the house nearest the kitchen door. He beckoned me over.

What now?

As I walked up, the ghost hunter said, 'Your running friend left a present outside the kitchen window. Come and check this out.'

McKay and Baxter were standing by a pile of rotting timber planks and old paint tins under the kitchen window. McKay appeared more anxious than deadly now. She had retrieved the laptop, I saw. Now the producer was itching to get the hell out of there.

'Come on, Lester,' she said. 'We need to go.'

'Give me a minute,' Jericho said. He pointed at some objects sitting on one of the old cans. 'Take a look, Jack.'

I walked over and took a look. Three shiny black

stones, each about half the size of a fist, sat on top of a tattered piece of grey cloth. I looked back at Jericho.

'Could be tribal objects,' he said. 'You know, to ward off evil spirits.'

I frowned. 'You think so?'

'It's a possibility. I think the guy may have been trying to help.'

McKay said, 'Does it even matter now? Let's go.'

Jericho shook his head. 'We need to get this on video, Liz.'

'Lester, we need to get the hell out of here. Now.'

'Two more seconds. That's all.'

She glared at him. 'Mate, there are some seriously fucked off people around here. And they look like the sort of people who might have guns.'

'They do have guns,' I said.

McKay gaped. 'I'll be in the car. You have thirty seconds, Lester. Then I'm gone.'

'Thank you, Liz.'

Jericho watched her hurry away. He ran his soaked handkerchief over his forehead. He asked Baxter to film the stones.

'That it?' Baxter asked when he was done. He seemed a little edgy himself.

'Thanks, Gerry. We'll catch you back in town.'

'No worries,' the cameraman said. He gave me a little nod and left.

In a moment, Jericho said, 'I have no idea how hard they'll go on this, Jack. Might be an idea to expect the worst.'

'I already am expecting the worst but don't worry about it. Whatever they do isn't going to be your fault.'

'Right.' He offered me a glum smile. 'Well, best be off, then. Thanks for your input last night. Despite the way things went I really did appreciate the company.'

'No problem,' I said. 'There is one more thing I need to quickly ask before you go.'

'What's that?'

'Can I have your autograph?'

After they had gone, I went back inside to look for Nicky. Lance was back at the coffee table, alone. He appeared to be staring into a corner at nothing in particular. I assumed the others were all keeping to themselves in their respective rooms, mulling over the morning's events. I cleared my throat.

'Seen Nicky?'

Lance turned with an oddly disconnected look on his face. It took a moment for him to register I had just spoken to him. He *was* stoned. I was sure of it.

'Uh. I think she went upstairs.'

'Thanks.'

I stood there for a moment looking at him.

'Crazy morning,' I said.

He nodded. 'Yeah, it's pretty fucked up.'

'Do you think Deb is behind this thing?'

He shrugged. 'Looks that way, hey.'

'Yep.'

I gave him a nod and went upstairs. Nicky was in her room, sitting on the edge of the bed. She was crying. I stood watching her from the doorway for a moment, unsure what to do. It took her a moment to realise I was there. She looked up and wiped her nose with the back of her hand. I went to her. Crouched in front of her. Placed my hands on her knees. A bubble of snot expanded from one of her nostrils and popped. She wiped her nose again.

'Are you okay?'

She looked at me as though I'd just said the stupidest thing ever, which possibly I had. I realised she was crying not because she was upset, but because she was angry.

'What the fuck do you think?' She pointed at the door. 'Why did she do that?'

'You heard her. She thought they didn't believe you.'

She shook her head. 'Well she totally fucked that up, didn't she?'

'Yes, she did. I'm sorry.'

'No need for you to be sorry.' She waved again, sniffing. 'I've had it with this place. I need a break.'

'What can I do?'

'Get me the fuck out of here, Jack.'

25

Friday afternoon.

Driving home.

To Nicky Chen.

Even though she had been with me almost a week I still couldn't get used to the idea of having somebody else in the house. She was, simply, *there,* and eating and drinking and smoking and snoring and farting as though she always had been. I wasn't entirely convinced this was a good thing. Nicky seemed to be dead broke as well, which was probably something we would need to discuss at some point if it turned into an extended stay. In just seven days, the household budget had become a prime issue but I had no idea how to best approach it, worried that we'd end up having some sort of scene. For now, though, there was an upside to having her around and that, naturally enough, was the sex. Nicky had half-heartedly done some of my washing too, which was an added bonus.

Apart from some brief phone calls to Kath and Murph, she hadn't spoken to anyone out at the house. The morning after *Hard News* aired their piece, Shane and Deb had packed some bags, collected the kids and taken off somewhere, leaving most of their belongings behind. Nobody had heard from them since. Lance had muttered something about leaving too. Brett had wanted to take off as well but Kath had argued they didn't have the money to go anywhere else, so they were stuck there for now.

Murph, meanwhile, had barely emerged from his shed. He had found the dog. Nicky hadn't said anything about its bashed-in skull, so maybe he didn't tell her about that. If Nicky did eventually decide to go back out there, I thought, it appeared increasingly likely that she would be returning to a mostly empty house.

Hard News had gone in hard. The whole thing was a nightmare. Nicky had refused to watch it, which was probably a good thing. Thanks to some crafty editing, the show portrayed the occupants of the house in the worst possible light. The thing was a hoax. They were in it for the money. They may have been drug users.

I didn't come out of it entirely unscathed either. There was a sly hint of my relationship with Nicky, and an even slyer hint that I might be complicit in the hoax as well, an accusation that saw me explaining myself to Mike Cooke and Murray Dowd the following morning. I denied everything and told them *Hard News* was simply indulging in a little payback for my scooping them on story. I had written it at home on the Sunday for the Monday paper, beating them to it by a good twelve hours. Mike and Murray seemed happy enough with that scenario, so they let it go. Mike was happy with the autograph for his kids, too.

I listened to the *Gurus*, tapping my fingers on the steering wheel. Traffic was at a crawl. An accident had closed off two of the three lanes leading outbound to the suburbs. Police, fire brigade and ambulance lights pulsed up ahead, wobbling in the heat haze over the line of barely-moving vehicles.

On the passenger seat, my mobile rang. I turned down the music and answered.

'Jack Jackson.'

'Jack. It's Lester Jericho.'

I was so surprised it took me a second or two to reply. 'Lester?'

I hadn't expected to hear from him ever again.

'Yeah,' he said. 'Listen, I've got something I want you to listen to if you've got a minute. *Hard News* may have jumped the gun with the whole hoax thing, mate.'

'What?'

The line moved. I progressed a further three car lengths.

'I need you to listen to something,' Jericho said.

'Okay. Sure.'

'Great.' I detected a slight tremor in the ghost hunter's voice. 'Now, just quickly,' he said, 'when we wrap up an investigation the whole team sits down to review the evidence, even when we think we haven't caught much. Or think that it's a hoax for that matter. We go through the motions simply to ensure we haven't missed anything. A lot of this stuff can happen real quick, so we're pretty methodical. We go through all the DVD footage, as well as the audio stuff, including the EVP sessions. It usually takes a couple of days to get through it all.'

'Okay.'

He paused for a moment. 'Jack, we caught something while we were in the bathroom, something we did *not* hear at the time.'

The lined chugged forward again.

'We caught something? What do you mean?'

'Remember how the K2 lit up?'

'Sure.'

'Something was speaking to us, Jack. Let me play it for you. I'll hold the recorder up to the phone. It's so good we're going to use it on the show. We'll be airing it in a couple of weeks.'

'Okay.'

I heard a hiss of static, and some tinny crackling noises, like clothes rustling. Then I heard Lester Jericho say, *'Please come forward.'*

More hissing and, after a beat, two or three deep, hissing words I couldn't quite make out. It was an unmistakably male voice, deep and disconnected somehow, like someone speaking loudly in another room. The hair at the back of my neck stood up. On the recording, I heard Jericho say, *'Whoa, the K2s going off like a bitch'* just before he clicked off the recorder.

Jericho came back on. 'Did you hear it?'

'I heard something. Play it again.'

I listened again, frowning.

It sounded like *air iss ee.*

'I can't make out what he's saying,' I said.

'It's probably not translating too well over the phone,' Jericho said. I heard him breathing. 'We think it's saying *Where is he?'*

'What?'

'It's asking a question. *Where. Is. He.* It's looking for somebody, Jack.'

Do you believe in ghosts, Jack?

'No, Lester Jericho, I don't.'

My eyes opened. Had I just said that aloud? And why in God's name was I dreaming about the little pink man anyway? The voice I'd heard over the phone had given me the creeps, for sure, but I concluded after we'd ended the call that Lester Jericho – or Gerry the cameraman for that matter - could easily have faked it. Despite that, it seemed simply hearing that deep, disembodied voice was enough for it to slip into my dreams, along with the scarlet ghost hunter.

I peered over at Nicky. I thought, perhaps, that I *had* said it out loud but she hadn't stirred. In the darkness, I could just make out the shape of her head on a very clean pillow, and a pale, uncovered shoulder. Her back was to me. She was snoring like a boozy little engine. I hadn't told her about the call from Jericho.

I sat up in the bed and peered out through the bedroom door, which I'd left open because the kids were in their room across the hall. Inside, a tiny orange night light sent a feeble glow over the floor. Max and Susie shared the bed. Nothing moved. I cocked my head to one side, listening to the dark. I thought I'd heard something, barely audible beneath the quiet swish of the ceiling fan.

A tiny *click,* maybe.

Something.

Most of the time we're chasing shadows and creaky floorboards.

'Shut up, Lester,' I whispered.

Still listening, I swung my legs from beneath the sheet and sat on the edge of the bed, an anxious pang suddenly pulsing deep in my belly.

I'd heard another small *click*.

What *was* that?

I held my breath for a moment, leaning forward with my hands on my knees, waiting for the noise to repeat. It didn't. I exhaled and looked up at the vague blur of the fan. The air was cool – the humidity had eased right off, and there was a touch of the coming dry season in the air, creeping through the blinds like an almost forgotten promise – but there was something else, too, like a subtle, atmospheric shift, as though some disturbance might be slowly swirling in the air.

And, I thought, there was a strange odour, too.

Heavy and sort of dusky.

Earthy.

I reached over for the bedside table, groping for my watch. I squinted at the luminous dial. It was quarter to three. I bit my bottom lip, thinking.

I had completely forgotten it was my weekend to have the kids, which was a mistake. I'd been in the shower when Ernie and Margaret had turned up to drop them off earlier in the evening, and that was a mistake too. As I towelled off, I heard Nicky answer the door with a surprised 'Oh Fuck Hello', which would have gone down exceptionally well. She was dressed in tiny shorts and a see-through singlet. I imagine that would have gone down well too. Five minutes earlier, Ernie, Margaret and the kids would've caught us going at it like over-sexed demons on the lounge room floor.

I'd managed to hop out there without breaking my neck as I slipped into some shorts, but it was a close thing. I said *hi* to the kids and formally introduced my in-laws to Nicky Chen. I could tell they were impressed. Ernie was all pink and flustered, possibly embarrassed by Nicky's magnificent breasts. Comically, he attempted to look everywhere but. Margaret kept glancing at him as though she might be waiting for some signal to scoop up Max and Susie and make a run for it. The whole scene was bad news.

In the end, they left without protest but I knew Ernie would probably bear the brunt of a furious ear bashing on the drive home. Oh, well. Nicky and I slipped into some less comfortable but more appropriate clothing, ordered in pizza and put the kids in front of a DVD, which had kept them happy until bedtime. I promised to take them swimming at Eric's in the morning, after pancakes for breakfast. We would have to go out for those. They were happy with that, too.

Sitting on the edge of the bed, I couldn't shake the feeling that something was wrong.

I got up, crossed the hall into the kid's room and slipped Max's cover back over him. A true Darwin boy, he was forever kicking them off. Susie rolled over but didn't wake up.

I looked around the room. Originally, it had been Susie's. Max had had the room now filled with Jessica's things. These days, they didn't seem to mind sharing. Pre-school finger paintings hung on the walls. Dolls and robots lined one shelf. Two soccer balls, a tennis racquet and a cricket bat sat on top of the wardrobe. I hadn't thrown anything out and Max and Susie seemed to like it like that, maybe because it somehow connected them to their lost mother. I didn't know.

Everything seemed fine, so I went back out into the hall. I stood there for a moment, peering towards the darkened lounge room, and listened. Apart from the whir of the ceiling fans in the bedrooms, there was nothing to hear. The weird smell seemed to be dissipating now as well. I went into the bathroom, closed the door and peed in the dark. Back in the hallway, I decided to check the house anyway, just to be sure. I padded along to the lounge room, reached for a light switch.

The lights came on and I drew in a sharp breath. There was a word spread out on the floor.

A word made of gravel.

Right there on my lounge room floor.

A chill iced up my spine and clutched at my scalp like an electrically charged skull cap. The word was:

CUNT

26

Nicky placed a hand on my shoulder. I hadn't heard her come up the hallway. I jumped. Maybe I squealed. I can't be sure.

Still half asleep, she said, 'What are you doing?'

I pointed at the word on the floor. Nicky looked. Her eyes widened and a hand went to her mouth.

'Holy fucking shit,' she said, but the words caught in her throat, coming out in a hoarse cigarette whisper.

That made me move.

'Stay here,' I said.

Stepping around the word, I went to check the front door.

Locked.

Next, I checked the back doors. Locked, too. Lifting bamboo blinds, I worked my way around the windows. The glass louvres were intact, the insect screens untouched. There was no sign of a break-in. Another chill coursed along my spine. I ran my fingers through my hair.

No way. No fucking way is that word on my floor.

I looked at Nicky. She had backed off down the hall a little, a hand clapped over her mouth. I motioned for her to stay where she was and went into the kitchen. After a few moments, I found what I was looking for. The biggest, sharpest, don't-mess-with-me-or-I'll-stab-you-in-the-face knife I possessed.

I gestured for Nicky to come into the lounge room.

'I need to check the bedrooms,' I whispered, pointing down the hall with the knife. 'They could still be in the house.'

She nodded, but said nothing. Her hands were shaking. So were mine.

Slowly, I made my way down the hall, first checking the office. Heart pounding like a piston, I flicked on the light.

Nothing.

Next, I went into the bathroom even though I had just been in there. The shower curtain was drawn. I couldn't remember if it was like that when we had gone to bed or not. I stared at it.

'You've got to be kidding me,' I whispered to it.

I drew back the knife, ready to plunge it into the intruder's head, and reached out with my other hand. I tore back the curtain and waved the knife at empty space.

'Shit.'

I moved into the kid's room, checked under the bed. It was the only place to hide. I saw nothing but dust in the glow of the night light. The hunchback had missed that. I would have to mention it to her.

Back in the hall, I stood before the closed door of the spare room, where Jessica's things were, and listened. I heard nothing but my own breathing, little short gasps as sharp as the knife I was holding.

I swung open the door and turned on the light. No movement. No sound. I went a little way in to make sure nobody was crouching behind any of the cardboard boxes. They weren't, so I went into my room to check under the bed. Nothing but dust there either. I went back out into the lounge room.

I shook my head at Nicky, who dropped her hand and waved at the word.

'How?'

'I don't know.' We looked at each other for a moment. I laid the carving knife on the kitchen bench. Then I said, 'We need to get the kids out of here. Now.'

It was all I could think to do.

Get the hell out of there.

Nicky nodded. 'Okay.'

We hurried back into the bedroom to dress. Then I grabbed my keys and phone and headed for to the kid's room, where I gave Max a few gentle taps on the shoulder.

'Max. You have to get up. Now, mate.'

He grumbled and rolled over. I shook him. He grumbled some more but sat up, rubbing at his eyes.

'Dad?'

'Sorry, Maxie. I have to take you back home. To grandmas.'

'What?'

'Come on mate. Grab your things.'

They had each brought a backpack. I slung Susie's over my shoulder and scooped her out of bed.

Behind me, Nicky said, 'Should I carry him?'

I grunted, hauling Susie up to my shoulder. 'No, he's too heavy. He can walk. Right, Max?'

Max shook his head. 'Uh,' he said.

'Come on, buddy. We need to go.'

Bleary-eyed, he swung out of bed and slipped his backpack on. I steered him out along the hall and past the gravel, holding a hand at the side of his face like a blinker, and unlocked the front door. Susie hadn't woken up. Nicky was staring at us as though she didn't know what to do.

'Come on. You're not staying here,' I said.

'Fuck, no.' She swept up her shoulder bag.

Half asleep, Max headed down the front stairs first. My free hand was on his shoulder to steady him but he fell anyway, tripping over his own feet about a third of the way down. He tumbled down face first, slamming into the concrete treads in a sickening series of thuds as he bounced from one to the next. I heard a loud *crack* as he came to a juddering halt a good six steps from where he'd started.

Max screamed, probably more from the shock than anything else. I hoped so, anyway.

'Fuck!' I said, turning to look up at Nicky. I held out Susie.

'Take her! *Take her!'*

Nicky took Susie, who was starting to struggle now, waking up. I scrambled down, dumping Susie's backpack over the side on the way, locked my arms under Max's, lifted him up and carried him down to the bottom of the stairs. I sat him down, ripped off his backpack and tried to get a look at his face. Even in the dark, I could tell it was slick with blood.

'Fuck fuck fuck.'

He was crying now, in loud, heaving sobs, turning his head this way and that.

'Max. *Maxie.* Calm down, mate. I need to get a look at you.'

He wouldn't stop crying so I held him close. It was too dark to see where the blood was coming from anyway. It seeped into my clothes, warm and wet.

Nicky struggled down with Susie, who'd also started to cry. It was chaos. I imagined lights coming on up and down the street. Maybe someone was already on the phone to the cops.

'Jack?'

I turned to look. Backlit in streetlight, someone was standing at the head of the drive, peering into the darkness. I tensed.

'Jack, what the fuck is going on?'

It was Eric. He trotted in, thankfully wearing boxers and a T-shirt and not his tiny porno pants.

'Max fell down the stairs,' I said.

'Jesus Christ. What's going on? It's three o'clock in the morning, for fuck's sake.'

I shook my head at him. 'Get the light, will you?'

Eric disappeared under the house and fumbled around for a second or two before the fluorescent light over the laundry tubs flickered on.

'Jesus,' he said. 'Is he alright?'

There was blood everywhere. On the driveway. On the stairs. I didn't know if Max was alright. It didn't look very good, at any rate.

'I don't know. I don't *know*,' I said.

Eric slipped off his T-shirt and squatted beside us. He made to wipe the blood from Max's face but Max wouldn't stay still.

'You've got to get him to hospital,' Eric said. *'Now*, Jack. That's a head wound. Hold the shirt on it.'

'Where?'

'On his forehead, Jack. Looks like he's cracked it open.'

I balled up Eric's shirt and pressed it to Max's forehead.

'Get going,' Eric said. He made to help us up.

'Yes, yes, yes.' I said, digging into my pocket for the car keys. I looked up at Nicky. She was stroking Susie's hair and rocking rapidly, trying to calm her down. It wasn't working. I held up the keys.

'Put her in the back. You drive.'

Nicky's mouth opened and closed a couple of times before she said, 'I don't have a license.'

'Fuck, Nicky. It's an *emergency*. Just do it.'

'Okay. *Okay.* '

Eric helped me get into the front seat with Max, and then threw his backpack into the rear with Susie. He spotted Susie's backpack in the garden by the stairs, went over to retrieve it, and threw that in the back as well. I said, 'Thanks, mate. Thanks.'

'No problem,' Eric said. He shut the door and banged twice on the roof. 'Go.'

Nicky started the car, jammed the gearshift into reverse and we whined backwards out of the driveway like a missile.

The hospital, like everything else in Darwin, was just ten minutes away but the drive was the stuff of nightmares and seemed to go on forever. Orange streetlight swept into the car in wildly revolving monochromatic flashes, turning the blood a glistening horror-movie black. Max continued to sob, shoulders heaving. In the back, Susie screamed inconsolably, over and over. Nicky did her best not to crash. Luckily, at this time of the morning the roads were relatively clear, so there wasn't much around to slam into.

Eventually, Royal Darwin rose ahead of us with all the austerity of an Eastern Bloc apartment building. Nicky wheeled into the car park with a squeal of rubber. Feral cats scooted out of the way before she could squash them flat. She found a spot reserved for the disabled and swung in, braking so hard we almost all ended up pressed flat into the windshield. We bundled into the emergency department, sobbing and bleeding, and wavered just inside the front door for a moment to take in the scenery.

Darwin's emergency department is one of the busiest in the country. Unlike other Australian capital cities, there are no other hospitals around to send excess patients to when things get busy. This was it, and it was bedlam. The army used to send field surgeons out here for training, I'd heard. Apparently, some of the wounds coming through Darwin's ED are as close to battlefield injuries as you can get without actually being in combat. Looking around, I thought that sounded about right.

The waiting room was packed and there was a queue at the counter. Two or three nurses were working the room, offering pain relief to those who seemed to need it most, which was just about everybody. One of the nurses spotted us hesitating at the front door, or maybe she heard Susie crying over the general din. She spotted all the blood and trotted over on squeaking rubber soles, expertly whipping a penlight from a pocket at her thigh on the way. After a quick assessment of Max's wound, she ushered us to the counter, cutting into the queue. We were through the doors to triage in less than two minutes. A pasty-looking asylum seeker in handcuffs occupied one of the three beds inside. Two burly security guards lounged around the bed, playing with their phones.

The male triage nurse snapped on gloves and started firing questions at us. I told him the story, and about that loud *crack*. Listening and nodding, he went about his business with urgent professionalism. Some localised swelling. Possible concussion. The wound was bad – an inch-long gash to the forehead just above the right eye – but not as bad as the amount of blood would indicate. He sent us through to the ED proper anyway. Nicky and Susie, he suggested, might want to wait outside.

'Sure,' Nicky said, giving me a look. She rolled her eyes downward. Susie had wet herself. Nicky was soaked.

'I'll call Ernie and Margaret to come get her.'

'Okay. No problem.' The door in was not the door out, and Nicky had trouble getting her bearings. She rounded a corner, came back, went down a corridor, came back, rounded another corner and then didn't come back.

The emergency department was so crowded that several curtained cubicles contained more than one patient. Max was shown into one already occupied by a teen girl with a knee was the size of a watermelon. She was on her phone, shouting to someone in a nightclub. When I finally got around to calling Ernie and Margaret, I had to do it with one hand pressed to my ear to shut her out.

They turned up fifteen minutes later, hurrying through the ED like an assault team. Margaret had Susie. I vaguely wondered if she had been civil to Nicky during the waiting room handover. Ernie spotted me by the end of Max's bed and marched up to the cubicle, barking.

'What the fuck happened?'

Ernie was a chest-puffer too. He pushed it at me. Before he'd retired, he had spent 25 years as a firefighter. He was well built, still fit, and in that regard reminded me of Eric. He was nowhere near as friendly, though.

I took a deep breath. 'He fell down the stairs, Ernie. Someone broke into the house.'

'Have you been drinking?' Margaret wanted to know.

I stared at her. 'What? No. Of course not. Fuck.'

Ernie huffed into my face, close enough for me to see the pores on his nose. They seemed to be opening and closing like dark little eyes. 'Don't speak to her like that.'

'Fuck, Ernie. I'm trying to explain what happened.'

'Don't take that tone with me, mate.'

I threw up my hands. 'I'm not taking a tone with you, Ernie. You're the one who marched up fucking swearing at me. I'm *trying* to tell you what happened.'

Over Ernie's shoulder, I could see doctors and nurses turning to look at us. A security guard on the other side of room was starting to take an interest too. He put his hands on his hips and stared at us.

'Look,' I said. 'They need to do some x-rays and stuff but it looks like he'll be fine. It's *fine.*'

Eric's face had gone a deep shade of red. He looked about to burst. Then he did. With a surprising swiftness, the grandfather of my children lunged forward and slammed two hands into my chest. I fell back onto a plastic chair by the bed, and the back of my head cracked against something hard enough for a white starburst to explode across my eyes.

'It's not fucking *fine!*' Ernie shouted.

I was too dazed to argue. Through the pain, I saw the security guard bounding towards us, along with a few of the larger nurses, male and female.

'Hey! Hey! Hey!' the guard shouted, as though that might sort things out.

Latching firmly onto Ernie's shoulders, the guard spun him around, away from me. Ernie shrugged him off and backed away, his face redder than ever, as though blood vessels might be popping all over the place just below the skin. The guard held up his hands to him. *Stay there.*

'Are you okay?' the guard asked me.

I nodded, clutching the back of my head. Watermelon girl was breathlessly describing the scene to her nightclub friend.

'No, no! There's a fight *right* next to me! I kid you not, *bitch!*'

'This is a *hospital,*' the guard said, stating the obvious. 'You want to have domestics, take it outside.'

Margaret was now standing by Ernie, talking to him. She was white, not red. In a moment, she walked over. Thankfully, Susie had fallen back into a deep sleep and missed the show.

'Just go, Jack,' Margaret said. 'Just go.'

That wasn't such a bad idea. I got to my feet and leaned over Max. I shrugged at him. 'I'll come back and see you in the morning.'

He nodded at me with a faint smile. Then I looked up at Ernie, glowering at him as best I could. It didn't seem to have any effect. To Margaret I said, 'I'll call you in a few hours.'

I left.

'He hit you?' Nicky said when we were back at the house.

We had driven home silence, me at the wheel this time. My brain whirred, processing data received. Margaret had once thrown a Hello Kitty cake at me during one of Susie's birthday parties, but this was way worse than that. It was the nastiest blow-up we had ever had.

'It was more of a shove,' I said, running my fingers over the back of my head. There was an impressive lump there now.

The foul word was still on the floor. I had half expected it not to be, hoping beyond hope that it might have vanished as mysteriously as it had appeared.

Nicky and I looked at each other.

I waved at the gravel. 'This just isn't possible,' I said.

She nodded, almost absently. Her clothes had dried but the smell of Susie's urine clung to her like a bittersweet cologne.

I studied her for a moment, and then said, 'Nicky, I don't believe in ghosts. And it doesn't look like anybody broke into the house. The doors and windows are fine.'

She blinked, not understanding where I was going.

I said, 'I know *I* didn't do it.'

She shook her head. I spelled it out for her.

'That leaves you.'

She blinked a few more times and then her eyes flashed with anger.

'I beg your fucking pardon?' she said.

I pointed at the word. 'I'm asking if you did this, Nicky. It's the only explanation. Or maybe you let one of your mates in.'

'Fucking *what?*'

'It's the only thing I can think of,' I said. 'Somebody wanted to send me a message and maybe you helped them out.'

Nicky stared at me. 'Somebody wanted ...' She shook her head and waved down at the word. 'What the fuck makes you think this is about *you?*'

I blinked. 'Well, it has to be, right? I've obviously pissed somebody off.'

Nicky's mouth opened, hung there for a moment. Finally, she said, 'Maybe this thing's after *me.*'

I ran a hand over my chin. 'I don't think so.'

Nicky stood there for a moment, seething, and then leaned forward, jabbing at my chest. 'Fuck you, Jack. *Fuck. You.*'

She suddenly swept up her bag and stormed for the front door. I tried to block her but she shoved me aside.

'Nicky. Wait.'

'Fuck off,' she said, sliding the door open. A second later she was gone with a slam, and thumping away down the stairs in the dark, in much the same way Jessica had five years earlier.

27

For the next few hours, my mind was in a state of mental fog. Fractured moments replayed over and over, blending into a continuous loop: the horrific *crack* of Max's head on the stairs, Susie's endless sobbing, the way the orange streetlights had flashed into the car to make the blood look black, Nicky thumping away into the night, the horrific *crack* of Max's head on the stairs.

All that blood.

Jesus.

I had wheeled my chair out of the office and parked it in front of the word on the floor. I sat there chain-smoking, staring down at it, until the sun began to rise behind the bamboo blinds. Something about that soft light angling into the room finally broke the loop. I got up and went over to the back doors. Outside and in, they could only be opened with a key. I unlocked the doors and swung them open to inspect the lock. No tool marks. Next, I went to the front door and did the same.

There *were* a few gouge marks around the lock and along the edge of the door frame but they were old ones. A few years earlier, someone had tried to break in during the first heavy downpour of the wet season. The attempt had failed. The sliding screen door, my first line of defence, was a triple-lock job, security-screened and almost impossible to prise open unless you were Mr Universe. I had called the cops anyway. They suggested the thief had been waiting for the rain. A heavy tropical shower hammering down on a tin roof provides excellent cover. You wouldn't hear a damned thing, not even breaking glass.

I frowned. There were no fresh marks on the door.

I looked down at the word again. By now, I had convinced myself that Nicky had had nothing to do with it, by simple virtue of the fact that it would have been impossible for her to get this much gravel into the house without me knowing something about it. She would have needed a bucket. Maybe two. There was still a possibility, I supposed, that she had let someone in, but her own shocked reaction at seeing the word on the floor seemed to rule that out as well.

Damn.

I closed the door and picked up my phone, deciding to take some photos before scooping up the word with a dustpan and brush and pouring it away somewhere. I took a dozen pictures from different angles.

When I was done, I phoned the hospital switch. It took a while for the friendly woman on the end of the line to track Max down. He'd left emergency and been admitted to the kid's ward, so she put me through. Max was sleeping. His grandfather was with him. He was going to be fine. No stitches, just glue. They would keep him under observation for a few more hours just to make sure. I disconnected just as a shadow fell through the screen door.

'Jack?'

'Hang on, mate.'

I let Eric in. Again, he had clothes on. Coming through the door, he said, 'Just wanted to see how Max ended up. Is he okay?'

'He's going to be fine. Major crack on the head but it looked a lot worse than it is. They're keeping him in for observation for a few more hours. They didn't give me your shirt back.'

Eric nodded. 'That's good news. Don't worry about the shirt.' He saw the word on the floor. 'What the fuck is that?'

'That,' I said, 'is why we were in such a hurry to get out of here last night.'

I filled him in. He listened, occasionally shaking his head and running a finger thoughtfully over his chin.

'Well,' Eric said. 'That's crazy. And there's absolutely no sign of forced entry?'

'None.'

'And nothing is missing?'

'I don't think so.'

Eric let out a chuckle.

'What's so funny?' I asked.

Eric waved at the word. 'Somebody broke into your house just to call you a cunt. That's pretty funny.' He shrugged. 'You've certainly pissed off somebody.'

'That much is obvious.'

'Who's that Chinese girl who was here?'

'Nicky. She lives out at the Mango Flat house.'

Eric gave me a sort of leery look. 'Got yourself a bit of Asian pussy have you, Jack?'

I didn't like the way he said that but I let it go. 'Not anymore. I think it's a safe bet to start referring to that particular relationship in the past tense. I accused her of...' – I waved my hand at the floor – 'this.'

'You think she did it?' he asked.

'I don't know. I'm starting to think not.'

Eric thought for a moment or two. 'You give her a set of keys?'

'No. And I don't think she let anybody in. She was just as freaked out as I was.'

'Does anybody else have a set of keys?'

You, Eric? Did Jessica ever slip you a set so you could creep over any old time in your tiny Speedos?

I said, 'Not apart from the cleaner, and she didn't do this. She's Vietnamese. She can barely speak English let alone spell out obscenities on the floor.'

Eric laughed. 'Yes, that almost certainly rules her out. What are you going to do?'

I took a deep breath. 'I don't know. I've had it with this whole thing.'

'Call the cops,' Eric said.

I looked at him.

Eric waved down at the word. 'Jack, whoever did this put Max in hospital. He might be okay but it could have been a whole lot worse. If it was me, I'd be doing my damnedest to find the person responsible.' He thought for a moment. 'You know, whoever did do this could come back, Jack. They got in once. They could do it again.'

My skin prickled. That was something I hadn't considered. Briefly, I pictured myself hiding in the dark with Max's cricket bat, ready to pounce. The only other alternative I could see *was* to involve the cops. I gave it some thought.

'You might be right, mate,' I said.

Eric smiled his movie star smile. 'I'm here to help, Jack. By the way, I saw you on *Hard News* the other night. You looked good.'

'Yes, that went well, too.'

Still smiling, Eric said, 'Yes. I thought so.'

Two uniformed cops turned up an hour later. I hadn't called them. Ernie and Margaret had. Thanks to my missing wife, my name would have red-flagged on the police computers, so it was no real surprise they turned up so quickly.

The uniforms wanted to know what had happened. By then I had cleaned up the floor and disposed of the gravel in a pile up near the back fence. I decided that part was too difficult to explain, so I left it out. I told them I heard somebody trying to break in. I showed them the gouge marks on the front door. I was worried for the safety of the children. What if they came back? We had to get out of there. Max lost his footing on the stairs. It was the middle of the night. He was half-asleep. End of story.

The cops seemed doubtful. I wondered what Ernie and Margaret had told them. That I'd been drinking? That I may have pushed Max down the stairs? That they were convinced I had killed their daughter and now I was maybe starting on the grandkids?

Before leaving, one of the cops handed me a card displaying a hand-written job number. Somebody from welfare might want to follow up, he said. The children's grandparents were quiet concerned for their safety, you know.

I knew. I had a feeling Ernie and Margaret may have resolved to angle for sole custody. That was something I'd always worried about. Until now, they hadn't had a real reason to go after me. I had played along, given them whatever they wanted. We had an uneasy truce. Now, it seemed, they had broken it.

Things, I realised, were coming apart.

I watched the cops go. They stepped over the blood on the stairs and stopped briefly to inspect the smears on the driveway. They said something to each other I couldn't hear. When they were gone, I went down and hosed the blood away. After that, I powered through half a container of disinfectant wipes cleaning out the car as well. I left the abandoned backpacks under the house so Ernie and Margaret wouldn't have to talk to me when they called around to collect them.

After wheeling my chair back into the office, I sat at the desk looking at the *Reporter* front pages, mobile phone in one hand and a cigarette in the other. It was my last one. I had smoked almost an entire packet in one hit, and my head was starting to pound.

MANHUNT was on top, Harry Hollis' bleak, black and white face staring up at me.

Eric was right. If I wanted to pursue this thing, I *had* to talk to the police. That might also give Ernie and Margaret something to think about before they went off half-cocked and called in the lawyers. But I wasn't going to do it with a couple of rank and file constables. It was too complex for that. I needed to go to the top, or as near to it as I could get.

I blew out smoke and keyed in the general number for police headquarters. I waited for them to track him down. Would he be there on a Saturday? Turned out he wasn't, but they would pass on a message. I asked them to get him to call me. He rang back within half an hour. Red flags again, no doubt.

'It's Hollis, Jack. How's your son?'

'He's fine, Harry. Thanks for asking.'

'Good. What can I do for you?'

I took a deep breath. 'Look, I've come across something that may interest you,' I said. 'It's in regard to Gary Tanner. Sort of.'

I imagined his eyes narrowing at that. Or widening. One or the other.

'Go on,' he said.

'I'd like to run you through it in person if that's okay.'

Hollis took his time and then said, 'What's this about, Jack?'

'To be honest, I don't really know. But I think you need to hear it anyway. Can you come out to the house?'

I wasn't too keen on simply turning up at the front counter. Cops gossip like you would not believe and I didn't need anything getting back to Paul Rankine. I could do without that particular headache. Besides, the Detective Inspector already knew the way. He'd been here before.

I heard him let out a breath. 'Fine. What time?'

I needed time to get my thought processes in order, so I said, 'Around eight?'

'Fine.'

He hung up, curt as ever.

Harry Hollis hadn't changed at all.

28

Thankfully, Hollis turned up in an unmarked car. In the immediate aftermath of Jessica's disappearance, police vehicles had lined the street for days on end: patrol cars, paddy wagons and, at one point, two forensics vans. Local media had parked all over the place for a while as well. Lawns were ruined. The neighbours went nuts.

The Detective Inspector looked tired, overloaded almost. He appeared a little pasty, too, as though he desperately needed some time in the sun. A long time ago, he'd had an admirable tan. I had wanted one just like it.

His name hadn't popped up in the paper for a while so I wondered if he still did any real police work. Maybe he simply spent his days shuffling paper in some airless office, which would be a pity. He was a good cop, no argument. Apart from a minor hiccup involving a bungled drug raid that left two cops wounded and a suspect dead, he had an unblemished record. In fact, he had scored an Australian Police Medal for commendable service in 2002. As far as police officers go, Harry Hollis was probably the most commendable around.

As I opened the door to him, we heard a grinding squeal out in the street. A car with a flat tyre shuddered past the house, sparks shooting up from the wheel rim. We ignored it.

I offered Hollis a beer. He declined. I popped the top off a bottle anyway and led him out to the back deck. I had already flicked on the overhead fans. The humidity couldn't make up its mind whether it was coming or going. Right then, it was as oppressive as ever.

We settled at the outdoor dining table, me on one side, Hollis on the other. The *Reporter* front pages rested on the tabletop, pinned down by my phone and an ashtray so the fans wouldn't blow them away.

Hollis said, 'Okay. You've got five minutes, Jack. My family is waiting.'

'That's all it'll take,' I said. 'Have you been following the Mango Flat story?'

He raised his eyebrows. 'I don't read the paper, Jack.' He wiped sweat from his forehead with his forefinger, flicking it away.

'Seriously?'

He shrugged. 'I have better things to do with my time.'

I looked at him. 'Okay. I'll give you the short version.'

He glanced at his watch. 'If you can do that in four and a half minutes, fine.'

'Right. Okay. There's an old farmhouse out at Mango Flat that the residents claim is haunted.'

I thought the Detective Inspector might roll his eyes at that but he didn't.

I went on, 'I've written a few stories on it. One of the claims was that something had left the name *Gary* on the bathroom floor. It was made of stones from the driveway.'

I let him digest that for a moment.

'Now,' I said, 'you and I both know there's no such thing as ghosts, so it follows that somebody out at the house left the name on the floor, right?'

Hollis sighed. 'Get on with it, Jack.'

I placed a palm on the pages. 'So, a little over a week ago these turned up in my letterbox. I think somebody from the house put them there, and that it's quite probably the same person who made the name.' I looked at him. 'These pages are in mint condition, Harry. Somebody has been keeping them very safe for a very long time.'

I lifted the phone, slid the ashtray to one side, and pushed the pages towards him. MANHUNT was on top. He picked them up.

'You haven't aged a bit, by the way,' I said.

Ignoring the remark, Hollis studied the pages. He ran a finger around one of the red circles. It didn't take long for him to work it out. In a moment, he set the pages down and said, 'You're wasting my time, Jack. This is fucking nonsense.'

I opened my hands. 'I thought so too but hear me out. We've pretty much established that the thing is a hoax. *Hard News* sent a crew up last week and caught one of them faking something for the cameras. Things went downhill after that. They started arguing amongst themselves, a few of them took off.'

'Get to the point.'

I picked up my phone and called up one of the photos I had taken that morning. I passed it over to him.

'Somebody broke in here last night and left that on the lounge room floor. That's how my son fell down the stairs. We were trying to get the hell out of here.'

Putting the pages down, he looked at the photo and frowned. 'You told the officers this morning that the offender hadn't gained entry.'

I blew out air. 'I know. It was too hard to explain, which is why I'm telling you now. Someone *did* get in. I'm just not sure how.'

Hollis looked at me for a long moment. The deck lights reflected in tiny pinpricks off the sweat on his brow. I waited for him to say something. When he didn't, I nodded at the phone and said, 'I'm taking that as a threat, Harry.'

Hollis put the phone down and leaned back in his chair. 'What do you want me to do?'

'I don't know, mate. I really don't. But there's something else. When I was out there last week, I found a dead dog. It'd been missing for a few weeks.' I leaned forward. 'Somebody had caved its skull in, Harry. Smashed it flat.'

I let him think about that for a bit. When he was done, he said, 'Fucking hell, Jack. What do you want me to say?'

'I don't know what I want you to say. I'm just passing on information, Harry. Draw your own conclusions.'

The big cop almost laughed. 'Jack, I can tell you right now Gary Tanner's killer is *not* out at Mango Flat bashing dogs to death.'

'I didn't say that.'

'No, but you're sure as hell thinking it.'

I leaned back in my chair. 'I don't know, Harry. For whatever reason, someone out there wants me to think that this thing has something to do with Gary

Tanner, and then I find a dog killed *exactly* the same way he was. *You* tell *me* what's going on.'

Detective Inspector Hollis drummed his fingers on the table. 'No idea, mate. But I can tell you one thing. You're chasing the wrong ghost.'

'What?'

Hollis looked out over the back yard for a moment. When he turned back, he said, 'Off the record?'

I nodded. 'Everything's off the record. I'm not after a story here, Harry.'

He pursed his lips, thinking, and then said, 'Garry Tanner's killer is dead.'

A mosquito buzzed into my ear. I slapped it away.

'What makes you so sure?'

He licked his lips. 'Look, I shouldn't even be discussing this with you. It's officially still an open case.'

'Harry, I'm not after anything here. I'm just trying to figure out what's going on. What makes you think he's dead?'

Hollis shook his head. I thought he might be about to get up and go but he said, 'Because the person responsible for Gary Tanner's death - the person who held him prisoner for three days, the person who repeatedly raped him, and the person who poured brake fluid down his throat before smashing his skull in – didn't do it again.' He looked at me. 'He got away with it but he never offended again.' He opened his hands. 'I can tell you right now these people don't just stop, Jack. He would have fantasised about doing this thing for years.

Being successful once would have emboldened him. He would've at least attempted to try something similar, and he never did.'

I blinked. 'He poured brake fluid down his throat?'

Hollis suddenly tensed, probably realising he'd said too much. 'Fuck,' he said. 'You repeat that to anyone and I'll charge you with hindering an investigation. I mean it.'

'Okay, okay,' I said. 'I know how it works, Harry. You always hold a little information back, right? I get that. It's fine. It stays right here.'

Hollis placed his hands flat on the table and leaned forward. 'I'm deadly serious, Jack.'

'I know.' I took a sip of my beer and then pointed the bottle at him. 'Maybe this guy has offended again and you just don't know about it.'

Hollis shook his head. 'No. We recovered so much DNA evidence from the scene that if this person had so much as sneezed anytime in the last fifteen years we would have him. We've got hair. We've got semen. We've got skin from under the kid's fingernails. We even have hairs from a dog we think belonged to the offender. DNA was the only thing this person overlooked, and we've got it all.' He paused to mop sweat from his face. 'Something took this guy off the radar. For good.'

I looked at him. 'Have you told the family that?'

The question threw him, and he hesitated before responding. 'Like I said, it's an ongoing investigation.' He looked at his watch again. 'I have to go.' He pushed his chair back.

I got to my feet and pointed at the phone. 'What should I do about this?'

Hollis drew in a deep breath. 'Someone's obviously fucking with you, mate, but calling you a cunt is not a crime.'

'Right. Thanks.'

'If somebody tries to get into your house again, report it. That's about the only advice can offer you.'

'I will.'

We walked back inside. Outside, the car with the flat tyre and sparking rim ground its way along the street again, this time in the opposite direction.

'You should go after that guy,' I said.

Ignoring the car, the detective inspector turned at the front door and said, 'You're not a good guy, Jack. You and I both know that.'

I sighed. 'I've never been a good guy, Harry. But I've never done anything as bad as you think I have.'

'We will find her, mate.'

'I know you will.'

He let it go at that. The big cop headed down the stairs. When he was gone, I dug the recorder from my pocket and switched it off. Then I went back out to the deck to finish my beer.

Later, I rifled through the filing cabinet for the old notebooks covering the weeks of the investigation. There was a lot of information in there, some of which I may not have used.

I selected two tattered notebooks at random from the top drawer and looked at the dates on the covers, which I'd scribbled in felt tip as each was filled, which sometimes takes a while. Once you reach the last page of a new notebook, you turn the whole thing over and start filling it up from back to front. It saves trees.

The first notebook was from 2007, as was the second. I flipped through the pages, frowning at my bad shorthand. Much of it was indecipherable. I retrieved a pair of reading glasses from my desk, which I only ever used in this room, and slipped them on. Putting the books aside, I slid out the second drawer. 2002.

I slapped my forehead. I had filled the filing cabinet from bottom to top. I opened the third drawer, shifted the shoebox aside, and started inspecting the covers one by one.

29

Gary Tanner's house was gone, bulldozed to make way for a southern-style mini-mansion with a complex roofline and double lockup garage. That's how it goes. Sensible tropical architecture is dead, and Darwin is starting to look like everywhere else. I closed the notebook in which I had written the address and leaned across the passenger seat for a better view.

The new house was both imposing and sterile, and took up most of the suburban block. Even though the place didn't look that old, patches of mould had taken hold on the exterior walls. Behind the electronically controlled security fence, the Tanner's trim front lawn had vanished, replaced with a paved courtyard, also spotted with mould. That's the tropics for you. A stone-lined feature wall leading to the front entrance doubled as a water feature. It glistened in the morning light.

I wondered if they knew that a murdered boy had once lived in this same spot. Maybe one of the neighbours had told them, not that it really mattered now one way or the other.

I pulled away from the curb and drove a couple of hundred metres down the street to the local shopping centre. It was a long, squat building housing an abandoned hair salon, a flashily decorated Indian restaurant, a fish and chip shop with greasy windows and a rundown supermarket closed up with dented metal screens.

I parked the Yiros around the side of the building in a space under a tree. The shops backed onto a small park beyond which spread the neighbourhood footy oval. I switched off the engine and sat looking through the windshield.

Gary Tanner had almost made it home.

I got out of the car and walked a little way into the park. Sunlight dappled over the leaf litter on the ground. I looked over my shoulder at the houses and flats across from the shops. They were as I remembered them, all grey brick and concrete. This was one of the city's older suburbs, and one of the hardest hit by Cyclone Tracy. Back in 1998, one of the houses still displayed a hand-painted message by the front door: *This house is occupied.* I had written that down for some reason.

On the day Gary Tanner didn't make it home, only one witness had reported seeing or hearing anything; a shirtless, arthritic old man preoccupied with drinking himself to death in one of the upper storey flats. Sally North had taken his photo. He had posed on his tiny balcony, pointing down at the park with a gnarly fist, a beer in his other hand, the good one. The photo had run in the *Reporter* the following day, on page two or three.

According to my notes, the old man had heard a car, or, more accurately, a tiny squeal of tyres. He had come outside to investigate. He often did that. There was always trouble in the park. Drinkers, mostly. Sometimes kids. He was forever shouting at them to shut the hell up. Anyway, all he saw that day was a backpack and a discarded bicycle under the trees. The front wheel was still spinning. He must have just missed the whole thing.

I squatted and picked up a stick, rolling it between my fingers.

Hollis was right. It *was* nonsense. It had to be.

Until somebody had decided to break into my house and call me a cunt, I hadn't really given much thought to Murph's dead dog. It was over. I was done with the story. But there was something about that word of stones and the way it looked on my lounge room floor that connected it in my mind to the awful savagery of smashing in a dog's skull. It was a bit of a stretch, for sure, but I couldn't shake the feeling that the same person was responsible for both acts. But had that person smashed Gary Tanner's skull in as well?

I shook my head.

Of course not. It's just not possible.

Those people out there? They were just kids themselves back then.

But then, as I rolled the stick: *Had a killer roamed around my house in the dark while my kids slept?*

A shudder ran through my shoulders. I threw the stick away and got to my feet.

Nonsense. It had to be.

Still, I had the feeling I was missing something. Back at the house, I stood just inside the door and looked down at the floorboards. The light coming through the blinds fell over a broad, dusty smear where the word had been. The hunchback would take care of that.

Or maybe not.

I remembered the dust under the beds. It should not have been there. Cam may have been a half-crippled hunchback but she was a fastidious cleaner. She wouldn't have missed it. I bent down and looked under the daybed. There was a thin layer of dust there too.

I scratched my chin. Nicky had been here on Friday – cleaning day - but hadn't mentioned encountering a Vietnamese hunchback with a mop, which meant only one thing. Cam hadn't turned up. I walked into the kitchen and lifted the lid of a small China teapot on top of the microwave. This was the agreed hiding place but her money was still there. That was a new one, and my first thought was that she must have taken seriously ill.

I thought about calling her, which would be problematic if her teenage daughter wasn't home to translate. That's how we'd had to negotiate the deal to start with. I decided to give it a shot anyway and called up the number.

'Hello?'

'Ah, hi. This is Jack Jackson. Who's this?'

'Karen.'

My luck was in. 'Hi, Karen. Listen, I don't know if you remember me but we spoke when I called to see if your mum could do some cleaning for me.'

'I remember,' she said.

'Listen, she didn't turn up this week. I just wanted to check that she was okay.'

There was a long pause before she replied. 'Please don't fire her,' she said.

'Karen, I'm not going to fire her. Is she okay?'

I heard Cam in the background, speaking in rapid-fire Vietnamese. Karen said something back and then to me she said, 'She's very sorry, Mr Jackson. Somebody broke into our house and stole the keys.'

It took a moment for that to register.

'Somebody stole the keys?'

'Yes. We had a break-in. They stole the keys from all the houses. Dad found most of them out in the street but he couldn't find for yours.'

I looked at the sliding door. My scalp tightened. 'Did the keys happen to have the addresses attached to them?'

'No,' Karen said, 'just the names of the people. My mum is very sorry. She was too scared to call you.'

'It's okay. It's okay.' I ran a hand through my hair. 'When did this happen?'

'Last Monday sometime. We told the police.'

'They didn't take anything else?'

Cam was speaking in the background again. Then Karen said, 'No, nothing else was stolen. Mum says she is very sorry for not calling you.'

'It's okay, Karen. Really. Thanks for letting me know. Listen, tell your mum not to worry. I'll call you in a couple of days about getting some new keys to her.'

'Okay.'

I disconnected. I thought it through. Whoever got into the house must have been watching the place. That was the only way they could know about Cam. They had followed her home, stolen the keys, and come back.

CUNT

And then: how many times had they been in the house since Monday? Had they come in on other nights? Stood silently in the bedroom doorway looking at us?

I shuddered, thinking about the house out at Mango Flat.

Who the hell *were* these fucking people?

I found a spare notebook in the office, selected a pen from the bowl by the front door and went out to the table on the deck. I wrote down seven names.

Brett Haverson
Kath Dunlop
Nicky Chen
Deb
Shane
Lance
Murph

What did I know about them?

Not a lot, as it turned out.

I looked at the names for a moment before writing SURNAME? beside *Shane*. I had no idea what it was. I had never bothered to ask. *Hard News* had aired their full names but for the life of me, I could not remember what Shane's was. It wasn't Smith or Jones. I knew that much. Without surnames, trying to hunt down background – or anything else about them - was pointless. And now, I was sure, I couldn't just ring up and ask.

I wrote SURNAME? next to *Lance* as well, before writing NOT HIS REAL NAME beside

Murph. What had Father Charlie said? Harry or Tony or something like that?

I stared at the notebook. After a moment, I drew a line of question marks to one side and underlined it three times. Below that, I wrote GARY TANNER. I circled GARY.

I leaned back and ran a hand over the back of my head. Ernie's lump was still there but it had softened and started to recede back into my scalp. I had spoken to him earlier that morning, when I'd called to speak to Max. I told my father-in-law I had called in the police to investigate the break-in. They were on the job. There wasn't much he could say about that, so he simply grunted. I was doing the right thing. Max was okay but the doctors had told him he would have a nifty little scar over his eye. It would be permanent. Max thought that was kind of cool.

I leaned forward again. I wrote *scar?* beside *Shane* and SURNAME, remembering the way it had looked bone-white under the mango trees. I twirled the pen, thinking.

Was that even possible? That you could lose your whole childhood like that? I had no idea. It happened all the time in soap operas but in the real world?

I went back into the office, opened my laptop and typed *memory loss* into Google. There were 117,000,000 results. I scrolled down for a bit, until I came to a Wikipedia entry for *Amnesia.* I clicked the link:

Amnesia *is a deficit in <u>memory</u> caused by <u>brain damage</u>, disease, or <u>psychological trauma</u>.*

I read:

There are two main types of amnesia: <u>retrograde amnesia</u> and <u>anterograde amnesia.</u> Retrograde amnesia is the inability to retrieve information acquired before a particular date, usually the date of an accident or operation. In some cases, the memory loss can extend back decades, while in others the person may lose only a few months of memory.

Okay. It checked out. I went back outside and sat for a while looking at the names. I had the odd sensation that something was staring me in the face but it took me a while to work out what it was.

1998.

I wrote it down. According to Nicky, the accident that had left Shane without a childhood had happened the same year as Gary Tanner's murder. I thought about that. And then, I realised, there *was* a way I could find out Shane's surname, and possibly Lance's too. Nicky had said the car had rolled and burst into flames. Getting out alive would have been a miracle. The *Northern Reporter* would have covered a crash that spectacular, and the story may well have been written by the very same reporter whose name looked great in a page one by-line.

30

Monday. *Today.* Well, yesterday now.

I'd slept through the alarm, so I was late into the office. Mike Cooke did not seem thrilled about that.

'What's going on with you, Jack? You're usually the first one in around here. Last week or so you've been all over the shop.' He waved a couple of media releases under my nose. 'I need you to look at these. The cops out at Maningrida are hunting a 4-metre rogue croc. It's eaten seven dogs in the last month. They're worried it'll go after a kid next. I've also got one on a drunk who bashed a bus driver with a watermelon.'

I took the releases from his hand. 'Where's Paul?'

Cooke glanced at his watch. 'He should be getting off a plane right about now. We flew him down to the Gold Coast over the weekend.'

'You flew him ...'

'To the Gold Coast. You look surprised. Murray said it was your idea.'

I had no idea what he was talking about. Cooke rolled his eyes.

'The dead kid,' he said. 'He went down to talk to the parents. It's such a good yarn we're looking at a whole series on unsolved murders. Turns out there aren't that many around here.'

Cooke didn't seem too thrilled about that, either.

'Okay. Right,' I said.

He gestured at the releases. 'See if anybody out there can send through some pics. Kids splashing in the water would be good.'

'No problem.'

'If it's a quiet day, that's tomorrow's lead.'

'Okay.'

He walked away. I dumped my phone, the notebook and my recorder on my desk. Next door, Beth Harvey hunched over her phone picking her nose. I slumped into my chair and picked up the phone. The Maningrida cops weren't around, so I called the community store and spoke to the operator, banging on my keyboard as we talked.

Rankine turned up a second or two after I got off the phone, an overnight bag slung over one shoulder. He had a brief conversation with Cooke and then stood at his desk going through his phone messages. One in particular seemed to intrigue him. He picked up his phone and called someone. He started nodding, and then looked over at me. Our eyes locked in a there's-going-to-be-trouble sort of way. I turned back to my screen, pretending to read. From the corner of my eye, I saw him slip his bag to the floor and start walking towards the front desk.

My desk phone rang. I scooped up the receiver without thinking about it.

'Jack Jackson.'

'Jack, you were right about the Mangrove Club,' my licensing commission contact said.

'What?'

'They've got two hidden cameras in the lady's toilet,' he said. 'There are two more in the staff change rooms out the back. We've busted their security guy.'

I blinked. 'Did he record anything?'

'Not that we can tell. The cameras aren't hooked up to any recording equipment, at least. Looks like he just sat in his office having a good old perve. Anyway, we got him and he's in big trouble.'

I blinked again. 'Glad I could help.'

'Yeah, thanks,' my contact said. 'We'll have a release ready to go in about half an hour. It'll go out to everybody, I'm afraid.'

'No problem,' I said.

We finished the call and I pushed back my chair and stood up.

Harvey was off the phone now and done with her nose.

'I've just got to duck downstairs for a minute,' I told her.

She looked up in surprise and said, 'Uh. Okay.'

I smiled at her but she recoiled almost imperceptibly back in her chair, so maybe smiling at her wasn't a good idea. I turned and headed for the stairs.

The *Northern Reporter's* picture library is a long underground vault half-carved into the hillside below the newsroom, so crankily guarded by its current keeper she'd been dubbed Conan the Librarian behind her back. Her real name was Dotty. She was getting on a bit, so the name was becoming increasingly apt.

I knocked on the door on the way in. Most of the time, the buried library had the quiet atmosphere of a morgue. For some reason, knocking first always seemed the respectful thing to do. Dotty never yelled at me for it, at least, so it must have counted for something.

Hunched at a desk at the back of the room peering at her screens, Dotty was scratching at her grey head like some wizened creature in a cave. Huge rolling shelves, of the kind you move by turning a creaking handle, took up two-thirds of the room, stretching all the way to the back wall. Theoretically, these shelves held every *Northern Reporter* photograph ever taken, from the mid-50s up until the time everything went digital. When she wasn't busy chasing around after reporters who didn't bring things back, Dotty methodically scanned the pictures into a central database. The remaining space in the library was jammed with scanners and copiers to help her along, although Dotty, I suspected, might be long dead before the job was done.

She looked up at my knock. Her hearing was fine. 'Yes, Mr Jackson?'

I waved and started walking down to her. 'Hi, Dotty. I need to look at the papers from 1998.'

'They'll be in the cage.'

'I know. I need the key.'

She inspected me over her glasses. 'Are you going to put everything back where you found it?'

'Of course.'

She looked doubtful but started hunting in a drawer for the key anyway. After much rummaging around, she finally held up a fraying lanyard.

'Guard this with your life. There are supposed to be three of these but I'm down to one.'

I reached out for it. 'Trust me, Dotty. I've never lost a key in my life.'

'I don't believe you.'

'And I'm sure you have your reasons for that,' I said. 'I won't be too long.'

She waved me away. 'I don't believe that, either.'

I went out into the corridor and headed deeper into the building, past two abandoned photographic studios and a series of maintenance doors. The cage was located just inside the paper store directly below the print room, behind a door at the end of a short corridor marked *Authorised Personnel Only* and plastered with pictures of industrial earmuffs. From here, the huge reels of virgin newsprint were hoisted up to the two-storey press hall above. For obvious reasons, the place was strictly off limits during print runs.

The bottom of the access door was badly warped and it scraped across the concrete floor so loudly it reverberated around the cavernous interior like a shriek. There was nobody around, so it didn't matter. At this time of day, the machinery was silent and, beyond the next-to-useless fluorescent light burring away over the door inside, the store was in darkness, although a vague wash of light fell from the press hall above through the opening in the ceiling. Most of the lights were off up there, too. Down here, I could barely make out a forklift parked nearby, and several rows of stacked newsprint reels rising like grey pillars in the gloom. Thick chains hung from a series of greasy pulleys. The air smelled oily and seemed filled with slow swirls of paper dust.

I found the light panel and fooled around with it until the fluorescents in the cage flickered on. They were next-to-useless as well. I closed the door – it squealed again - and went in.

Located just around from the door, the cage was a deep, shelf-lined bay, recessed even further into the hillside. Entry was via a padlocked steel gate centred in a rusting chain mesh barrier. At one point, it must have been some sort of storage area for the pressmen. Now it held copies of every edition of the *Northern Reporter* up until the late-2000s, when they had given up keeping physical copies. These days you can call up a whole edition with a mouse click - and print it too, if you like - so why bother?

Swinging the key, I went over and slipped it into the padlock. It opened with an easy clunk. I hadn't been down here for a few years, so it took me a while to work out the filing system again. Bound in slim weekly volumes, the paper files had the dates written on their spines in black felt-tip. I didn't have to wander too far into the gloom to find what I was looking for. The later issues were closest to the gate.

The first week of 1998 was so high up I had to stretch to reach it, tottering on my toes. I slipped it out and quickly flipped through the pages, scanning the headlines because they were pretty much all I could make out in the bad light. In the first week of January, there *had* been one or two bad accidents but they weren't Shane's. I slipped the volume back and took down the second. Same story. I worked my way through. After a while, the tips of my fingers turned black from the newsprint.

The paper store door opened with a sudden squeal. The light from the corridor outside threw a long black shadow over the floor.

'Jack?'

I recognised the voice. Rankine.

After a second or two, I said, 'I'm in here.'

The police reporter came in, closing the door behind him. That was a bad sign. In a moment he appeared at the open gate, smiling. That was a bad sign, too.

'What are you doing down here, Jack?'

Typically, he reeked of aftershave.

I closed the file and held it up, making sure to hide the spine from his view. 'Oh, the paper's sixtieth anniversary is creeping up on us. Just wanted to refresh my memory on what we did last time. You know, get a head start on it. What are *you* doing down here?'

Rankine waved a hand at the shelves. 'Oh, I'm doing a feature on an old murder. 15-year-old kid bashed to death, still unsolved.' He lifted his chin at me. 'But you know all about it, right? Cookie tells me you suggested the idea to Murray.'

'Oh, right. Yeah, I was thinking we hadn't looked at it in a while.'

Abruptly, Rankine took a step or two into the cage, his smile vanishing. 'Jack, Jack, Jack,' he said with just a hint of menace. 'If there is one thing you don't want to do, it's fuck with me.'

'I don't even think you're attractive,' I said. 'So your luck's out there, I'm afraid.'

Rankine glared and his chest puffed out. 'Fuck you, Jackson. I know you've been speaking to Harry Hollis about it. The cops tell me everything, mate. I am the fucking police reporter, you know. This is my story now, mate.'

Now I took a step towards him. 'Paul, the conversation I had with Hollis was about my missing wife, you dumb prick. We talk about it all the time.'

That threw him. He blinked, perhaps suddenly considering the real possibility I might be about to whack him over the head with the file.

'Now,' I continued, 'during our most recent discussion the subject of the Tanner boy's murder *did* come up, but I think Harry mentioned it first.' I shook my head at him. 'I'm not sure who's fucking with whom here but it's not *me* fucking with *you*.'

Rankine held up his palms. 'Maybe I misunderstood what was going on.'

'Sure fucking looks like it, mate.'

He looked at me for long moment, and then said, 'I apologise.'

'Go back to work, Paul.'

Rankine drew a deep, deep breath and released it in a mouth-washy wave. He said, 'I'll see you upstairs,' and turned away. I watched his long shadow exit the storeroom. He didn't close the door on his way out.

Turning back to the shelves, I slotted away the file and took down the next. My hands were shaking. I worked my way through the files up to October, and it wasn't until I'd replaced the last week that I noticed some of the November volumes were missing. Rankine probably had them. Shit. I skipped to December.

Cyclone Thelma took up most of the first week. The storm had formed off the coast to the northeast of Darwin on December 3. By the end of the week, it was a slow-moving category 5 system, the worst there is – more powerful, even, than Tracy. That, I recalled, had put the willies up just about everybody, including me. Luckily for us, Thelma eventually whirled away to become somebody else's problem.

I replaced the volume and took down the second, and almost immediately found the 'MIRACLE ESCAPE' story. It was front-page news. Nobody could believe the teenagers had survived. I squinted at the by-line. I *had* written the story. No surprise there. Back then, I was writing maybe two or three bad crash stories a month. After a while, they take on a terrible sameness that makes one accident indistinguishable from another, unless it involves some celebrity or Princess Diana.

I studied the accompanying black and white photo. Sally North had taken it. Even when you're brilliant, it's hard to do much with a crash photo, especially at night. The car was so mangled it looked like a smoking, black lump by the roadside, and it was difficult to tell what was what. I did recognise a scorched mag wheel sitting beside the wreckage like a twisted bottle top, but that was about it.

I slipped the volume under my arm while I locked the gate. After dropping the key back to Dotty, who was quite surprised that I'd even bothered, I headed back upstairs to the newsroom.

As I walked up to my desk, Beth Harvey wheeled away from hers, head down so she could talk around the cubicle wall without being seen.

'Excuse me, Jack?'

I frowned down at her. 'What's up?'

'Paul just rifled through your desk. I think you should know that.'

I looked down. My notebook was gone.

I said, 'Thanks for letting me know,' and looked towards the front of the room. Rankine was in Dowd's office with Cooke, waving the notebook around like a crucial piece of evidence. He was jabbing a finger at a page, probably where I had written down Gary Tanner's name under the question marks. In a moment, all three men turned to look at me.

'Beth, if anyone is looking for me, tell them I've had to go out for a while.'

'Where are you going?'

'You're a journalist. Make something up.'

'Okay.'

I slipped my phone and recorder into my pocket and grabbed my car keys. Taking the 'MIRACLE ESCAPE' volume with me, I turned and trotted for the stairs.

31

I drove around town looking for a quiet place to park. On the passenger seat, my ringing mobile shuddered around like a beetle on its back. The calls were from Dowd. He gave up after the fourth attempt. After a while, I pulled into a tree-lined public car park on the esplanade, not far from the city's cenotaph. The lawns of Darwin's esplanade run atop an escarpment overlooking the harbour, but the cliff face is so bushy with vegetation you can barely see the water.

The *Reporter* volume sat in the gap between the passenger seat and the centre console. I looked at it for a while before picking it up, resting it against the steering wheel and flipping it open.

The accident had happened around one in the morning, just out of town on an isolated stretch of road that dead-ended at some kind of defence force listening station. Word was that the ultra-secretive Defence Signals Directorate ran the place, and its primary function involved monitoring regional satellite communications, Indonesian in particular. Navy personnel manned the post, and an officer had alerted the cops after hearing the crash. He had been outside having a smoke.

The rest of the story was straightforward enough. Two fire crews had arrived within minutes. The vehicle was ablaze. The occupants had managed to get out just in time, and had collapsed by the roadside in a bloody mess. One was in critical condition with head trauma. The other wasn't so bad. It had been obvious to everyone that excessive speed was a major contributing factor. The car had rolled several times, leaving a trail of glass and twisted metal scattered along the road like a plane crash on a runway.

The article did not name the boys, so I didn't bother reading it all. I flipped to the following day's edition, searching for a follow-up. It was on page three, accompanied by a Bill Garwood photo of Shane's elderly-looking parents sitting shell-shocked by his bedside. Shane lay surrounded by medical equipment, swathed in sheets and bandages, tubes and wires criss-crossing all over the place. Underneath it all, it was difficult to tell that he was a person at all. To one side, sitting on a plastic chair and half-cropped from the photo was a skinny, teenage Nicky Chen. Somebody else was sitting beside her but only the lower legs showed. I guessed it might be Deb.

I read the story. I had written this one too. I had spoken to Shane's parents at the hospital. Ronny and Evelyn King were praying for their son's survival. It was a lesson for everyone with children. Love them. Watch them. Keep them close. The usual thing.

Lance's name didn't appear anywhere in the story. Legally, he couldn't be named. He was underage and facing a string of traffic charges. By the following morning, the police had established beyond doubt that the unidentified teenager had been behind the wheel. Lance had been driving Shane's car. It wasn't looking good for him.

I flicked back to the original story, this time reading it all the way to the end.

I blinked. I ran a finger over my chin.

Buried in the last paragraph was the fact that crash scene investigators had recovered the body of a dog from the vehicle later that same the night. It had been burned beyond recognition. It hadn't stood a chance.

The hairs on my scalp tightened. I closed the folder, dumped it on the passenger seat and dug my recorder from my trouser pocket. I rewound, clicked, held it to my ear.

... king hell, Jack.

I clicked forward.

... makes you so sure?

Forward again.

... semen. We've got skin from under the kid's fingernails. We even have hairs from a dog we think belonged to the offender.

I gripped the steering wheel with my free hand, listening.

In a moment, Harry Hollis said: *Something took this guy off the radar. For Good.*

I clicked. Went back. Played it again.

Something took this guy off the radar.

I looked at the date written on the spine of the *Reporter* volume. The crash had happened just two weeks after Gary Tanner had been found between the burned boats. I switched the recorder off. I let go of the wheel and ran a hand through my hair.

Shane.

I massaged my temples, trying to work it out. Was I *really* on to something here? In my mind, I saw the spinning wheel of Gary Tanner's bicycle.

I glanced back at the file. A horrifying image

flashed before me: a boy bound and gagged in the boot of the car, his eyes wide with fear.

Jesus.

And then: the car growling through the night, Shane grinning in the wash of light from the dash, Lance laughing his mad laugh beside him, the girls in the back, drinking and giggling and smoking weed in the dark, with Gary Tanner, terrified and unknown, mere inches away.

Is that where he kept him for three days?

Inside the car suddenly felt claustrophobic, as though some invisible force outside might be pressing against the windows trying to get in. I opened the door, got out and walked into the trees at the edge of the car park. Construction noise drifted to me over the manicured lawns. Across the road, a new apartment block was going up. I took a couple of deep breaths. I closed my eyes and saw the name of stones on the bathroom floor. Behind my eyelids, my mind drew a glowing red circle around it.

It didn't make any sense.

The name on the floor. The old *Reporter* pages. Two dead dogs.

CUNT

What the hell did any of this shit mean?

Somehow, it had to come together. It all made sense to somebody. But who? Shane?

I stood there, looking out across the lawns, disjointed thoughts shooting off in all directions, some flaring to life, others fizzing into nothing. For a brief moment, I thought I saw, away across the lawns and shimmering in the heat, a boy in school uniform, watching me. I shook my head. Looked again. He was gone.

I went back to the car, started the engine and sat for a long time with the air-conditioning playing over my face. After a while, I fished my mobile out of my pocket and scrolled through the contact list until I found her. I chewed at my bottom lip, thinking I should probably be calling Harry Hollis instead. I had an idea that might turn out to be a waste of time. I had nothing but some old newspaper stories, two dead dogs and a wild theory. A child-killer with amnesia? Give me a break, Jack. This is the real world, mate, not fucking Hollywood. Give Russell Crowe a call, not me.

I looked at Nicky's number for a long time, *CALL?* pulsing below the digits on the screen like some kind of illuminated dare. Eventually, I touched my finger to the screen.

She didn't answer. I imagined her glaring at my number and telling it to fuck off.

I tried a second time, and then a third.

Finally, she answered and said, 'What?'

'Can I talk to you?'

'I'm not fucking interested, Jack.'

'Nicky, I'm sorry.'

She didn't reply.

'Are you there?' I said.

'Yes. Jack, I don't know if you realise this or not but you looked fucking crazy the other night, like you were about to go super fucking nuts or something.'

I said, 'Look, I know and I am really, really sorry about that. We were both a little freaked out by the whole thing.' I paused, looking out through the windshield. 'Somebody else has a key to the house. I know this sounds crazy but they broke into my cleaning lady's place to get it.'

After a moment, she said, 'You have a cleaning lady?'

'Ah. Yes, I do.'

'Then why the fuck were you letting me clean your house?'

'Sorry, what?'

'I cleaned your fucking house for you. What the fuck did you think I was doing all day long? Sitting around on my arse?'

Somebody started talking to her in the background. I recognised Deb's voice. Nicky said, 'We'll work it out later. I'm on the phone.'

There was silence for a moment before she came back on. 'How's Max, by the way?'

'He's fine. Was that Deb? Are they back out there?'

'Yeah, Deb's here. She's just packing up the rest of their stuff. Shane's coming out later to pick it up. '

'They're leaving?'

'Yeah. Tonight, as soon as Shane gets in from work. They're moving into a flat somewhere in town.'

I suddenly recalled the way Shane had so easily dropped Brett with that double-punch under the mango trees. Despite that, I said, 'What time do you think Shane will be there? I need to talk to him.'

'What for?'

'Nicky, I can tell you about it later. I need to talk to him first.'

She was silent for a moment. 'Probably around

five-thirty, six.'

'I need to come out there. Is that okay?'

'I suppose so. You can bloody apologise in person.'

'I'll do that. I promise.'

'You'd fucking better.'

We fell silent for a moment. Then I said, 'Listen, I have a quick question for you. It may sound a bit weird.'

'You're sounding pretty bloody weird anyway, Jack.'

'I know. Do you remember telling me about Shane's car accident?'

She didn't reply straight away. 'Did I?'

'Yes, you did. That first night you came back to my place.'

'If you say so. I was pretty pissed.'

'Right. Anyway, there was a dog in the car the night of the crash. It didn't get out.'

'What?'

I took a breath. 'Do you know if Shane had a dog? Back when you were kids?'

'Oh. No, that wasn't Shane's dog. It was Lance's.'

'Lance's?'

'Yeah. Fucking thing used to stink like you wouldn't believe. I don't know why Shane even let it into the car, it was that bad. They used to take it out hunting.'

'Hunting? For what?'

'Fucked if I'd know. Jack, what's this all about? You're starting to freak me out.'

'Sorry,' I said. 'I'll talk to you later, okay?'

'Right. Sure.'

We disconnected. I looked at my watch. It was already past noon. I tapped my phone again and called up Murray Dowd's number.

'Murray, it's Jack.'

'What the fuck is going on with you, mate?' he said. 'I've got enough problems getting this fucking newspaper together without my reporters fucking off whenever they feel like it.'

'Murray, I may be on to something. I just need this afternoon to chase it.'

I heard him sigh. 'It had better be fucking worth it, mate, that's all I can say. If it's not, I'll let Paul punch your lights out on my behalf. On second thought, he'll probably do it anyway. Then I'll fire both of you.'

'Thanks, Murray. I'll call you later.'

'You do that.'

After he was gone, I sat staring out through the windshield again, thinking about Lance's burned dog. I processed information. Eventually came to a conclusion. I shuddered. In the end, it was the only scenario that made any sort of sense.

Everything seemed to fit.

Shane *and* Lance.

Two kids and a dog.

Hunting.

I leaned over and opened up the *Reporter* volume to the photo of the smoking wreck, a single word forming in my mind.

Truro.

Not one killer.

Two.

32

The drive home seemed unreal, almost dreamlike. I was still in control – my brain was diligently sending signals to my hand on the gearshift and my foot on the pedal – but the world whizzing by outside the windows seemed disconnected somehow, as though I was inside some weird cocoon.

As soon as I decided I knew everything I started having doubts. The thing was simply too bizarre. It was unbelievable. I had no idea what I was going to do, or say, when I got out there. What if I was wrong? What if I was right?

I thought about Murph's dog and its crushed skull and the knife in the wall. The person responsible for all that was crazy. They had to be. How about that, Jack?

Almost mechanically, I pulled into my local shops to buy cigarettes, figuring I needed to smoke 57 of them before heading out to Mango Flat. Six or seven Aboriginal men started exiting single file through the shop door as I got out of the car. They were loaded with booze. The high sun picked out the sweat on their dark skin, dotting their faces and arms and legs with microscopic sparkles as they one by one emerged into the light. Their eyes were downcast, their faces expressionless. Outside my cocoon, they seemed to glide into the afternoon heat like a single entity.

With a start, I realised one of them wore a stained red football jumper. Halfway out of the car, I froze, staring. The man shuffled slowly away cradling a carton of beer and in a second or two, I could see the number on his back.

18

It had to be a coincidence, but just as I thought that, he half-turned to look over his shoulder. Our eyes met. He inclined his head slightly, as though in acknowledgement, and slowly turned away again. I stared after him. My scalp prickled, and I had a momentary sensation that the ground beneath my feet was vibrating, as though some machine had come to life deep below. In a moment, the group rounded the corner of the building and disappeared from view.

I was losing it. The ground wasn't vibrating at all. The red jumper I'd glimpsed through the mango trees did not have an 18 on it. It could have just as easily been a 19 or a 13. Or anything else. You didn't really *see* it, Jack, did you?

No. I did not. I went inside and bought a pack of 50s.

Back at the house, I drifted upstairs, showered, changed and prowled around chain-smoking for a while, my stomach gurgling with uncertainty. For a time, I considered doing nothing at all – *just let it go, Jack* - but I kept hearing Max's face crack on the stairs.

All that blood.

Eric was right. That could have turned out a whole lot worse. And somebody had to answer for it. He was right about that, too.

By 4.30, I was ready to roll. I slotted the *Reporter* front pages into their envelope, went downstairs, got into the Yiros, and backed out of the driveway, still unable to shake the odd sensation that I was separate from the rest of the world.

When I was a boy, I fell off the house my father was building. It was a stupid thing. We had land in Sydney's western suburbs. The block fell away, so that while the front of the house sat at ground level, tall brick pillars supported the rear. On the day I fell all the pillars were in place, crowned by shining sheet metal termite shields. A few of the timber floor joists were in too and, while my father was busy helping to unload more from a flatbed truck, I climbed onto the skeleton of the house and began to jump from one to the other. It went okay for a while, until I mistimed a jump. I fell through the wide gap between two joists, slicing my leg open from knee to hip on a corner of one of the termite shields on the way down. I landed with a dusty thump, thought I was okay, and tried to stand up. My leg opened up as though it had been unzipped. I fell over again.

When my father found me, he swore. It was the first time I had ever heard him do that. He scooped me up, threw me into our car and drove me to the local doctor's surgery. It wasn't as bad as it looked, although I still bear a thin, almost invisible scar.

By the time I reached the top of the drive at Mango Flat, I had the feeling I was about to do something just as stupid. I almost stopped to turn around and go home, but that strange mirage of the schoolboy on the lawns suddenly popped shimmering into my head. What would Lester Jericho make of that?

Something was speaking to us, Jack.

Waving the thought away, I slowed the car and pulled into the drive.

Halfway down I met a car coming the other way, the Commodore with the different coloured doors. Brett was behind the wheel, Kath in the passenger seat. The car bounced over the wheel ruts, jerking them from side to side in their seats. We each had to pull a little way into the scrub to make room for the other.

As he drew alongside, Brett nodded to me and made a window winding gesture. His was already down, or maybe there wasn't a window there at all.

I pressed a button and my window slid down with an electric hum, letting in a blast of warm, heavy air.

'How are you going?' I said.

'Good, mate. You going down to see Nicky?'

'Yes,' I said. 'I've got some explaining to do.'

He nodded. 'Yeah. She told us what happened. Crazy stuff, right?'

'Sure is. Where are you guys headed?'

Brett cocked his head back in the direction of the house. 'Shane just rocked up so we're just off for a little drive until they're gone.' He grinned. 'I don't want to give him any last minute chances to punch me in the bloody guts again.'

I tried to smile. 'Fair enough, mate. Is Lance around at the moment?'

Brett frowned at that but said, 'Yeah. He's down giving them a hand to pack.'

'Okay. I'll go find Nicky.'

'No worries. If that goes well, we might see you later.'

Kath waved as they bounced away. I caught a glimpse of a baby capsule on the back seat. I wound up my window and headed down to the house.

Out the front, the rear door of the station wagon was open. The interior was empty but a couple of bulging cardboard boxes sat on the ground by the back of the car. All three roller doors over at Murph's shed were open. Intermittent blue-white flashes lit up the interior beyond the caravan, stuttering over an impressive collection of farm machinery and floor to ceiling storage shelves. I couldn't see Murph but a long shower of welding sparks arcing out from behind a tractor told me where he was. The sparks spat and died as they hit the concrete floor, sending up little wisps of smoke.

I pulled in under the frangipani tree, turned off the engine and looked at the house. The front door stood open. Envelope in hand, I got out of the car and crunched through gravel and heat.

Before I made the little porch, Lance emerged carrying another box. He gave a little grunt of surprise, as though I'd startled him. He was drenched in sweat.

I didn't say hello. 'Is Shane around?'

'Uh, yeah. He's just inside.' He glanced down at the envelope. A flicker crossed his face, a tiny contraction of muscles. It was enough.

He knew what was inside.

I pictured him running his finger around the red circles. I saw him following me home. Saw him outside my house. Saw him *inside* my house.

Deep inside my gut, something tightened.

We stood looking at each other for a moment before he heaved up the box to get a better grip and said, 'I'll be back in a second.' He strolled away towards the station wagon without looking back.

I watched him for a moment before stepping inside. Somebody was clattering around in the kitchen. Shane and Deb's kids sat in the TV room, mesmerised by something on the screen. They didn't notice me come in. Overhead, the ceiling fans churned through sluggish, smoke-filled air.

I went into the kitchen. Nicky was standing on a wobbly-looking dining chair, banging about in one of the overhead cupboards. I cleared my throat to get her attention. She jumped. She almost fell from the chair. She clutched at a cupboard door to steady herself.

'Fuck, Jack' she said. 'Are you trying to give me a bloody heart attack or what?'

'Sorry.'

She stared at me for a moment before climbing down and standing in front of me with her hands on her hips.

'Is that it?' she said.

I took a breath. 'Nicky, I *am* sorry. I can't say it any other way.'

She pointed at the envelope. 'Please tell me you haven't written some weirdo letter to me, Jack. I've had one of those before. That guy was a fucking nut.'

I shook my head. 'No, it's not a weirdo letter. It's something I need to show to Shane.'

She cocked her head to one side. 'What is it?'

'Where is he?'

Nicky frowned in annoyance but said, 'Him and Deb are cleaning their room before they fuck off out of here. Least they could do.' She jutted her chin at the cupboards. 'I was just checking that Deb's got all her shit out of here.'

I glanced over my shoulder into the front room. Lance was standing at the front door, backlit by the lowering afternoon sun, his skinny shadow falling into the house. He leaned to one side, trying to see what was happening in the kitchen. Instinctively, I felt for the phone in my trouser pocket. I could call the cops in a flash but it would take them at least half an hour to get here.

What the hell was I thinking?

I turned back to Nicky, a sudden knot of new anxiety balling low in my stomach. 'Can you go let Shane know I'm here to see him?'

She gave me a serious look. 'What's going on, Jack?'

I took another breath. 'I'll tell you all. Together. Go get him.'

She stood there for a moment, searching my face, before pushing past into the front room. I followed her, keeping an eye on Lance. He scratched the side of his face and took a few steps into the room.

'You like a beer?' he said.

I shook my head, wondering if I could take him, if it came down to that. Maybe. Maybe not. I felt for the phone again.

'No, thanks,' I said. I held up the envelope. 'You know what's in here, don't you?'

He let out a little snort. 'No fucking idea, mate. What's in there?'

I didn't answer. Nicky led Shane and Deb into the room. They too were drenched in sweat. Puzzled, the couple looked from me to Lance and back again.

Shane wiped his face with a sleeve. 'What the fuck do you want?' he said.

I held up the envelope and waved at the coffee table with my other hand. 'Have a seat. I've got something to show you.'

Lance took a couple of steps further into the room. 'Think I'll grab a beer. Anybody else want one?'

Shane glanced at him and said, 'Sure, mate.'

Lance offered him an odd grin and went into the kitchen. The others stood their ground, ignoring my invitation to sit.

'What do you want?' Deb said.

I didn't answer her. Instead, I looked into the kitchen. I had heard the back door open.

'Hang on,' I said. I stood listening for a moment longer, and then went to take a look. Lance was gone. The back door was ajar.

Shit.

I peered out through the window but could not see him, and then I looked down at the wooden block of knives by the sink.

The carving knife was gone.

33

I felt like I had just fallen off another house. And that odd vibration was back. It coursed through the floorboards beneath the tattered kitchen linoleum. My knees almost buckled. I grabbed the kitchen bench for support and looked over at the wound by the light switch.

Shit.

Nicky appeared in the doorway and a second later so did Deb.

'What are you doing?' Deb said.

I straightened, locking my knees so I wouldn't crumple to the floor, and waved at the back door. 'Lance took off. He's got a knife.'

The women stared at me.

'What the fuck?' Nicky said.

I took a breath and looked at Deb. 'Get your kids into your room and lock the door. Fuck, lock all the doors.'

Nicky shook her head. 'What the fuck is going on, Jack?'

Now Shane was behind them. He threw back his shoulders. 'Yes, just what the *fuck* is going on?'

I waved at the open door again. 'I need to go after him,' I said.

Shane suddenly pushed between the two women and came towards me, clenching his fists. 'Mate, you tell me right now what the hell is going on here or I'll drop you like a sack of shit.'

I lifted up the envelope and pressed it to his chest. 'Look at these.'

He simply stood there, trying to stare me down. His face reddened beneath a film of sweat. The scar was turning white. I held my ground, half-expecting one of his piston fists to ram into my stomach but in a second, he relented, snatching the envelope from my hand like a testy kid.

I said, 'Lock the doors. I need to go after Lance before he does anything stupid.'

Shane looked over my shoulder at the back door. His brow crinkled. 'He's got a knife?'

I pointed at the wooden block. 'Yes. He's got a knife.' I looked into his face. 'Lance has been behind everything going on out here, mate. Right from the start.'

He held my gaze for a long moment. 'And why the fuck would he do that?'

'Because he's fucking crazy. Now, lock the bloody doors. I'm going out to find him.'

I turned to the back door but Shane gripped one of my shoulders, his fingers digging deep enough to hurt.

'You're not going fucking anywhere.'

I shook him off and shouted at Deb, 'Get your fucking kids *now!*'

That made her move. Shane half-turned to say something to her but Deb had already darted back into the front room. Beside him, Nicky stared at me open-mouthed. While Shane was looking the other way, I pushed him back with two hands and almost threw myself at the back door, slamming it behind me on the way out.

One, two, three steps and I was past the little laundry and outside. I pulled up, looking around, expecting Shane to come slamming out hot on my heels. He didn't. Maybe he'd gone after Deb instead. Nicky didn't follow me out, either.

Down at the work sheds, nothing moved, and beyond them, Lance was not running away through the shadows under the mango trees. I listened for a moment, wondering if he had gone for his vehicle. I couldn't hear an engine, so I trotted a little way down the slope, glancing back at the house as I went, trying to get a look around the side of the building. I saw nothing.

Up in Murph's shed the blue-white flashes had stopped. The yawning interior was dark and silent. I didn't like the look of that. I slowed to a walk and headed cautiously back up the slope, breathing hard.

In the first bay, shelving full of equipment towered over a parked cherry picker and a couple of quad bikes. In the next was the tractor Murph had been working on, and beside it stood a large motorcycle. A welding mask sat on the oil-grimed concrete floor in front of the machines. A few feet away, the carving knife lay glinting on the floor, discarded.

Over in the third bay, something suddenly thumped around inside Murph's sagging caravan. It wasn't Murph. As I watched, Murph's bearded gnome-face rose from behind the tractor's front fender. He clapped a stubby hand on the fender for support, trying to haul himself up. With one eye on the caravan, I hurried over, hooked an elbow under his armpit and helped him to his feet. He wavered unsteadily for a moment and then stared at me, blinking.

'Did you just fucking clock me?' he said.

'No. Are you okay?'

He rubbed at the back of his head. 'No.'

Something thumped inside the van again. We turned to look. Lance appeared in the doorway, a double-barrelled shotgun in one hand and a handful of shells in the other. Looking at us, he started shoving the shells into the pocket of his shorts. When he was done, he seemed to consider things for a moment and then stepped out of the van, walked out of the shed without shooting us and started casually strolling back towards the house.

'What's he doing?' Murph said.

'I don't know.' I swallowed, hard. 'Do you have a phone on you?'

'It's in the van.'

I dug into my pocket for mine. Without taking my eyes off Lance, I handed the phone to Murph. 'Call the cops,' I said. 'Tell them you have an armed man on the property. Tell them to get out here right now. Then turn the phone off or they'll keep trying to ring back. I don't want Lance knowing we called them.'

'What the fuck is going on?'

'We're in trouble, that's what's going on.' I turned to him. 'He killed your dog. Call the cops.' I looked back. Lance had rounded the corner at the front of the house. I heard him crunching over the gravelled yard. Heart pounding, I said to Murph, 'Stay here,' and walked out of the shed.

I considered my options. If I could get close, I could probably take him down. Or, alternatively, I could try talking to him, which seemed the better idea. Both scenarios, though, could end in one of two ways; one killer caught or one dead Jack Jackson. I liked the first outcome better.

I walked around to the front of the house. Lance was at the now locked front door. He knocked on it, almost politely.

'Shane,' he called. 'We need to talk.'

Lance heard me coming. He glanced over and held up a hand for me to stay right where I was. With his other hand, he briefly waggled the shotgun in my direction, so I got the idea. I stopped five or six metres from him. From that distance, my chances of tackling him to the ground were non-existent.

Lance knocked on the door again, this time with the business end of the shotgun. 'Shane,' he repeated. 'We need to talk.'

No response.

Lance looked my way again. Murph had come up behind me, doing his best to go unnoticed but it hadn't worked. I glanced over my shoulder at him. Murph's hands were behind his back, probably so Lance wouldn't catch sight of the phone. He looked like he might be standing at a bus stop. He gave me a tiny nod. The cops were on their way.

Ignoring us, Lance knocked on the door again. 'Mate, if you don't open the door I'm going to blow a fucking hole in it.'

He waited. We all did. A long way off, thunder rumbled.

In a moment, the door opened. Just a crack. I could see Shane peering through the gap. He said something I couldn't hear. Lance, raising the shotgun as he went, took a step or two back and said, 'We need to talk, mate.'

Shane opened the door all the way and stood in the threshold, his bulk almost filling the entire frame. This time I heard what he said.

'Just keep that thing away from my kids.'

Behind him and out of view, Deb said something but her voice crackled and I couldn't understand her. I heard one of the kids bawling. Shane quickly waved a hand at the gloom behind him, motioning for them to get back.

'I'm not going to hurt anyone,' Lance said. He looked from Shane to Murph and I and then over at the cars. 'Got your keys on you?'

Shane tapped at the side of his shorts, almost absently. 'Yes, mate. Stop pointing that thing at me.'

Lance said, 'Sorry,' but did not lower the gun. He waved it at the yard. 'Get in your car.'

Shane shook his head. 'What's going on with you, mate?'

'Get in the car.'

Shane held up his hands. 'Okay, mate. No worries.'

A trickle of sweat coursed down the side of my face.

Move. Go for him now. Give Shane a chance to take him.

I couldn't move. The thing was playing out in front of me like a slow motion film and I couldn't move.

Walking backwards and gesturing with the gun, Lance motioned for Shane to get moving. Once away from the porch, Lance circled behind him and they were treading through the gravel toward the station wagon.

I took a step or two forward. 'Lance,' I said.

He turned and pointed the shotgun at me. 'Fuck off, you dopey cunt,' he said.

Shane opened the car and slid in behind the wheel while Lance circled around to the back, the whole time pointing the gun through the windows. He slammed the rear door shut and slipped into the back seat.

In a moment the car started. With the gun trained at the back of his head, Shane backed up, grinding the cardboard boxes standing at the back of the vehicle into the gravel. Then he shot forward in a spray of stones and they were bouncing away up the drive, trailing a low cloud of dust, lit gold by the afternoon sun.

Unable to move, I stood there watching them go, dumbstruck at the speed with which everything had gone so completely pear-shaped. Overhead, thunder growled across the deepening sky. Now clutching her crying children at the open door, Deb screamed at me, *'What have you done?'* and her words almost drowned out the noise of the approaching storm.

34

In the doorway, Nicky appeared at Deb's shoulder, trying to get a look outside.

'What the hell just happened?' she said.

I looked at her but didn't move. Murph did. He trotted past me, holding up my phone.

'The coppers are on their way,' he said.

I looked over at the long drive. I was certain Lance was going to tell Shane what they had done. What happened after that was anybody's guess.

'Jack,' Nicky said. 'You need to tell us what's going on. Right now.'

I ran a hand through my hair. That was fast becoming my signature move. I started for the door and said, 'Inside.'

Murph let me go first and the women backed into the room as I thumped up the steps. The kids had stopped crying, so Deb let them go. They stood uncertainly by her side, looking from one adult to another as though they wanted to know what was going on too.

Three steps into the front room I stopped. Scattered over the coffee table and the floor around it were a dozen strips of torn newsprint. The *Reporter* front pages. Kicked along by the ceiling fans, one of the strips skittered across the coffee table and fluttered to the floor.

I turned to Deb. 'Did Shane do that?'

She said nothing.

'Did he even look at them?'

No response. I looked at Nicky.

'Who tore up the pages?'

Nicky waved a hand. 'Well, Deb did.'

'Did Shane look at them?'

Nicky said, 'He didn't get a chance to. She ripped them out of his hand. Seriously, what is going on, Jack?'

Ignoring her, I looked at Deb. She lifted her chin at me. 'So fucking what?' she said.

I stared at her. I suddenly recalled the way she had almost jumped out of her seat when Lance had guffawed that first night I'd come out here. I remembered the look on her face. The way she had seemed to recoil from him. She *had* been frightened. Of Lance.

It hit me like a slap.

What have you done?

'Jesus Christ,' I said. 'You *know.* '

She said nothing. A hand flitted up, searching out that strand of hair.

'Fuck. You know what they did.'

Nicky finally erupted. She stamped a foot on the floor. 'Jesus Christ, Jack! Will you *please* tell us what the fucking *fuck* is going on here?'

The children jumped. So did I. Holding Deb's gaze, I said. 'Fifteen years ago a schoolboy named Gary Tanner was abducted, raped and murdered. His killer was never found.' I let that sink in. 'The killer smashed the boy's skull in.' I glanced at Murph. 'You know your dog was killed the same way, mate.'

Murph opened his mouth to say something and then closed it again when nothing came out.

Turning to face Deb, I said, 'I think Shane and Lance killed the boy. Together. The problem is

Shane can't remember doing it. They crashed Shane's car two weeks after the murder.'

Deb suddenly scooped up her little girl and screamed at me. *'I don't need to listen to this shit!'* She turned away, grasping her boy's arm as she did so, twisting it hard enough for him to yelp in pain as she dragged him away. In a moment, she had stormed off into the hall in a whirl of whimpers and writhing limbs. A second later, a door slammed.

I looked at Nicky. Her mind was working. One of her jaw muscles pulsed. She shook her head in disbelief, or confusion, or a mixture of both.

I waved an arm at the room.

'Lance has been pulling all this shit for one reason and one reason only, to try to get Shane to remember what they'd done.'

Now Murph was shaking his head in disbelief. He didn't know what to make of it. I pointed at the torn pages.

'Lance has held on to those newspaper pages all this time. The night we ended up in the Mangrove Club, he left them in my letterbox. I think he expected me to write a story about Gary Tanner haunting you. He wanted to plant the idea in Shane's head, like some weird subliminal message. Or maybe he just wanted to get you guys talking about the murder. That's why he left the name on the bathroom floor, but none of you made the connection. He wanted Shane to *remember.'* I glanced out through the open door. 'But things didn't work out the way he thought they would. I didn't write the story.'

I let them think about that for a second or two.

Nicky ran a hand over her mouth. 'Jesus, Jack, are you sure about this?'

'I am now. Lance's behaviour sort of makes me think I'm on the right track here.'

Nicky frowned. She rubbed at her chin. 'Let me work this out for a minute.'

I let her work it out.

In a moment, she said, 'So what you're saying is that Shane and Lance killed this kid and then had their accident and Shane couldn't remember fucking doing it?'

'Correct.'

'Bullshit. These guys are our fucking *friends*, Jack. There's no way they'd do something like that.'

I looked at her. 'Nicky, I am 99.9 per cent certain about this. I think Lance came back here to try to reconnect with Shane.'

'Why?'

'I don't know.'

'That's right. You don't know.' She shook her head. 'It's too fucking crazy. Why would he move all our shit around in the night? Why'd he stick a knife in the fucking wall?'

'I don't know, Nicky. I really don't. I'll tell you something, though. I've been in newspapers a long, long time and I've covered a lot of crazy shit. Hell, this place is the murder capital of the world. I've seen people hacked to death with machetes over a spilled beer. I've seen people shot dead for mowing their lawns on a Sunday. I can't pretend to know what goes on in Lance's head any more than I can tell you what went on in the heads of the people who did those things. Nobody can.'

'Right. Fuck. Okay.' She glanced over at the hallway. 'And, what, Deb fucking *knew* about this?'

I blew out air. 'Her reaction would indicate that, yes. Maybe Shane told her before the crash, or she figured it out somehow. I don't know. That's for the cops to work out.'

We fell silent for a moment. Then Murph slotted the hand not holding my phone deep into a pocket. 'Why'd he kill my dog?'

'I don't know,' I said, not looking at him. I'd spotted something on the floor. 'Maybe it barked at the wrong time, or just got in his way. I don't know.'

Murph grunted. 'I knew that guy was an arsehole,' he said.

I took a step forward, leaned down and retrieved a triangle of ripped page from the floor. I flipped it over. It was a section of the BODY ON BEACH MAY BE MISSING BOY page. I flipped it over again. The lead story spilled onto page two, and on page two was a map showing the location of that tiny beach, hand drawn by one of the *Reporter's* artists. We don't have artists anymore. Computers and budget cuts have all but killed them off. We do still have a cartoonist, but he doesn't even bother coming into the building.

Thunder grumbled overhead. I studied the map, thinking. I ran a finger around the coastline, picking out landmarks. There wasn't much out there back then so there weren't too many, but one in particular caught my attention.

'I think I know where they're going,' I said.

Nicky came up and looked over my shoulder. 'Where?'

I showed her the map and said, 'Mud Point.'

She didn't understand. 'Why?'

'Because it's quiet, it's isolated, and it's where you guys used to hang out when you were kids. And the beach where they found Gary Tanner's body is just around the corner.' I pointed. 'Mud Point could be where they killed him.'

She shook her head. 'This is too fucking crazy,' she said again.

'Yes. It is.' I looked back at the map and said, 'I'm going after them.'

'What?'

I reached into my trouser pocket for my keys. 'I'm going after them. I've started something here. I need to see the end of it.' I snapped my fingers at Murph. 'Give me the phone.'

Handing it over, he said, 'Shouldn't we just wait for the cops to get here?'

'You two can fill them in.' I slipped the phone into my pocket. It clanked against the recorder.

Nicky took hold of my elbow. 'I'm coming with you.'

'No, you're not.'

'Yes, I fucking am.'

'Shit,' Murph said. 'You're not leaving me here by myself with the cops.'

I looked from one to the other. 'Okay. *Okay.* I'm not going to stand around arguing about it. Let's go.'

As the Yiros bounced up the driveway Nicky said, 'So Lance got into your house that night, right?'

'Yes.'

I looked at the dashboard clock. 6:15. Another forty minutes or so and night would fall. I gave the accelerator pedal an extra nudge. We bounced some more.

'But why did he do that? It doesn't make any fucking sense.'

I shrugged. 'I think he was pissed off things weren't working out the way he thought they would. Shane and Deb had taken off. So had you. Things were falling apart and I think he was blaming me for it. He was sending me a message, not you.' I took a breath. 'He must have been following me for a while. He probably wasn't even going to work. I mean, how else would he know about my cleaning lady? He broke into her house and stole my fucking keys, so he must have followed her too. Christ knows how many times he's been inside the house.'

Nicky leaned back in the passenger seat, thinking about that. In the back, Murph farted.

'Sorry,' he said. 'I'm frightened.'

A spattering of rain slapped across the windscreen as I pulled out onto the road. I flicked on the wipers and tried to remember the way to Mud Point. This time of day, the highway would be choked with evening traffic but it was the only way to go. The turn-off, I thought, was maybe a twenty-minute drive back towards town. I sped up, taking the rural back roads a little faster in the rain than I should have, until we came to the T intersection with the main road that would lead us past the Mango Flat Tavern and that cowboy crocodile and onto the highway.

It started raining quite hard. I could hear thunder over the hum of the tires. We had to stop at the intersection to let a flurry of vehicles flash by in a whoosh of swirling wet spray - people heading home to their properties and chooks and dinners and beds. What a life. Briefly, I considered simply hitting the highway and going straight home. I liked the idea, but by now that old ambulance-chasing adrenaline rush was back and, gripping the steering wheel a little tighter, I realised how much I'd fucking missed it.

We turned right onto the main road and immediately caught sight of a pulsing band of blue and red lights in the distance, heading our way through the rain. None of us said anything. The police vehicles sped past us just outside the tavern - two patrol cars, one four-wheel-drive and one large armour-plated Bearcat. They weren't using their sirens. The Bearcat was probably full of heavily armed tactical response group officers. Deb was in for a big surprise.

In the rear view mirror, I saw Murph turn around to watch them go.

'Do you think you should call to tell them they're going the wrong way?'

Speeding up again, I said, 'Not yet. I'm working on a guess here, Murph. They'll be pissed off if we get them out to Mud Point and there's nobody there.'

Murph snorted. 'They'll be pissed off when they get to the house and there's nobody there.'

'Yep.'

Beside me, Nicky had fallen into a gloomy silence. I figured she was still trying to work it out. One minute she had been cleaning out a cupboard, the next she was driving through the rain chasing after a couple of killers. That's probably a difficult thing to get your head around.

I had to slow down again as we approached the highway. Traffic had banked up ahead of us, waiting for the lights to change. The rain started to ease off, almost as quickly as it had started. The storm had blown over, and it turned out to be the last one the city would see until the following October.

The lights finally turned green and I took off, heading back towards the city, weaving in and out of traffic and doing my damnedest not to get us killed.

'What happens if they *are* there?' Murph wanted to know.

'Then we call the cops,' I said.

'Right. That's good.'

We fell silent, which was good too, because I really needed to concentrate. Darwin drivers are not the most considerate around, especially when happy hour's on.

Ten minutes later, I made a sharp left off the highway, taking a two-lane road that sliced through a scarred landscape of half-built houses before winding away in a flat ribbon through mostly untouched bushland. High voltage electricity pylons ran along one side of the road; it eventually terminated at the city's main power station. On the way, the road and the power lines passed by the site of the old hospital at Mud Point, which was never really a hospital at all. It was more like a prison.

35

Leprosarium. Another unhappy place. Possibly the unhappiest of them all.

The Mud Point Leprosarium had been abandoned to weeds and vandals back in 1982.There wasn't much to see down there now - a jumble of brick walls and a few decaying, weed-covered concrete floor slabs where the buildings once stood, all of it now almost lost to the dense vegetation that rambled down to overhang the muddy foreshore. Down by the water, rotting timber pylons - all that remained of the leprosarium's jetty - marched into the harbour as if they were trying to get away. I didn't blame them. If anywhere around here was truly haunted, it was this place.

The ruins now stood in a conservation zone, protected from the approaching housing estates and gas plants by a buffer of thick bushland. A couple of years earlier the government had erected a small monument to those who had worked, lived and died at the Mud Point Leprosarium. I'd covered the official unveiling, slapping at mosquitos with my notebook, which is how I knew the way.

I pulled off the road and parked along the shoulder at the head of the single lane dirt track leading down to the ruins. A pair of metal poles stood to one side of the entrance. The sign informing curious visitors that there was something interesting to look at down there was gone. Past the poles, trees closed over the path in a brown tangle of interlocking branches, gathering in the growing darkness. Down there, nothing moved.

'I don't see the car,' Nicky said.

'I'll go down and take a look,' I said.

In the back, Murph said, 'How about we just call the cops anyway, eh?'

I turned to look at him, digging out my phone again. 'I'll take a quick look first.' I handed the phone to Nicky. 'You two stay here. If I'm not back in five minutes, call them, okay?'

Staring at me, Nicky took the phone. Our eyes met. 'I don't like this,' she said.

'Neither do I.'

I clicked my seatbelt off and opened the door. To both of them, I said, 'You see or hear anything, get on the phone.' They both nodded. I slid from my seat and stood by the open door for a moment, looking down at the track. The ground fell away from the road in a gentle slope, the track winding down through the trees like a cave.

Before closing the door, I leaned back down and said, 'Back in a minute.'

The heat beneath the trees closed in. The ground was bone dry. The storm hadn't made it this far. More sweat trickled down the side of my face. I felt like I was being cocooned again, separated from the rest of the world. As I walked, I reached into my pocket. I passed by two more signposts without signs.

The authorities weren't too big on the upkeep around here, I thought. Maybe they no longer had the budget for it, or maybe, given that the signs were gone, they had simply given up on the place. Whatever the case, there was a brooding air of something so long forgotten that I had the odd sensation of going somewhere nobody was supposed to go.

I looked back just once, half-hoping Nicky and Murph had decided to follow me. I couldn't see them, and the car was long lost from view. I kept going.

An ancient, graffiti-covered water pipe ran along one side of the overgrown road, dipping and rising with the terrain. Crushed beer cans and broken glass were scattered here and there along its length. Kids. I wondered if any of them knew the terrible history of Mud Point. Would they still come down here if they did? Probably. Kids are still kids.

After a few minutes, the track widened and opened into a small parking area, now wild with weeds and covered in broken glass and rubbish. Off to one side stood the remains of a decaying building, its battered brick walls now reduced to a waist high jumble. The roof was long gone. In places, you could still make out where the windows and doors had been. It had been the leprosarium's administration block. The small memorial cairn stood at the front of the building, spots of green and black on its brass plaque. Parked a little way beyond the building sat Shane's station wagon. The driver's door was open.

I stopped, listening. I heard a distant outboard motor, burbling away out on the harbour. In a moment, it faded away and there was no other sound.

I should have turned back then.

Gone back to Nicky and Murph.

Called the police.

But I didn't.

Why? I don't really know. Looking back, it probably had more to do with some reckless desire to see the story through than anything else. News *is* news, and a boy was dead. I needed to know why. Maybe Gary Tanner's ghost was egging me on, although I kind of doubted that.

Whatever the case, I walked through the gloom down to the car and looked in the windows. Two children's booster seats in the back. A couple of toys on the floor. Nothing else.

From here, I could make out more roofless buildings straddling either side of the track further along, all broken walls and clinging vines. In places, the snarl of overhanging tree branches reached down over the rotting complex like claws. One of the smaller buildings featured the vine-covered remains of a leaning brick chimney. You wouldn't need a fireplace around here, so I guessed it must have been the kitchen.

Lumps of concrete and discarded bricks littered the entire area. Given how close this place was to where Gary Tanner had been found, the cops *must* have searched here for the object used to cave in his skull. Looking around, I could see how mammoth a job that would have been, and there was no way to know whether the killer had simply tossed it into the harbour or not. No wonder they'd never found it.

The track continued like a tunnel between the buildings and the trees, all the way down to the festering jetty. I started walking. A mosquito whined into my ear and out again. I took a zigzagging path, peering into the ruined buildings one by one, seeing nothing.

I stopped to listen again, and did not hear a thing.

There was one building left to check. I walked towards it. One of the window openings was still there, as was the doorway. The far wall had fallen over, scattering bricks into the shadows under the trees. The remaining three walls jagged around the floor slab at roughly chest height, blocking my view of anything inside. I took a step forward, peering through the doorway. The internal walls were gone but a grid-like pattern on the floor defined the room layout. Bricks and lumps of concrete and broken glass lay here and there. At first, I didn't see the blood, and when I did see it, it took me a moment to work out that it *was* blood. In the gloom, it looked like a long, black smear on the concrete.

The bloody trail started in the middle of the floor slab and led off behind the front wall. I couldn't see where the trail ended. Stepping forward, I followed the blood with my eyes. Another step and I saw work boots on the ground; one toe pointed up at the trees, the other off to one side, as though their owner might be enjoying a good lie down. Another step revealed legs and a pair of shorts, both spotted with blood.

I went into the ruined building.

Shane was sitting with his back to the wall, hands in his lap. I stared at him. Blood covered the upper half of his body, soaking his shirt. The earth seemed to tilt beneath my feet and for one desperate moment, I thought I might fall over.

Half his face was gone. The remainder folded down in a massy pulp to rest on his chest like a bloody beard.

No.

I half collapsed, my legs folding at the knees and taking me down into a sort of squat. Time slowed. The total absence of sound began to ring in my ears, buzzing in an electric hum. I don't know how long I stayed that way, staring, before I heard the noise.

Click.

I tensed. My heart did a savage little flip-flop. The metallic 'click' hung in the dense air behind me, weighty and terrible and frightening. In the bush a nearby a scrub fowl called out, happy as a lark.

Slowly, I turned to look over my shoulder. Lance – toothless, damaged Lance - was standing a few metres away, at the edge of the blood-smeared slab where the wall had collapsed, holding the shotgun across his chest. Low sunlight, orange and dying, found a way through the trees and speckled over him in a grouping of tiny spotlights.

Where the hell had he come from? Had he been standing in the shadows the whole time? I focused on the gun. I wondered if he'd reloaded it. Maybe that was the click. Then I noticed his hands, smeared with blood. He'd dragged Shane across the floor.

My eyes drifted up to his face.

He was crying. He looked at me.

'I didn't want to kill him,' he said, almost matter-of-factly. 'He was my friend.'

I nodded as though I understood that, and slowly got to my feet, which was a struggle. As I turned to face him, Lance took a shuffling step onto the concrete, stepping over bricks, coming closer.

'He didn't want to listen,' he said. 'I told him what we'd done and all the other things too.' He managed a thin, gummy smile. 'How we used to fuck. How we used to suck each other's dicks. You know, how fucking *close* we were. How we fucking *loved* each other.' He raised the shotgun, pointing it at my chest. 'How can you just *forget* all that?'

The enormity of what was happening struck me like a physical blow. Two people were dead. Their killer was aiming a gun at me. Once more, my knees threatened to give up the ghost. I fought to stay upright. I raised my palms to him and said, 'Hey.'

'This is your fault,' Lance said. 'You just had to come along and fuck it all up, didn't you?'

'I didn't mean to.' My voice cracked as the words came out.

'No. Nobody ever means to do anything, do they?'

Something small scrabbled through the bushes behind him but he didn't turn to look. I caught sight of that happy bird, clawing and pecking at the dirt, oblivious to the drama.

Lance sniffled and ran a tattooed forearm across his face, wiping away tears and mucous. He rubbed it away on his shorts.

I waved my hands at him, hoping he would lower the gun but he didn't.

I said, 'But you left me those old pages for a reason, right? You wanted Shane to see the boy's name in the paper, yes? So he would remember. You wanted me to help. Mate, you dragged me into this thing.'

He nodded his head, quickly, dismissively.

'Yes, yes, but it doesn't really matter now, does it?'

By now, my heart was pounding with a ferocity that shook my entire body. I had to keep him talking while I looked for a way out. I pictured myself dashing forward to scoop up a loose brick, and maybe throwing it at him.

'It happened here, right?' I said.

Lance looked at me and then looked around. He nodded thoughtfully and scratched at his hair. His brow furrowed, as if he might be trying to remember something.

In a moment, he simply said, 'Yes. We liked it here.'

I asked, 'Why did you take the boy?'

One of his shoulders lifted in a half-shrug. 'I don't know. It just happened. Shane thought we should try it. I don't know why.' He shook his head, mystified. 'I didn't know he would end up dead.'

'It was you who killed him, though, right?'

Lance waved an arm, almost wearily. 'Yeah. Shane wanted me to do that.' He shook his head. 'He was done with him. Did all kinds of sick shit to him and then he was finished. All over, red rover.' He looked at me. 'I never did anything sexual to him, you know. That boy.'

'Okay. I believe you.' I swallowed hard. 'You tried it with brake fluid first, right?'

Lance nodded, slowly. 'Yeah. That was Shane's first idea. Didn't fucking work though.' He ran his free hand over his greasy head and then pointed at the body. 'Why the fuck couldn't he just *remember?*'

I shook my head. 'I don't know, mate.'

Lance looked at me for a long time. He wiped at his nose again. Then he took a couple of halting steps forward. His work boots scraped on the concrete. He waved the gun at me, or at Shane, and said, 'I just wanted him to love me again.'

I nodded, slowly, as if that made perfect sense.

Tilting his head back, Lance looked up into the trees for a moment and let out a deep sigh, as though he might be weighing up his options.

He looked back down and said, 'I'm sorry.'

He raised the shotgun to his shoulder.

Taking aim.

At my chest.

I said, 'No,' but Lance simply shook his head.

By rights, I would be dead now if not for the brick that went sailing past his nose at that precise moment. The brick smashed to the concrete in a series of tumbling clunks. Lance shuffled back in surprise, swinging himself around. My neck cracked as my head snapped around too.

Nicky stood behind a half wall. If she had been a better shot, I decided later, things may have turned out a little differently. A few feet behind her, Murph threw his hands in the air as Lance pointed the shotgun at them. How they had managed to get this close without us knowing was a major miracle.

'Don't shoot!' Murph said.

At that, Nicky abruptly ducked down behind the wall. A second later, she shot back up again, armed with another brick. She glanced at Shane, drew back her arm.

'Drop the fucking gun, Lance,' she said.

I stared at her. A patch of waning light lit her face. Her eyes were wide. Her nostrils flared. She looked magnificent, and I decided to love her.

In a moment, I turned to look at Lance. He was backing away, swinging the gun this way and that. At me. At Nicky and Murph. Back at me.

I took a step towards him. 'You can't shoot all of us,' I said. 'It's over, mate.'

Lance stopped. He lowered the gun.

Slowly, his head turned, and he looked down at Shane in a sort of wonder.

'Yes,' he said.

Then the tall, skinny, toothless killer of a small boy turned his back to us, flipping the shotgun as he went. Firmly planting the weapon butt first on the ancient concrete with one long arm, he leaned over it so that the double barrels pressed hard into his chest. Then he reached down with his other long arm and pulled the trigger. The blast erupted from his back in a deafening detonation of smoke and blood, and the smoke and blood mixed into an orange mist that went swirling up into the failing light.

As he toppled over – in that still, claustrophobic afternoon heat under the trees it seemed to take forever - I finally fell to my knees, feeling the warmth of his blood drift over me in a soft rain, the sound of the blast rattling around inside my head in a series of reverberating thunderclaps. Beneath me, I thought, the ground again began to tremble with that strange subterranean vibration.

And then Nicky was next to me, screaming something I couldn't hear, and Murph was there too, dragging me away from the dead men.

Interview – Part 3

What have you done?

'I didn't think he was going to kill him, you know. That's the trouble with people. Most of the time you don't know how they work.'

For the moment, the two men said nothing. I toyed with my plastic cup. The coffee was long gone and the detectives had only once taken a break to get more. Tezuka, after punctuating the conversation with just one or two questions of his own, sat implacably as Knight scanned his copious notes. The only sound in the interview room was the steady, overhead hum of the air-conditioning.

Finally, Detective Sergeant Knight twisted his head to one side so that an audible *crack* popped from his neck into the silence, looked up and said, 'So, Lance admitted to you that he killed the boy?'

I nodded wearily, looking at my watch. It was closing in on four in the morning.

'He did,' I said. 'But he made it clear that only Shane had sex with him. I'm guessing that whatever DNA evidence you still have might back that up.' Leaning forward, I slid my digital recorder across the desk towards him. 'It's all on there.'

Tezuka leaned forward to inspect the device. 'You recorded your conversation with him?'

I waved one of my blood-speckled hands at him. 'I did. I switched it on as I walked down to the ruins.' I looked at Knight. 'You'll find my conversation with Harry Hollis on there too.'

I figured Detective Sergeant Knight might be just as tempted to glance up at the camera as I was, but we managed to hold ourselves in check. I had no idea if Hollis would be in trouble for talking to me – or, indeed, ignoring me - or not. I kind of hoped so. Throughout the night, my own growing sense of responsibility had increased exponentially. Two men were dead. And, monster or not, one of them was father to two small children. Spreading the guilt around seemed like a good idea.

We fell silent again, until Tezuka adjusted his big glasses, flipped over a couple of pages and rubbed a forefinger over his chin. He looked up at me and said, 'You mentioned another name earlier this evening. Truro. Who is that?'

I looked at Knight. He waved a hand in a go-ahead manner. He wasn't going to tell the story.

'It's a place not a person,' I told the Japanese detective. 'It's a town in South Australia. Back in the 70s, the bodies of several young women were found in nearby bushland. They had been dumped there over a two-month period by two men, a young guy and an older man. The murders only stopped when the older guy was killed in a car accident.' I shook my head. 'I can't recall offhand how the younger man was eventually caught. I think he blabbed to someone. Whatever happened, the similarities to this case are pretty striking. In Truro, the younger man was infatuated with, and dominated by, the older one. They shared a sexual relationship as well.' I paused, thinking. 'It's obvious that Shane was the dominant personality here, which is why Lance sort of wandered off after the accident, I guess. He didn't know what to do. What he's been up to for the last fifteen years is your job to work out. Maybe you'll come across something that can explain why he came back after all this time.'

Tezuka nodded, thinking about that. 'He wanted to be loved,' he said, more to himself than anybody else.

I leaned back in my chair. 'You know, the problem you lot had was that you were looking for one psycho, not two. And you most certainly weren't looking for a couple of kids. I can see how this thing got away from you.'

Neither detective reacted to that.

I went on, 'Christ knows what would've happened if they hadn't crashed the car that night. It's a real possibility they would've kept going.'

Detective Sergeant Knight drummed his fingers on his notes. 'You believe Shane's wife knew about the killing?'

'Well, no, I don't know for sure. The way she tore up the news pages before Shane could get a look at them does sort of suggest it.' I shrugged. 'That's up to you guys to work out. What'll happen to her if it does turn out she knew?'

'I can't really say at this stage.'

I could see Knight's mind ticking over. He wrote something down and then closed his folder.

'Well, Jack,' he said. 'I'd like to thank you for being so cooperative with us tonight.'

I blew out air. 'I didn't have much of a choice, detective.'

He inspected me for a moment and then said, 'I think we're done for now. That doesn't mean we won't be talking to you again. We *will* need to follow up with you again at some point over the next few days. As I said, we may have more to talk about once the forensics come in.'

'No problem. Should I bring a lawyer?'

'That's entirely up to you.'

'Okay.'

'About the forensics, we'll be needing your clothes, mate. If you agree to that, we can have the paperwork ready for you to sign shortly. Then we'll organise for a couple of officers to escort you home.'

'Naked?'

'No. We'll give you a disposable forensics suit to wear.'

'Okay. That isn't a problem.' I nodded at the desk. 'You can keep the recorder.'

'Thank you.'

'Can I go back out there to get my car at some point?'

'We'll bring it in for you. You can pick it up from the compound, probably later in the week.' Knight looked at me for a moment. 'It goes without saying that we'd like you to hang around, Jack. Don't go anywhere.'

I opened my hands to him. 'Where am I going to go?'

36

Bali, of course.

We were staying in small, one-bedroom villa located at the end of a winding *gang* off Jalan Double Six, where the tourist chaos of the Kuta/Legian strip starts to blur into the relative tranquillity of the slightly more urbane Seminyak. In two days of wandering narrow, shop-lined streets, I had already burned to a crisp, and was now so dangerously pink I might give Lester Jericho a significant run for his money.

Kicking back on the sunlounge, I looked over my bargain bin novel and watched Nicky slip naked into the pool. She started doing lazy laps, her pale buttocks rolling from side to side in time with her unhurried strokes. In the morning light, swirls of acrid smoke rose over the villa's high back wall, beyond which was a vacant lot. Over there, somebody was burning a stinking pile of rubbish. That's Bali for you.

The villa was not exactly high end and the fares over had been reasonably cheap but the trip was managing to burn a smoking hole in my wallet just the same. Nicky was still out of work but she had her licence back now and had promised to hunt for a job when we got back home. Luckily, I still had mine. I was at the centre of the biggest crime story in years, so that probably helped. Paul Rankine wasn't happy about that, but that's how it goes. Ernie and Margaret, by the way, were letting me see the kids again, which was good. Everything, I told myself, would turn out fine.

I'd been surprised when Nicky had first suggested the break, and even more surprised that she possessed a passport. Nicky Chen had only been out of Australia once before, on a family trip to China three years earlier, the highlight of which was her 'going tits up on the Great Wall.' One of her brothers had posted video of it on YouTube.

Me, I'd been overseas too many times to count. Jessica had been big on Bali, even after the terror attacks. We had been here dozens of times, so I knew my way around. So far, I had studiously avoided taking Nicky to any of the places we used to go.

After a while, Nicky sidled up to the edge of the pool, rested her chin on folded arms and looked at me for a long moment, as if she had something on her mind.

'What?' I said.

'Nothing.'

'Not nothing. Something.'

She frowned and said, 'I still don't understand why Deb chucked that toy into the kitchen. You said she probably figured out what Lance was up to when he made the name on the floor, right?'

I rubbed at my chin. 'I think so, if she *did* know about the murder. There aren't too many dead kids around named Gary, you know. She would have joined the dots fairly quickly, I'd say.'

'Then why play along with the whole spooky shit thing? I mean, why would she do that?'

'It was about the money, Nicky.'

'You think so?'

I waved my book at her. 'Sure. Do you remember asking me if *Hard News* still had to pay you even if they caught nothing on film?'

'Did I?'

'You did. Maybe Deb had the same worry. If she *did* figure out what Lance was trying to do, that money was their ticket the hell out of there. She needed to get Shane away from him. Just in case he suddenly *did* remember something.'

Nicky looked down at her hands for a while, thinking. Then she looked up at me again.

'Okay,' I said. 'What?'

Water dripping from her face, Nicky pursed her lips for a moment and then said, 'While the cops had me locked up they told me you killed your wife.'

I put my book down. 'Do you believe that?'

She thought about it. 'After what we've just been through I'll believe anything.'

'I didn't kill her, Nicky. She walked out on me. It's that simple.'

'What happened?'

Inside the villa, my phone rang. I held up a finger as I slipped from the sunlounge and said, 'That's a story for another time.'

'Sure it is.'

'Nicky, I'll tell you all about it one day, okay. Not now. We're on holidays.'

Nicky nodded as though that was okay, and then slid back into the water.

I went inside and looked at the phone. I didn't recognise the number on the screen but answered the call anyway.

'Jack Jackson.'

There was a slight echo on the line but I heard him just fine when he spoke.

'Hello, Jack. It's Father Charlie.'

That was a surprise.

'Uh, how are you, Father?'

I glanced back out at the pool. Now Nicky was floating on her back, her breasts bobbing up and down on the surface like fleshy buoys. I turned away.

'Oh. Good, Jack, good,' the priest said. 'Sorry I haven't been in touch earlier. I know you've been through a lot lately but the newspaper wouldn't give me your number and I've only just now found your business card again.'

'Oh. Well, it's great to hear from you but I'm fine. Really. Taking a bit of a break. You know.'

'Yes, they told me you were away. It's a good idea.' He fell silent for a moment, and then, 'Jack?'

'I'm here.'

'I think there's something you should know. It's about Murph.'

I looked back out at Nicky, my heart suddenly leaping into my throat.

'Is he okay?'

Murph – whose real name was Alan Harris - was last man standing at Mango Flat. Everybody else had cleared out. Nicky had been the last to go, packing everything she owned into a couple of cardboard boxes and a battered suitcase, the contents of which were now scattered in glorious disarray around my house. Giving up on Darwin, Brett and Kath had decided to drive back to Adelaide. Deb and the kids had been spirited away to an unknown location in

Queensland by her elderly parents. We would all meet up again in a few months' time to give evidence at a coronial inquest or two. Nicky and I had caught up with Murph for drinks a couple of times since the afternoon at Mud Point. For now, he wasn't going anywhere. He still had work to do.

'Oh, yes, sorry, he's fine.' I imagined Father Charlie's wet eyes blinking behind those big glasses. 'I went out to see him the other day.'

I relaxed, blew out air, and slumped onto the cushions on the lounge. 'Phew. For a minute there I thought you had bad news.'

The priest chuckled. 'No, sorry, Jack, no bad news but I do have a story to tell you. Not for publication, of course. I just think it's something you'd be interested in hearing.'

'Father, I'm off duty, and I am all storied out at the moment anyway, so go for it.'

'Well,' he began, 'as I said, I went for a ride out to see him the other day. He was sitting out under that big frangipani tinkering with one of those four-wheeled bikes in the shade.'

'A quad bike.'

'Yes. A quad bike. Anyway, he looked happy to see me, told me the Norton seemed to be burning a bit of oil so he'd drop by the church to have a look at it for me. He's a good man.'

'I'm not going to argue with you there.'

'Indeed. I asked if he was okay staying out there by himself but he said it was fine. The owner is paying him a little extra to hang around. Apparently there has been some trespassing, gawkers mostly, wanting to get a look at the house. They're getting ready to demolish it. Apparently the place is full of asbestos, so they need to get rid of that before the bulldozer goes in.'

'Well, that's good news in a way. Nobody will want to look at something that's not there.'

'Yes. I hope so. Anyway, we sat under the tree chatting for a while and then Murph started stroking his beard the way he does when he's got something to say. He told me something I don't want repeated, Jack. Murph will never confide in me again if he finds out I told you.'

'Father, I understand.'

'Thank you.' He hesitated before going on. I heard him smack his lips together. 'So, Murph told me a story about the shoes. He thinks that's what gave this Lance fellow the whole haunting idea in the first place.'

I frowned. 'The shoes?'

'Yes. That was right at the beginning, you remember. You know how they were moving around, lining up on the steps, that sort of thing? And do you recall how no-one could work out how anyone could get into their locked rooms to get them?'

I'd forgotten all about that. 'Yes, I remember.'

'Murph told me it *wasn't* Lance who did that. He says it had nothing to do with Lance or the dead boy at all.' He took a deep breath. 'Jack, *it was all about Murph.*'

'All about Murph?'

'That's right. He told me it used to happen at *his* house when he was a kid. Every now and then his family would wake up to find their shoes lined up outside the damned house.'

'You're kidding.'

Father Charlie snorted. 'I think I told you I don't kid, Jack. Anyway, Murph copped the blame for it all. Things would move around inside the house as well. One day his father's wallet went missing and Murph's dad eventually found it in Murph's room, and gave him a hiding for taking it. Apparently, this sort of thing went on for years, until somebody smashed up the house and Murph ended up in detention. Murph told me he didn't do that either. He told me this thing had been following him around all his life.'

I felt skin tighten beneath my sunburn.

They haunt people, not places.

'What are you saying, Father? That there really *is* some kind of ghost and it's following Murph around?'

I suddenly recalled that deep, disembodied voice Lester Jericho had played for me over the phone.

It's looking for somebody, Jack.

'I don't know what I'm saying, Jack. I'm simply relaying what Murph told me. But I'll tell you something else. As we were sitting there, I noticed some movement out of the corner of my eye, over at the house. And I have to admit it sent a chill up my spine, let me tell you.'

'What was it?'

'Well, the front door opened. By itself.'

'By itself?'

'Yes, by itself. There was nobody else around out there, Jack, and there most certainly was not anybody inside the house. And I'd noticed a fairly hefty padlock and bolt fixed to the front door when I'd arrived. The padlock was gone. Forgive me if I sound dramatic, but for the briefest of moments, I thought I saw something moving in the darkness just inside. Some kind of shadow. It looked like ... It may have been a trick of the light but I'm not ... sure.'

'Looked like what?'

I looked back out at Nicky, a low gurgle coursing through my gut.

Where. Is. He.

'A shape, I suppose,' Father Charlie said. 'Sort of darker than everything else. By now, Murph had noticed I was staring at the house and he turned to look. Said he must have forgotten to lock the door, but he didn't sound too sure. We got to our feet and he told me to stay where I was while he went over to take a look.'

'What did he do?'

I heard Father Charlie cluck his tongue. 'Well, he leaned in to pull the door shut and told whatever was in there to fuck off and leave him alone.'

* * *

Jack Jackson (and Nicky) will return.

CAULDRON BY *COLIN WICKING*

Unstoppable Nazi Zombies in Outback Australia. Yep.

Two men stand guard over the entrance to a forgotten Cold War bunker. There's something down there. Something locked behind ancient steel doors. Something that scrapes around in the dark. If you come looking for it, you die.

Naturally, somebody comes looking for it...

Not so best-selling author Ross Vittachi becomes convinced a lost Nazi artefact – a golden cauldron once in the hands of Heinrich Himmler – may be hidden somewhere in Outback Australia, and he's on a mission to find it.

Teaming with newspaper reporter Larry Kirby and Larry's no-nonsense girlfriend, Jasmine 'Jazz' Reilly, Vittachi embarks on an unlikely hunt for Nazi treasure – a hunt that will soon see them chopping their way through hordes of ravenous, reanimated corpses and straight into the malevolent heart of the Third Reich's darkest secret.

Bon appétit.

www.vividpublishing.com.au/cauldron